The Reluctant Incubus
Alvin Alonso's Secret Files
Book 1

Alex Woolfson

Cinnamon Roll Press

Copyright © 2025 by Alex Woolfson

Published by Cinnamon Roll Press

San Francisco, CA

First Edition, November 2025

All rights reserved. No part of this book may be reproduced in any form or by any electronic or mechanical means, including information storage and retrieval systems, without written permission from the author, except for the use of brief quotations in a book review.

This is a work of fiction. Names, characters, places, and incidents are either the product of the author's imagination or are used fictitiously. Any resemblance to actual persons, living or dead, events, or locales is entirely coincidental.

ISBN: 978-0-9857604-5-8 (paperback)

For inquiries, visit alexwoolfson.com

Cover design by www.trifbookdesign.com

For my husband, Fernando

1

I am being hunted in broad daylight by an elven knight.

Of all the fae, elves are supposedly the fiercest warriors. They have the finest weapons, centuries of training, and a relentless drive to win. Mom always said if you want someone powerful dead, find an elf.

But in my case, he probably just wants to mug me.

I clocked him shortly after I left my local hipster café, carrying my boss's Nitro Cold Brew with Bulletproof Upgrade in a cardboard tray. (I got myself an iced soy milk with a shot of vanilla, which should give you a hint of exactly how *not* badass I am.) It's 8:30 a.m. in the Tenderloin—way too early for the drug dealers and hustlers to clutter the sidewalks, but all the regular working folks are out and getting ready for their day. I probably would have missed a normal tail in all that human noise, but an elf has so much magic, it's like being snuck up on by a tornado of lightning. It doesn't hurt that he has his sword out. And that it's made of sharp, glittering ice that flurries a trail of snow. That kinda draws the eye.

I wonder for a second what the normals are seeing. The dude's in actual shining armor. This *is* San Francisco, but he's gone full snowy Renaissance Faire and not even the suits are giving him a second glance. His glamour must be on point.

But he's not doing anything to hide from me, which is a flex—that kind of selective filtering takes some real power. He wants me to know he's coming. He wants me to be scared.

I'd ask *Why me?* but the answer's easy: Somehow he's picked up on my incubus nature, and elves are notorious bullies. (At least according to my mom. I've never actually met one before, but the pointy ears and flawless skin are a dead giveaway.)

My apartment is between the coffee shop and my boss's office. It's only a couple blocks away, and he's still several yards behind. If I booked it, I could probably make it to my lobby. Maybe I'd even get the door closed before he was through. But a bunch of families live in my building, and their kids hang out on the stairs. He'll almost certainly be faster, and something tells me that Elf-With-Blade-Unsheathed wouldn't want witnesses. And what's a few dead humans to someone who can literally make himself invisible?

I know what my boss, Ms. Stryker, would do. She'd stop, turn, and confront him, right here, right now. Demand to know his purpose and give him hell if she didn't like his answer. That's what you're supposed to do with bullies. Call their bluff. Make them put up or shut up.

I throw the cardboard tray down onto the curb and run like my ass is on fire.

I sprint past my apartment building toward Market Street. All the stores on this block are still closed and gated. Some restaurants are open, but there's nothing to stop him from hurting people in there, either. My one chance is to get to the police station on Eddy Street. Almost no humans can use magic, and tax dollars don't actually show up to work in my neighborhood, but San Francisco is a big city. They might have someone trained to handle supernatural threats. And anyway, it's the freaking police! I don't care how arrogant Lord-of-the-Rings-dude is, he's still a paranormal—even he wouldn't want *that* much attention, right?

A fed incubus can supposedly run over a mile a minute. A hungry one about half that. I've never fed, not even once, so my speed is the same as a normal human. A normal, kinda chubby, can't-afford-a-gym-membership human.

I dodge around the actual normals, who don't bother to get out of my way, and make it to Eddy. Without looking over my shoulder once (which takes serious willpower!), I even get around the corner. I focus fully on getting my short, little legs to pretend they're Olympic material and kick into overdrive.

And it doesn't matter in the least, because somehow the elf is already there. His hand slams into my throat, and he swings me up like I'm nothing. Rams my whole body against a brick wall. The friction yanks the fabric of my

Old Navy polo shirt tight around my neck and causes one of the front buttons to rip halfway out. I'm five-foot-six in shoes. He's well over six feet, and all of it looks like lean muscle. Wonder what gym *he* goes to?

At least he put his sword away.

"Alvin Alonso," he says, his voice smooth as silk. "I need you to do something for me."

My back's on fire. The wind's knocked out of me. He's literally choking my throat. And he's talking to me like I'm his secretary and it's just another Friday morning. *Of course, I'd be delighted to help you, Mr. Big-Strong-Fae—how can I offer you excellent service today?*

Did I mention elves are notorious assholes?

I try to speak, and nothing but click-like choking noises come out of my mouth. It's only then that he realizes his hand is stopping actual air from reaching my lungs.

"Oh. Yes. Of course," he says, pouting like he's just noticed gum on his shoe.

He releases my throat and drops that hand to my chest, letting my feet hit the ground. He's still pinning me, but at least I can speak again. If I were Ms. Stryker, I'd be asking how the hell he knows my name. I mean, I've never met the dude, and that's kind of a big deal, right? But the police station is just across the street. There are even three cops walking to the parking lot right this second. So instead, I yell my head off.

"Help! Help! Someone help! I'm being attacked! *Help* me!"

The police don't look over. They don't even slow their steps. The fae must have glamoured us both so tight, I could spontaneously combust and no one would notice. But the moment I start yelling, Elf Boy rears back his head and loosens his grip.

Well, heck, those pointy ears of his must be *sensitive*.

So I belt out full-blast, right in his face. "Get OFF me, you big fat jerk!" Then I knee him right in the balls.

Or, at least, I try to. I miss by at least several inches, and he has a codpiece anyway, but I am still able to get out from under him.

I start to run, but four steps in, he grabs me by the back of my khakis and yanks me up against the wall again. *Wham!* Then he's on me, pinning me against the rough red brick with his whole body. You'd think that would really hurt, but it turns out elven plate mail is actually not pokey at all. I swear I can feel his muscles flexing through it. Just like I can feel his sweet, cool breath against my ear when he says, "*Stop* that."

Despite being born a literal sex demon, I'm short and thick, with a moonlike face. He's got the sleek silver hair, chiseled jaw, and drop-dead, conventionally gorgeous movie-star features of all the Winter fae. (Because there is no justice in this world.) This is as close as I've gotten to an attractive man in a long time, or *ever*, and I'm honestly so desperate it might be possible to find this whole thing kinda hot.

If he didn't have a dagger pressed against my throat, that is.

He cocks his head to the side. "You're very weak, even for an incubus, aren't you?"

Nice.

Ignoring my glare, he continues. "I need you to get

something for me. A watch. And I need you to do it tonight."

"Oh, yeah? Why don't you go get it yourself?!" (This is me trying to act tough.)

"I'm elven nobility, and that presents an insurmountable challenge for this task. My beauty and power attract notice wherever I go. If I were captured, the bounty my kidnappers could ask for would be immense, which makes me a constant target. The sheer power of my aura would set off the wards before I even reached the front door. Not to mention the fact that the current owner of this watch likely hid it in some deep hole that would be physically difficult for someone of my frame to navigate."

My eyes narrow. "Wait. Are you saying you're just too handsome, rich, powerful, and tall to do this?"

The elf smiles, pleased. "Yes. Exactly! And I need someone who is *none* of those things."

"Screw you, Lord of the Rings! I'm not a hobbit!"

I try to twist out from under him without nicking my throat on his dagger and have as much success with that as you'd think I would.

Whatever. If what Mom's goblin friend told me is right (and he wasn't just making fun of me—real possibility), I should have a get-out-of-magical-bullshit-free card. One that even the fae are bound to obey.

I glare at the elf and try to sound like I mean business. "I don't have to do anything for you. I've chosen to live a human life."

The elf cocks a skeptical eyebrow. "You've chosen to become a *wizard*. For money."

Huh. So he knows I'm interning for Ms. Stryker. I

haven't even told Mom about that. I should probably find out how he knows so much, but I'm still hoping to talk my way out of this.

"Humans can use magic! A few, anyway!" I protest. "And it doesn't matter. By royal decree, you aren't *allowed* to mess with me."

He smirks like I'm an amusing child, his green irises literally twinkling with mischief. "Your objection is noted. I'll be sure to pass that on to the Dragon King the next time I see him." He then presses his body harder against mine. "But I'm afraid my needs can't wait."

"Let go of me, you—you—!" I fumble for the biggest insult I can think of, but even though I might talk big in my head, the last time I actually swore out loud was, like, six years ago when I broke my toe against the bathroom scale.

"Or you'll do *what*?" he asks, bringing his icy lips next to my ear, practically cooing.

He has me completely trapped. And even if he didn't, he's a million times stronger, and he knows it. I don't need to speculate what a fae warrior like him thinks he's entitled to do with an incubus like me to know how bad this could go.

My cheeks start to burn, and hot water stings my eyes. But I'll be damned if I give him the satisfaction of bursting into tears.

Instead, I look away and mumble helplessly, "But I've chosen a human life…" The words choke against the rawness of my throat, barely a whine.

The elf's tone is cool. "And I've chosen something *better* for you."

He steps back, releasing me. I guess he knows I won't run away now. What's the point?

I stare down at my shoes, defeated. "I'm not a thief. I can't actually cast any spells, not yet. I have no real training, even as just a PI. I don't know why you think I can get anything from anyone."

"The watch is at a private residence, and the owner is... distracted. He will not be there tonight, and the doors will be unlocked. The only wards are noisemakers, and they are designed for big fish. Someone of your level won't trigger them. To accomplish this task, all that is needed is an ability to *detect* magic, and my understanding is you are quite good at that. The enchantment in this watch is very special. You won't have any trouble tracking it down."

"What does it do?"

"It solves problems well above your station. You would be wise not to trouble yourself with such details."

Right.

God, elves really are assholes.

"And what if I say no?" I gesture at the dagger in his hand. "You kill me?"

He chuckles and holsters the dagger in its scabbard at his waist. "Stars, no! I'm not a *monster*." He glances over at the police station. "I'd merely turn you in to the authorities as a 'malignant paranormal.' My understanding is they've become quite *thorough* nowadays when it comes to locking down supernatural threats."

Yeah, that would completely screw me over, all right. Until recently, governments didn't know paranormals even existed, but about ten years ago that changed, and they aren't happy about it. I haven't dared to tell Ms. Stryker or any other human what I am. Even if I could convince the Feds I wasn't an actual demon from hell—and that's a big if—I'm sure I'd be kept on a short leash my entire life. I'd never be able to get a real human job. Best-case scenario, I'd have to work for them or something, locked away. More likely, considering how weak I am, they'd just use me for some kind of lab experiment, the kind where you dispose of the bodies after.

I don't even bother asking him how he would turn me in and not get caught himself. He's in full armor, assaulting someone in front of a police station. He's not going to have any trouble staying off their radar.

I must look as miserable as I feel because he says, "There, there, Alvin. That's merely the stick. Of course, if you're successful, I will compensate you. When you bring me the watch, I will pay you thirty thousand US dollars. Nothing glamoured—real currency. Enough, I imagine, to get you that camera you've had your eye on, along with a fair amount of independence from your mother. At least for a time."

Okay. Wow. I'm flat broke and my internship with Ms. Stryker is unpaid, so thirty thousand dollars would be a life-changing amount of money for me. There's *a lot* that I'd do for thirty thousand dollars. Even though my boss thinks I'm too weak-sauce to teach any spells to, she did say that if I had my own camera, I might be able to help with the more normal PI cases. And that kind of cash could definitely get me out from under my mother's thumb, which would be an even bigger deal. But how does *he* know all that?

"How do you know so much about me?"

He contemplates me blandly, like he's reading a shopping list. "You take the same route back and forth to your internship every day. Go to the same grocery store every Saturday. Gaze longingly at the consumer electronics in the same Chinatown shop windows every Sunday. And you talk to your mother on the phone beside your open kitchen window at the end of every month when you become desperate for your next rent check. You are a creature of habit and desire, Alvin Alonso, and for my kind, that makes you a very open book."

I grit my teeth. Maybe he is an asshole elf, but it might as well be Ms. Stryker lecturing me on security hygiene. I'm a paranormal with a lot to lose if I'm discovered, and I haven't been careful. Of *course* I'm easy to blackmail!

Whether I learn how to cast spells or not, if I'm even a little bit serious about becoming a real paranormal investigator someday, I'll need to get smarter. A lot smarter. That is, *if* I survive this insane heist I've gotten myself roped into.

The elf extends his hand, his smile broad. "So, do we have a deal?"

And there it is. Fae are legendary for their unbreakable bargains, and humans are terrified of accidentally getting trapped into one. (At least the few on the Internet who suspect such things exist.) But while you can be coerced, you can't actually get *tricked* into a real Obligation—if you don't truly understand what you're agreeing to, it doesn't count. And anyway, most humans don't have enough magic to feel consequences if they did break a fae deal.

But for paranormals, like me, it's another matter. Even

if we're never able to do anything with it, magic is intrinsic to what we are. Mother barely has a protective bone in her body, but she did make me swear up and down as a kid to *never* accept a deal with a fae. Not even for something small.

Well, looks like I'm going to find a whole new way to disappoint her. Yay.

I can at least try not to be completely stupid about it.

"You say the guy is not going to be there, and the doors are unlocked. You mean I can just walk in and take it? No guard dogs, security, or anything?"

"Well, I'd certainly recommend being more discreet than you usually are. You never know if the neighbors might be watching. But there should be nothing in the house that can cause you harm. I *do* need the watch, and I have no illusions about your ability to defend yourself."

"Fair enough. Do other fae or anyone else you're associated with know about me?"

"No. I've kept that information to myself. For now."

"Great. Then if I do this, you have to promise you will never reveal my identity to anyone, or ever use what you know about me against me in any way. You get to play this blackmail card once, and never again."

The elf smiles, mildly impressed. "That's a very reasonable and wise addendum to our agreement, Alvin. I accept that stipulation, *if* you get me what I've asked for."

It's at least something. Supposedly the fae can lie, but they can't break a deal. Ever.

I extend my hand. "I'll get you your damn watch."

We shake, and then I immediately feel it, like heavy chains falling onto my shoulders. The *Obligation*. I have knowingly given a fae my word, and now all the magic inside me (what little there is) has been bent to that purpose.

He hands me an address written in fine calligraphy on the back of a fancy hotel napkin. And before I can even ask him his name and how I'm going to get the watch to him, he vanishes into thin air.

Typical.

Whether I like it or not, I'm in it now. Normally, after a boring day sorting Ms. Stryker's mail and answering her phone, I'd go home to scarf some Lean Cuisine on the couch and fall asleep in front of the TV. Looks like tonight, I'm going to steal a magical artifact for a fae.

And the weird thing is, there's a part of me that's actually looking forward to it.

2

My newfound enthusiasm for danger and adventure doesn't last long. By the time I ride the rickety brass elevator up to Ms. Stryker's small eleventh-floor suite in the Aston Building, I'm flashing through all the ways I could wind up shot or worse if this little heist goes pear-shaped. It doesn't help that my butt crack still stings from when the elf yanked me by the waistband of my pants against the wall. God-tier wedgies—apparently just a taste of what life is like when you get mixed up with the fair folk.

But there's no point in dwelling. If I don't comply, the fae Obligation will make me horrifically sick. Supposedly, over time, it can even kill you. I have to steal that watch tonight whether I like it or not.

I unlock the door to the cramped reception area of Ms. Stryker's two-room office and scoot behind the cheap particleboard desk she got me last month. Right now what I need is distraction, so I force myself to focus on the little work Stryker actually lets me do. First, there's the thin stack of envelopes I grabbed from the old-school copper mailbox in the building's 1930s art-deco ground-floor lobby. I shuffle through each one, visually scanning for curses. (It's the only real magical thing I can do.) All of it is junk without a trace of spellcraft, so they go straight into the trash. Then I power up the office's ancient beige PC, hit play on the landline's cassette-tape answering machine, and log the night's messages in a Word 97 doc. (It can't run anything newer. Stryker isn't much for tech or for buying new things to make my job easier. The computer was gathering dust in a corner. I was lucky to get the secondhand furniture.)

The messages are mostly spam and crank calls, but one is from a previous client whose family in the country had been threatened by a feral werewolf pack. He wants a meeting sometime next week. He doesn't say for what, but I still highlight the text in bold, copy-paste it to the top of the document, and print out the call log on her dot-matrix printer. Doing that at least feels vaguely useful.

I just get started entering the few receipts she left me into an expense report when the woman herself bursts through the door, carrying a horned demon head in a clear plastic bag. She casually tosses it on the desk in front of me, and I barely yank the printout away in time. Ms. Stryker's dark brown skin gleams with sweat.

"*Coffee…*" she growls. She doesn't even look at me as she slips off her thick black jacket and throws it over the back of the plastic "client" chair on the side of the desk opposite me. There's a vibrant splotch of yellow blood on the collar.

She always works nights, and she always wears full

motorcycle leathers on her jobs. I think it's because it makes good armor, but I haven't worked up the courage to ask. Of course, it also makes her look badass. (As if having runic tattoos around her throat and wrists, a shaved head, and the ability to shoot lightning from her fingertips left any doubt.)

I slip the call log onto a safe corner of the desk and quickly turn to get her the Nitro Brew when I realize I left it splattered all over the sidewalk on Larkin.

Oh, no.

I immediately leap to my feet. "Oh! God! I'm sorry, Ms. Stryker! I, uh, had it, but then, uh, stuff happened and I dropped it, and then I totally forgot! But I'll go get you a new one right now!"

I round the table at speed when she stops me with an iron palm against my chest. Her amber eyes pin me in place like I'm a bug.

"It's not like you to forget things, Alvin. What 'stuff' happened?"

She's planted her grip over my racing heart, and she's so intimidating, I instantly feel a compulsion to tell her. It's not like she couldn't help me. According to leaked government reports, less than 0.001% of the human population can use any magic. Apparently that represents a huge uptick in just the last ten years, and that's still mostly parlor-trick stuff. Stryker's a human who's been practicing since the late 1800s, and she doesn't look a day over forty. (Powerful magic apparently keeps you young!) She easily commands primordial elemental forces violent enough to take out an entire platoon of SUVs. And on top of that, she's a member of some kind of elite wizard council that dates back to Merlin's time and has only twelve members.

There's no way I could stand up to that elf, but Ms. Stryker practically eats the fair folk for breakfast. Even the Winter Queen takes her calls. If anyone could get me out of a fae Obligation, it would be her. And it would be so good to not have to do this.

I open my mouth to beg for her help just as a fat drop splats next to my shoe. Then another. The loosely-wrapped demon head has toppled to the side and rivulets of yellow goo are sliming their way over the metal lip of the faux-pine Ikea desk. It's the blood from the paranormal she just killed. She kills a lot of paranormals for her cases, because most of us are predators, one way or another.

Right. If Stryker confronted him, Lord of the Rings would almost certainly tell her what I am. Of course, I always planned to do that myself someday. When I was sure I could convince her I was "one of the good ones." When she wasn't fresh from a fight with an evil monster. When I didn't just totally screw up and forget her coffee.

Today is not that day.

Instead, I punt. "Oh, uh… It was stupid. I slept through my alarm, and I was rushing, and then I tripped and spilled everything and banged my knee, and I— Well, I was already late, and so I just booked it here. I meant to go get another, but then, uh… I got caught up with work… So yeah, I did forget… I guess…"

My voice spools down into a mumble as her eyes narrow. She's got six inches on me. You'd think after lying about what I am my whole life, I'd be good at it. You'd think wrong. And Ms. Stryker has a world-class bullshit detector.

"You tripped, spilling everything…" she says. "And then you *forgot* about the coffee—" Her eyes flick from the three receipts she left me, perched on a still-clean corner of the desk, to the handful of junk mail I threw in the trash. "—Because you were so *busy*…"

She's using the same tone on me she uses with clients who try to get out of paying her day rate.

"Um, yeah," I say, doubling down, weakly. "I'm sorry."

When I look up from the waste bin, her attention is on the torn button on my polo, and I can only assume the sour expression on her face represents profound disappointment. It's not like the look Mom gives me. That's just about what a complete failure I am. This is tinged with suspicion, which makes it more dangerous.

I have the insane impulse to fold my arms to hide the button, but she has me trapped and there's probably fricking red brick dust or something all over my shoulders, anyway. The only thing I can do at this point is push through, so I unfurl my most helpless, innocent smile and try to pivot my body toward the door. "But I'll get you that coffee right now, boss! It won't take ten minutes!"

There is a pause of a fraction of a second before she drops her hand, but it's long enough for her face to shutter into cold stone. Whatever she thinks I'm hiding, it's beneath her notice. At least for now.

"Don't worry about it. I'm going to be off-world for a few days while I help an old friend with a favor." She brusquely turns from me and strides the five steps to the door of her private office. "Put that head in cold storage.

Get my jacket cleaned. And if anyone calls, we aren't taking on any new cases for the foreseeable future."

I nod, not skipping a beat when she mentions going "off-world." That's just another day at work for her. (God, I'd do anything to be half as cool as she is!)

I quickly clutch the slick top of the plastic sack with the scarlet-skinned head and follow as she steps through the door into her office. My little reception area might look low-rent, but she's got an oak Humphrey Bogart desk hulking in front of a high-backed swivel chair of fine Corinthian leather. Shelves with rare vellum-covered books line the walls. There's a crystal decanter with thirty-year old scotch on a silver tray. Even a stuffed raven, eyes glowing with cold moonlight, on a high shelf, frozen-winged in flight. If you come looking to hire a wizard PI (and you're worthy enough to make it in here), she looks *legit*.

Sweeping forward, she whisks a spare motorcycle jacket off the freestanding coat rack by the entrance and slides it on. She then lifts a sheathed obsidian sword from the side of her desk, buckles its belt around her waist (complete with actual utility pouches, like freaking Batman), and finishes her ten-second prep by hoisting a waiting tactical black Cordura Go Bag over her shoulder.

All this time, I'm just standing awkwardly in front of the doorway, freaking out because I'm dripping demon goo on her hardwood floor, but not wanting to move in case she has more orders for me. When she turns, I stiffen my back, determined to appear confident and reliable.

The suspicion in her gaze hasn't completely gone, but there's now something else. If I didn't know better, I'd say it was concern. "Alvin… You *would* tell me if something happened that could use my attention, right?"

"Of-of course!" I say, still lying, badly. (And feeling even worse about it since it now seems like she might actually be worried about me.)

She nods, frowning. "All right. It's Friday. Once you drop off my jacket at the cleaners, you should knock off work and close the office."

My face falls. Usually, she wants me to be here for the full eight hours, just in case a client stops by unexpectedly. That hasn't happened yet, but it still made me feel useful. Like, on some level, she trusted me to handle important things. But what if I've just completely blown that trust? What if this is a prelude to her firing me?

Naturally, she notices my reaction. She looks away, impatient—she's not big on other people's normal emotions, let alone my innate catastrophizing—but then she returns to me, pursing her lips, like she's rallying her strength.

"You still want to learn how to cast spells, right?"

My eyebrows shoot up. "Uh— Yes! I do, boss!"

"Well… Your first lesson is that magic needs triggers to activate. You have to feel things. Not stress, not fear… You need to feel strong, because you need to *believe*."

I have no idea why she's saying this to me now, but it's the first actual magical advice she's given since I met her two months ago, so I just nod quickly, hoping she'll continue.

"What I'm saying is you need to live a little. I get the impression you don't do that much."

She's not wrong. "Well, um, I guess you could say I'm not really a, uh—"

Her hand flicks up, stopping me. "I want you to step outside your comfort zone this weekend. Get drunk. Get laid. You said you had a hard time feeling your own magic. Well, let's see if making out with a stranger doesn't open something up."

The fact that she remembers anything I told her about myself is front-page news, but that hot lede is buried under what she's actually telling me to do. It takes me a solid moment to get my mouth working again.

"Are—are you saying you want me to, uh…?"

"I don't have time to spell this out for you. You're a healthy twenty-two-year-old boy in the most libertine city in the country. What I'm asking you to do shouldn't feel like a chore, but this is your homework. Can you do it or not?"

I can't. She might as well be asking me to soft-shoe my way up the cables of the Golden Gate Bridge. I've never dared to let myself anywhere near alcohol. And if I do *anything* sexual, there's a very good chance I'll kill someone.

But any protest will just invite more questions, and her expression makes it clear that she's in no humor for excuses. At least for this, though, there's a way I don't have to outright lie.

"I… promise I'll step out of my comfort zone tonight, Ms. Stryker."

"*Good*." She's pleased with me, which is a rare event. She gives a quick nod like she, herself, has leapt a hurdle. "I think this could be your way in. I want you to feel for your power while you're having fun—really pay attention, keep your focus around your solar plexus, the third chakra, *that's* where mana pools—and I expect a full report when I get back."

Mana. That's the part of myself I've been desperate to access. Incubi have a number of specific, intrinsic magical abilities—but they're vicious by nature and you have to feed to be able to use them, and I'm not down for either of those. There's another form of magic, though: mana. It's wildcard power that can be used for practically anything, if you know the right spell. Stryker is one of the rare humans who possesses any—it's what makes her a wizard—but supposedly every living paranormal has a reservoir of mana inside them, to some degree or another. I've just never been able to find mine, no matter how hard I've looked.

It's the satisfied smile on her face that finally clues me in to what might be going on here. My boss is gruff, and hard, and hella scary. But all this time, when I assumed she'd forgotten I even asked her, it looks like maybe she's been trying to think of some way to teach me how to access my magic—or at least get me started. Sure, what she came up with is not actually going to help me, but it's still the closest we've come to her taking me under her wing, letting me in—exactly what I've been working so hard for. And of course, now that it's finally happening, I deserve her trust less than ever.

"I won't let you down, boss," I say, knowing that's exactly what I'm going to do. Here she is, thinking of me as this innocent human kid in desperate need of life experience, when I've literally just conspired with another paranormal to break into someone's home for $30,000.

She gives me another pleased nod and strokes an index finger over a line of tattooed runes on her wrist. It causes a green-glowing portal to spring open in the air beside her. She gives me one final glance before stepping through—I swear to God, it looks almost proud—and when the portal closes and she's gone, all light in the room fades away.

Which feels downright poetic. Until I met Stryker, I hated what I was. Being paranormal meant only one thing—being a predator. But then I saw how magic could be used to help people, to save lives. I watched her use the same power that's inside me, that makes up what I am, to fight a monster that was going to kill a dozen men. I begged her to teach me how to do that. I promised her she wouldn't regret it. And she took a huge chance on me because she thought I could be worth it. Because she believed that someday, maybe, I could be a little like her. But from day one, I've been keeping secrets, and now I'm piling on even more lies. And tonight I'm going to use what little magical ability I have to help someone I *know* for a fact is a predator become even more powerful and dangerous. All of which are choices I'm consciously making for selfish reasons.

I swear, it's almost like Mom's right and I was born to be evil.

3

My dark train of thought continues rumbling along as I lock the demon head into the magically refrigerated safe in Stryker's office and then grab a roll of paper towels to clean up the gobs of blood that I dripped everywhere. Becoming an actual good person feels further away than ever, and every time I think of that pleased look on Stryker's face, it's like a knife in my gut. So, after I finish inputting the last receipt, I decide to take my boss up on her offer of cutting out early, even though it's only 11 a.m. Being in her office just reminds me of how far away I am from who I want to be.

Right as I snatch up the soiled jacket on my way out, I'm startled by a soft rap against the frosted glass of the door. I hesitate for a moment, not sure what to do, until I remember that greeting potential clients is one of the few actually important things in my very short job description. (At least in theory, since it's never happened before.)

I stash the motorcycle leather into a discreet corner, plaster on what I hope is a professional smile, and pull open the door to find a middle-aged woman with tired eyes and disheveled hair. Even if I didn't recognize her from the building, her polyester blouse, slacks, and faded navy cardigan would tag her as a clerical worker from one of the low-rent businesses on our floor. She's my height, but I find her looking up and over me, clearly having arrived with higher expectations than I can fulfill.

Her gaze lands on the torn button of my polo. She purses her lips but doesn't say anything.

"Hi, um, can I help you?" I ask, shifting awkwardly, already not off to a great start.

The woman takes in the stenciling on the glass. SARAH STRYKER, PARANORMAL INVESTIGATOR.

"Your site says you're wizards. Is that true?"

It's true that I used one of those cheap builder apps to make Ms. Stryker her first website. It's also true that she wanted me to put "Wizard-for-Hire, $300/day plus expenses" on its single page along with our phone number, like some kind of classified ad from the 1980s. I'm pretty sure it's where all the crank calls have been coming from.

"Well... My boss is."

The lady glances down the hallway, like someone might see her. "You're right across from the bathroom. I've seen this door a thousand times. I wasn't sure if it was a joke or not."

I exhale, frustrated. It figures that my first chance to do something real for Stryker turns out to be some rando indulging her curiosity. "It's no joke. But we aren't taking any cases at the moment, and I'm actually about to go. So, if you want to learn more, maybe stop by some other time—"

Her fist darts up to the edge of the door, preventing me from closing it. The hand grips a wad of tissue, and her eyes are rimmed red.

"I'm sorry." She bites her lip. "It's my daughter. She's missing. And I… I really don't know where else to *go*." The last word comes out in a strangle.

"Oh," I say, softening my tone, and feeling like a total jerk. "Well, um, I'm sorry to hear that. Honestly. But we aren't taking new any cases right now, so the police—"

"They can't help me. Not with this. *Please*."

She leans in and her eyes cling to mine like she's drowning.

This woman is not going to find what she needs here. My boss doesn't take cases involving kids—too much heartbreak. And, of course, I don't have the power or the ability to find anyone. But, at this moment, I also don't have the ability to say no to this desperate mother falling to pieces in front of me. Not without offering her *something*.

I pull the door wider and gesture inside. "All right. Ms. Stryker is away, and I don't know for how long, but I *can* take a message and give it to her when she gets back. I'm afraid that's the best I can do."

"I understand. Thank you." She sniffles as she passes me. The protective runes around the doorway grumble slightly in their slumber, but do nothing. The woman has no hostile intent, and I only notice because my sensitivity to magic is so high.

She warily takes in the beige chenille couch Stryker uses for post-battle naps and then the plastic chair in front of my cheapo desk. She chooses the chair, perches her

Kleenex on the lip of the table, and removes a mobile from her frayed, quilted shoulder purse.

While she's distracted, I quickly glance into the trash bin to make sure the demon blood on the paper towels isn't glowing or anything. (It's not.) Then I remove a yellow legal pad from the lowest drawer and pluck a pen from its stained coffee-cup holder, before squeezing into my own chair opposite her. This might be pointless, but I might as well do it right.

"I'm Alvin, Ms. Stryker's assistant. Why don't you tell me what happened?"

"I'm Nicole. I work for Harry Jinny Accounting, down the hall? And… I think monsters have taken my daughter." She places her phone in front of me, turning it in my direction. "This is Emma. Her most recent picture."

The full-screen image shows a sturdy-looking girl in an orange corduroy work shirt and black jeans, standing alone in front of a wooden park picnic table.

"Monsters," I echo, trying to sound neutral while noting down both names on the pad. Emma looks to be in her mid-to-late teens. She's got short, cropped hair with frosted pink tips—the color matches the small triangle pin on her collar. Her scowl is fierce, aggressive even, but there's vulnerability in her eyes. It feels like the face of someone who doesn't fit in and is trying to learn to be okay with it.

I have some idea what that's like.

Nicole puffs out a helpless breath. "I know it sounds crazy. Maybe I am crazy! But you see things online. When I was growing up, it was UFOs, but now people are saying that the government's made contact with creatures from fairy tales. That magic is real."

A lot of our crank calls are based on what "people are saying." Actual details about what the US government knows about the paranormal are sketchy, but that hasn't stopped a ton of conspiracy theory forums from posting what they call "P-drops." The first emerged after "P-day" —a twenty-four-hour window ten years back when conspiracy theorists believe random Americans suddenly manifested magical abilities with no warning or ritual preparation. Spells like a businesswoman levitating across a busy New York City road, blue satin Manolo Blahnik pumps kicking in the air—or a burly construction worker blasting streams of rainbow light from his hands into the face of his nagging foreman. All these reports were subsequently dismissed as a hoax, and anyone who came forward claiming otherwise was immediately discredited. Regular folks moved on with their lives, but there were more than a few Americans happy to believe in a government cover up. The first P-drop claimed federal agents were reopening cold cases after discovering the existence of very real mythical beings eager to do people harm. Stories about monsters are still what gets the clicks.

The media and almost everyone else treat these reports as malicious fiction for the gullible, but Ms. Stryker told me P-day was real—she, herself, felt the extra magic in the air. And even if I haven't personally met many other paranormals, I know for a fact these P-drops aren't wrong—at least in the broad strokes. Elves, werewolves, vampires, goblins, even yellow-blooded demons do exist, almost all of them *are* looking to hurt people, and Stryker has confirmed a section of Homeland Security was created six years ago, specifically charged with rounding up supernatural threats.

But there hasn't been any official acknowledgement. And Mom says our numbers are so small that 99% of the "sightings" have to be total BS. That it's just human nature to look for an "other" to blame when bad things happen. So, while there might indeed be some kind of "monster" behind the disappearance of this woman's child, the chance of it being of the nonhuman variety is vanishingly slim.

Nicole takes in my skeptical frown. "I *know*. I wouldn't believe it myself, if I hadn't seen it with my own eyes."

I ready my pen. "What did you see exactly?"

"You should know Emma's a good girl. Kind, cares about animals, helps around the house even without being asked. But she's always looked for… *something*. Something that would help her feel strong. Something I couldn't give her, I guess. There's just the two of us. For a while, it was ninjitsu. Throwing stars, knives, she even got the mask and boots, and not just for Halloween… Then it was hacking, cracking codes." Her smile broadens. "She's really good at math." Her expression falters. "But this past summer, it became witchcraft."

I lean back in my chair. "A lot of kids get interested in the occult. It's not usual."

"That's what I told myself. It was just another phase. She's sixteen, so I try to give her the freedom to explore things. But then, a few weeks ago, when she had gone to the burrito place down the street to get our dinner, I heard a strange man's voice in her room. Calling her name. I knew it couldn't be her phone—she had that with her. I grabbed the kitchen knife and looked in, but there wasn't anyone there." Her expression hollows, blood draining from her face. "It was coming from a candle she had lit on her desk."

She reaches into her purse, removes a tall cylindrical glass tube filled with white wax, and places it on the tabletop in front of me. The front is imprinted with an illustration of a robed saint. He has a bright golden halo around his head and is holding a small brown book. I can just make out the title: "El Libro de San Cipriano." But that's not what captures my attention.

"Wait," I say, breath caught. "That has real magic…"

There aren't many actual magical items in the world. Stryker says they are exceedingly difficult to create and wizards like her have scooped up most of the old ones. The power on this candle is subtle and fading fast, little more than just residue at this point. Even my boss might have missed it. But I can just make out its metallic tang. I can't really explain why, but it tastes like *connection*, making me think of a door or window, so it's possible this could have been used as some kind of communication device, at least before its connection was severed.

"You can tell it's magic?" she says, looking more relieved than surprised.

I nod. "Or at least that it was. It feels broken. Even lit, I don't think it would work now."

"*Good.* I wish I could say I reacted as calmly as you. That I thought before I confronted Emma about it. My parents were religious and I was raised to see witchcraft as evil. When Emma got interested in this stuff, I tried to dismiss any fears I had around it as superstition, but this wasn't some trick. And there was something about that voice. Smooth, cloying, commanding. There's no other way to put it—it sounded like the voice of the devil. I immediately blew out the candle, and when Emma got home, I told her she needed to throw it away. The books, the pentagrams, the altar—she needed to throw it *all* away!"

"How did she take that?"

"Badly. We fought. Our first real fight in years. She said this was something she needed, that the man was teaching her, that she couldn't *live* without magic, and that made me more sure than ever that I had to keep her away from it. She got really upset and then all the pots in the kitchen started to shake and rattle, like something from a movie. It scared me and I—" She brings her fingertips up to her lips in hushed, anguished regret. "I told her she couldn't stay in our apartment if she was going to keep learning about spells. I thought that would get her to stop, but she wailed like she was in pain and ran out the door. And I didn't follow. I didn't go after my baby!" She squeezes her eyes tight and twists her head away, like she can't even bear to think of it. "That was last Wednesday. The last night I saw her."

My gut tightens with realization. "Which means she's been missing for over a week."

Nicole nods, retrieving the tissue and dabbing the corner of her eyes with it. "About an hour later, once I calmed down, I called her friend. She hadn't seen her. And Emma wasn't at school the next day. When I went to the police, they took a report, but they say they haven't found anything. I don't think they're looking that hard. They think she's just a runaway."

The police *are* the experts. The only thing I know about missing persons comes from the used private investigation textbooks I bought from Amazon, and nationwide statistics show that 90% of teenagers who leave voluntarily are back within a month. Considering the circumstances, it makes perfect sense why the police wouldn't assume foul play, especially of the supernatural kind. I know firsthand from working with Stryker how rare actual paranormal activity really is—reports to the authorities are almost always going to turn out to be something else.

But I can see for myself the candle had real magic. And from what happened in that kitchen, it sounds like Emma might have access to some, too. Mom's always kept me in the dark about the wider paranormal world, but Stryker has encountered human magic users who exploit regular humans for power. And since access to magic *is* so rare—that could make a vulnerable teen even more valuable. At least to those who knew what to do with it.

"You said she was taken by monsters…"

She indicates the candle with a meaningful tilt of her head. "There's a building in our neighborhood. The Benevolent Society of San Cipriano. The police say they're a Christian charity, but where else would she have gotten this thing? Last night, I went there after work."

Her fingers nervously twist the wad of tissue. "It was just before dark, and it was full of people. The man I talked to at the door, he wanted me to come in. He said he didn't recognize my daughter from the picture, but maybe someone else would. But there was something about the way he looked at me... I don't know why, but my heart started racing.... I just... I just knew something was wrong!"

"How did he look at you?"

"Like someone *hungry*."

A chill flutters through me. "It felt predatory."

She blanches and nods again, steepling her fingertips in front of her mouth.

"I made some stupid excuse, and once I was out of sight, I ran from that place as fast as I could. I know that sounds insane. Everything I'm saying sounds crazy, even to me. The Benevolent Society's a religious charity, for God's sake! It's been around for years and years. But I could tell that man was lying to me about not recognizing Emma. Just like I knew I had to get away from him as fast as I could."

A paranormal predator usually doesn't give a victim a chance to escape before they attack. And if this Benevolent Society were a nest of evil human wizards, there are probably a hundred things they could have done to stop Nicole from getting away, if they really meant her harm. I don't think she's making all this up, but a gut feeling from a distraught and exhausted mother isn't much to go on.

But what if she's right? No one else is going to believe her. The police sure don't. And in another few hours, the remaining residue on this candle will be gone. Even if she went to the Feds, without any actual magical evidence, they'd probably just dismiss her, too.

Which leaves me.

Nicole's phone dimmed but never went to the lock

screen. I glance down at Emma's broad, freckled face, now in digital shadow. Her vulnerable eyes. You could say they are hungry, too, but it's not predatory. It's like she's desperate for some kind of connection, to be understood. Stryker told me that for those who have access to magic, it doesn't come naturally, and the call to learn is nearly irresistible. You need training to use it and it's not like you're sent an owl or anything. I've denied my own power for years, and it's felt like living half a life. But I was lucky enough to run into someone good. Someone at least open to teaching me—and who wasn't a predator like my mom.

It looks like Emma was found by someone or something else.

The words are out before I realize it. "I'll help you."

"You will?" Her lips part in surprise as she leans forward. "You said you weren't taking on any new cases."

"That's true. But I can look into this 'Benevolent Society' on my own time and, if they really are evil magic users, I'll be able to tell. I won't be able to fight them or anything—I'm no wizard—but I can certainly gather evidence. Maybe even enough to convince my boss to get involved." I frown and try to think about what Stryker would do now, if she were taking on this case. She'd probably first want to make sure her client was safe. No point in saving the girl if the monsters get her mom! "Look, uh, do you have a place to stay? Not in your apartment. But somewhere else. Out of town, maybe."

She sucks in a breath. "You think I'm in danger?"

"It's just a precaution. Maybe these Benevolent Society folks really are just philanthropists. But in case they're not,

I don't want you anywhere they can find you. At least until Ms. Stryker gets back."

Her teeth worry the bottom part of her lip as she considers. "I have a friend in Daly City. He has a spare bedroom."

"Good. I want you to go straight there. Don't even stop at your apartment, and I'll see what I can find out. I promise I'll do my best." I hand her phone back to her. "Leave me your contact information and I'll get back to you one way or the other in the next couple days, all right?"

She tucks the mobile back in her purse before dabbing again at her eyes, but this time, there's at least a flicker of hope in them. "Okay. Thank you. Thank you for believing me."

I nod, straighten my shoulders, and meet her eyes with what I hope resembles quiet confidence. She's been through a lot, so I try to look like someone she could rely on.

It's, of course, another lie. There's no guarantee that Stryker will listen to me. She barely trusts me to go through her junk mail and, most of the time, she acts like I'm an annoying encroachment on her space. Even the "homework" she gave me before she left might have been nothing. Just a bone she decided to throw me for when I was looking all pathetic. Or a test she doesn't expect me to pass, so she can finally wash her hands of me. (The reality is, she hasn't said word one about training me before today. And there's no guarantee I'd feel anything, even if I could do what she told me to do. I've certainly never been able to feel any mana inside me before!)

But that elf was right. For whatever reason, I am extra sensitive when it comes to detecting magic, and if I could somehow show that a bunch of evil wizards had set up shop in her town, Stryker wouldn't dismiss it. She couldn't. I would have discovered something, on my own, that she truly needed to know about. I'm not going to be able to make out with a stranger, but this could be the exact thing I need to do to prove myself to her. To prove that I really am worth training.

And maybe, if I really am able to help this woman find her kid, prove to myself that I *can* be more than a monster.

4

AFTER NICOLE LEAVES, I PULL OUT MY OWN PHONE and spend the rest of the day doing a little Internet research about the Benevolent Society of San Cipriano. Turns out that Saint Cyprian of Antioch, the dude on the candle, was some kind of Turkish sorcerer who converted to Christianity in the 4th century. Even though the Catholic Church stopped recognizing him as a saint in 1969, he still has a "feast day" in the Eastern Orthodox Church. (October 2nd.) And in some parts of the world, like Spain and Latin America, he is directly petitioned for matters related to magic, protection against curses and, what would probably matter most to a teen trying to control her magic, to gain occult knowledge.

As for the Benevolent Society itself, there is only one, and it's located right here in San Francisco in Lower Nob Hill, not more than a fifteen minute walk from Stryker's office. According to their website, it's "a spiritual community inspired by the transformative journey of Saint

Cyprian of Antioch." They offer transcendental workshops and study circles and "believe in the power of redemption, the profound wisdom of ancient practices, and the eternal light of Christian teachings." They've been around for over a hundred years and, while they keep their activities private, they have made sizable monetary contributions to almost every one of City Hall's charitable efforts. Any mention I was able to find about them in the press have come from local politicians throughout the decades thanking them for their exceptional generosity.

Sounds like it could be legit. It also sounds like it could be a cult. Either way, they're definitely worth a visit.

But not today. Tonight, I have a magic watch to steal for an elf, and I can't afford any distractions. I get back to my apartment a little after 6:00 p.m., scarf down a couple Lean Cuisines, and try to distract myself with doom-scrolling the news on my phone while it's charging until I figure it's late enough that most people will be asleep. Then I get into the darkest clothes I own (black T-shirt, dark-wash jeans, dark blue windbreaker, and dressy black Oxfords I've only used twice), take a night bus, and walk the remaining ten minutes to the address the elf gave me.

Now it's almost 3:00 a.m., and I'm standing across the street from a large, charcoal gray, three-story Queen Anne wondering if I actually have the nerve to do this.

The house is in the ritzy Lake Street district, but it looks old, practically abandoned. The dark, gothic towers on its corners, blood-red trim, and arched, stained-glass windows completely clash with the renovated, high-end designs of the rest of the buildings on the street, but it figures I'd have to break into the freaking Haunted Mansion.

I'm sure the rest of the houses all have modern alarms. I bet there's a neighborhood watch, too. I briefly consider trying to be sneaky and making my way in through the back door, but I honestly can't see any way to get to the backyard from the street. The spaces between the house and its neighbors are blocked by tall iron fences with sharp, pointy tips. There's no way these stubby legs are going to get my tender bits past those architectural spear tips in one piece.

So I decide that rather than skulking around, it'd be better to just walk right up the front steps and into the house like I belonged there. Much less suspicious-looking, and the elf did say the door would be unlocked.

As soon as I get on the small porch, I'm confronted by a tarnished brass serpent-head knocker with open-jawed fangs. Its warning isn't limited to an I-will-devour-you glare—I can immediately see it's magicked, which as I mentioned is super-rare. The energy tastes crisp, like a sour apple, and it feels protective—defensive, even. Maybe it just triggers a loud alarm if it recognizes you as a serious threat, like the elf said. Or maybe it blasts a murderous flood of hellfire at intruders, which would make mine officially the shortest criminal career ever.

For a hot second, I consider calling the whole thing off, but then I feel the Obligation. I'd been completely unaware of it all day while I was going along with the plan, but now that I'm hesitating, it wraps its cold, boney fingers around my heart and squeezes.

Ouch.

Right. A promise is a promise. Especially to a fae. There is no turning back.

I take a deep breath, slide my fingers around the door handle, give it a small turn, and brace for impromptu barbecue. I practically wet myself when the serpent's eyes widen and flash gold, but all that happens is the sound of a bolt unlocking with an angry clack. Not from the latch I turned, mind you, but rather from a heavy deadbolt above and inside the door. Then another heavy lock turns. And another.

I cringe back, certain that the current owner of the house is about to confront me. But there's no motion or light coming from the space at the bottom. In fact, the whole house is still dark. And even after several seconds, the door doesn't open.

Which means the elf was right. No one's home.

It also means the door specifically unlocked, with magic, just for me. (And if that doesn't feel full-on "'Will you walk into my parlor?' said the Spider," I don't know what would.)

I wrack my brain, trying to think of some not-death-trap reason why a powerful spell would be in place to let a stranger enter someone else's home. Could the elf have planned this? A spell he cast on it at a distance or something?

There's no way to know for sure. What I do know is if the neighbors are watching, then the longer I stand out here, the faster I move from "looks like that guy could belong" to "you think we should call the cops, hon?"

I push on the door and go inside.

Just as I'd expect, the old hinges squeal, horror-movie style. So, I quickly close the door behind me and take advantage of the only other real party trick I have access to as an incubus who has never fed: low-light vision. I can see in pitch-black almost as clear as day. (Trust me, it's nothing special. Pretty much every paranormal has it. Creatures of the night and all that. But I'll admit, along with not getting colds ever, that is one of the few things I dig about what I am.)

I'm in a large foyer with a wide set of stairs leading up to the second floor. There are high ceilings with intricate but crumbling moldings. Tall windows covered by tattered lace drapes. Peeling wallpaper with faded blue roses. The smell of old wood—dusty pine.

Back in the day, this is where guests would have been received, but there's no furniture. I suddenly remember the door unlocking by itself so my eyes shoot up to the ceiling to make sure there's not a huge net or something ready to land on my head, but I only see a very expensive crystal chandelier. Nothing there.

I force an exhale. I can't keep freaking out. Not only is it way not cool, but any real PI will tell you that you always need to keep your eyes open. You can't do that if you're constantly cringing in fear.

I deliberately slow down and look at what's around me. There are doors to the left and right, both open, and both lead to large, empty rooms. My gut nags at me to try to figure out what the deal is with this house. It doesn't look like someone lives here. It's so empty, it looks like the place has already been burgled, and then meticulously cleaned up after.

But the longer I'm inside, the more time there is for something to go sideways. And if you haven't figured it out, I could easily be, like, the *prince* of sideways. I need to find this watch and get out. And the elf said it should be easy to track down.

There's no obvious magic in sight, so I move to the darkest corner of the foyer, take a deep breath, close my eyes, extend my mind, and try to *feel* if there's any magic around me. Other than the scary door, there's nothing else on this floor. Nothing special under the hardwood beneath my feet. Nothing in the side rooms. Nothing on the stairs. Nothing up—

Then, I see it. Like a beacon in my brain. Usually, I don't get visuals when it comes to magic, I just *sense* whatever is around. But this flares up in my awareness like a point so bright, it almost hurts to think about. And its taste— Well, I actually have no idea what it tastes like! All I'm getting is pure, cold power. It's like crunching down on unflavored ice, brain-freeze and all. Even working with Ms. Stryker, who owns some pretty badass toys, I've never encountered anything so strong.

This has to be what the elf is looking for. And it's in one of the rooms upstairs. Much *farther* into the big creepy house.

Yay.

I slowly make my way on tiptoes up the staircase, afraid of creaking a floorboard and alerting… I don't know what. Another automatic door? Ghosts? Flying monkeys? There really doesn't seem to be anyone here. And it doesn't even matter, because the old wood underneath the blue velvet carpet whines and moans regardless of where I step. It looks like I'll just have to suck it up and accept that I'm going to make noise no matter what I do.

I just need to get this thing and go.

I turn right at the top of the stairs and make my way to the room that's all the way down at the end of the empty hallway. There's more of that faded flower wallpaper along the walls. Doorways to vacant rooms that feel like gaping mouths. The intricate baseboards are chipped and covered in a thin layer of dust.

Like the rest of the hallway, the door ahead of me is also open, but unlike everywhere else, this room is fully furnished. I'm immediately faced with a large gray steel desk. A big gamer-style recliner is shoved to the side. Bookshelves are loaded with dozens of leather-bound books, with a few more spread out on the floor. In the far corner of the room is a closet with another wide-open door. It's completely empty except for one thing— embedded into the floor of that closet is a safe.

That's where the bright magic is coming from.

The safe door itself is about a foot and a half by two feet. Polished burgundy metal with intricate scrollwork. In one corner, the word "Diebold" is engraved. In the center of the safe's lid is an emblem—yet another serpent, but unlike the one on the front door, this one is gilded in gold leaf. And just like the door knocker, this barrier also has protective magic. Part of the reason I didn't sense it before is that it's eclipsed by whatever powerful artifact the safe contains. But the big reason is because the door itself has been torn wide open by God knows what. It's actually resting on its side against an inner wall of the closet. Whatever job that spell was supposed to do, it failed, and there are only sputtering remnants left.

I'd be worried that someone else got here first, but that bright point of light is still blaring out from just over the lip.

I cautiously peer over the side into the well of the safe to find the inside completely bare—except for an old-fashioned silver pocket watch resting dead center. It's latched shut. No chain. But in terms of magic, it blazes like a small, cold sun.

Bingo.

Okay. Time to be smart about this. The thing is clearly crazy powerful, so there's no way I'm going to touch it with my bare hand. I go and tear a page from one of the random books on the floor—it's written in a language I don't understand, even the alphabet is weird, but there's no magic—and then gingerly pick up the watch with it.

I give the artifact, resting in the crumpled paper, a quick look over. Engraved in gold on its front is a tree with a thick trunk and an expansive canopy of highly rendered leaves. Surrounding the tree, along the edges, is an intricate design of raised, interwoven silver lines and loops that looked vaguely familiar to me but I can't exactly place. Even through the page, I can feel some kind of pull, like it wants me to learn all its secrets.

Like I could stare at it for hours.

…

Okay! Yep, *that's* dangerous!

I shake off the bizarre compulsion, wrap the watch up in the torn page as best I can, shove it into the back pocket of my jeans, and turn for the door, ready to book it out of there.

It. Is. Time. To. Go!

Then two things happen.

The bright, blaring magic that hurt my brain collapses to the barest whisper.

And I hear a voice. Small, dry, and raspy.

"Please... Please *stop*... I'll tell you what you want to know... Just please... No more... No more..."

It's someone sobbing. Someone *in the room*. It's coming from behind the desk.

I freeze, still halfway in the corner alcove, kneeling in front of the safe.

Crap! There couldn't be anyone else here! I checked!

(*Did* I check? I think I checked! *Crap!*)

As slow as I can, trying to make zero noise, I peer around the open door of the closet and behind the desk. And there, sprawled prone on the floor, is a young man, close to my age, tears streaming down his face.

He's got wavy blond hair. Medieval-style clothes— we're talking a cloak, soft gray wool trousers, and a woven green shepherd shirt that goes down halfway to his knees. Bare feet. His face is covered with bruises, his nose is bleeding, and every inch of bare skin looks scratched up. Raw red nicks and cuts everywhere.

There's no way in hell I would have missed him! He simply wasn't there before.

At the sight of me, he immediately cringes away, scooting back, shoulders hunched up to his ears, like I might come at him at any moment.

But then he stops. His eyes—a striking bright blue I

can see from halfway across the room—scrunch with recognition.

"Alvin? What are *you* doing here?!"

My breath catches mid-inhale, while my brain tries to process that bizarre question. (This is the second complete stranger who seems to know who I am today. Is this guy in cahoots with the elf? But then why would he be surprised? And why does he look like he's been rolled through broken glass?)

The boy reaches up and grips the edge of the desk, trying to get to his feet. But not halfway up, he winces in sharp pain and his legs buckle. And since my brain is still in some kind of overflow loop, before I even think about it, I'm lunging forward, down onto my knees, to keep him from falling.

"Oh! Crap! Here, let me, uh…!" I blurt out, like I'm helping a sweet old lady with a bag of groceries that's slipping from her hands.

I get my hands under his armpits, and just like that, *my arms totally wrap around the guy.*

Before, I was freaking out over the smallest thing. Now, I'm rushing in close to someone who literally appeared out of nowhere—because he knows my name? (Or is it because he looks cute and vulnerable?) I mean, what for the love of all that is holy is *wrong* with me?!

I get that I don't have any real training as a paranormal PI, but I don't even have words to tell you how stupid I'm being right now. A "hot guy in distress" suddenly appears out of nowhere and acts like he knows who I am *while I'm in the middle of stealing a powerful magic artifact from someone's house.* (Someone who, for all I know, is a wizard as dangerous as Ms. Stryker.) This could be a trap. This guy could be a monster in disguise. Hell, why choose?! He could be both a trap *and* a monster in disguise!

But here I am! Pressed up next to him, like a total idiot. All my tender vitals right within easy claw-scooping distance. He grips both hands around my shoulders as we rise together. He's only, like, an inch taller than me, so we're basically face-to-face. I mean, he's close enough for me to *smell* him! (Cloves and campfire? Not unpleasant at all, to be honest.) (Oh, for Pete's sake, can I please focus?!)

This should be about when the fangs come out. You know, right before he swallows my head. But all he does is smile, new tears forming in his eyes.

"Jaysus. It really *is* you! Thank the Gods!"

Even through the blood and scratches, he has the most gentle face. Handsome in a sweet, boy-next-door kind of way. And he folds himself against my chest and belly like hugging me is the most natural thing in the world. Like he couldn't be happier. Like no one else has ever done with me before. And it feels—

Oh. My. *God!*

I really need to get it together!

I peel myself off his body and try to look stern. (Or, at the very least, not like an easy meal!) "Look. *How* do you know me? Who are you?" Actually, let's not beat around the bush! "*What* are you?!"

His eyes widen. "Right! Of course, you wouldn't—" He glances up and off to the left, and his eyes shimmer. (Accessing some kind of clairvoyance, maybe?) "Oh. Oh. I see! You were *sent* to find the watch. Ah, shite! My name is

Collin. And I promise I'll tell you everything, but you need to get out of here before—"

A loud creak sounds out from the lower floor, and the boy immediately tenses. But you don't need to be some kind of psychic to know exactly what made *that* noise.

It's the front door opening. Someone's home.

"Oh, no," he says. "It's too late."

5

WE BOTH FREEZE FOR TWO FULL SECONDS. NOT even breathing, just holding each other. And then Collin's eyes clear, and his face snaps tight with determination.

"Don't worry. We'll be grand! The front door has a magical alarm—that's probably why they're here. If they don't hear us, they'll search the downstairs rooms first. This way!" Collin grips my wrist and points down at the floor. His hand is warm and soft. I finally notice he's speaking with an accent. British? No, *Irish*. (I think.)

In the direction of his finger, glowing blue footsteps emerge on the carpet and go out into the hallway. The phantasms are shoe-shaped and look like what you'd find in an old-timey dance-instruction book. The projection would be an impressive display of spellcraft, except *I'm not sensing any magic at all*. Not from the shimmering guides or my new Irish buddy.

The boy gives my arm a tug, and meets my eyes, earnest and urgent. "You just need to follow the steps,

Alvin. Keep your weight centered on the middle of your foot, and the wood won't creak. I promise!"

Uh-huh.

So, yeah, it looks like I've got two choices. I do what this guy is telling me to—even though I have no idea how he knows me, how he's creating this glamour, who he is, or even *what* he is—and hope he isn't leading me to a dismal end. Or I can stand stupidly in this room, trying to come up with a better plan, all the while freaking the hell out, until whoever just let themselves in makes their way up here.

I start my little dance forward on those glowing shoe prints. *Cha cha cha!*

The steps are widely spaced apart. Apparently there aren't many places under the carpet that won't scream in protest, so I'm practically doing splits trying to follow Collin's directions. Meanwhile, even though his legs aren't any longer than mine, he's skipping on ahead of me, smoothly landing on each step like Fred freaking Astaire.

"Alvin, you need to hurry. They aren't going to stay downstairs for long. Oh! Shite! I can't believe I almost forgot! Once you get to the doorway, you'll trigger the defenses. You're going to need to—"

He's not doing anything to keep his voice down, and since I'm moving as fast as I can (at his urging!), I'm already *halfway through* the doorway, leg fully outstretched toward the next spot, before he even mentions it. But when I glare at him, I find his gaze locked on the doorway's upper beam. That's when I see a set of blocky runes above me flaring to life with serious crisp-apple-flavored magic that somehow I missed. This spell doesn't just feel protective, it feels ferocious, and it activates with a roar of power just over my head.

The good news is that nothing actually bad seems to happen as I jolt ahead. The taste goes from tart to sweet and its magic flutters away, like cherry blossoms in the wind.

The bad news is that I'm so freaked out by the sudden magic, I pitch forward awkwardly, and my knee crashes against the floor with a hard thud.

"Ow!" I exclaim, because I'm an idiot.

Creeeeeeak! the floorboards exclaim, because of course they do.

I freeze. The boy freezes. Maybe whoever's down there missed it. Maybe they were far enough away that they didn't—

Multiple footsteps from below start running for the stairs. It's not a whoever. It's a *bunch* of whoevers. And they are coming for me. Right now.

The dance steps on the carpet disappear, and the boy points at what looks like a small handle, painted the same color as the wallpaper, sticking out of the wall of the hallway about ten feet away. I probably would still have missed it, except there's also now a big glowing blue arrow blinking above it.

"This way!" he cries.

Well, crap! What else am I going to do?! I bolt for where the arrow is pointing, rip the handle back, and I'm shocked to find it pulls out a tall rectangular slice of the wall that reveals a completely *separate* set of rough-looking wooden stairs leading up and down.

"These are what the servants used to use," he says. "Quick! Lock the door behind you!"

On the other side of the door, there's a small exterior bolt lock. Like the rest of the house, it looks over a hundred years old. But it also has a small serpent's head on the lock case, and when I slam the section of wall back and twist the thumbturn knob, its eyes glow. Tart magic immediately spreads over the whole door, like a rolling wave.

I barely get my hand off the lock when something thunderously strong rams itself against the other side of the door with a guttural snarl. This side of the wall is completely unfinished, and the bare bricks between the beams that surround the entry cough out sprays of century-old dirt from the impact. The door still holds, but only because of the magic that just activated.

Collin tugs quickly on my hand with both of his. "You need to move, Alvin! Right now!"

"Yeah, okay!" I sputter, my heart pounding.

The wood in the stairwell looks thin and rotten—apparently protecting servants from occupational safety hazards wasn't really a thing in San Francisco back in the day. The blond dude easily trots down each of the sketchy-looking wooden steps, while I lurch from side to side on the narrow boards after him, trying to suss out the thicker parts of the wood while hauling ass. He's still Fred Astaire, and I'm clumsy as a freaking dancing bear. At this point, my fate is completely in this strange boy's hands. I have no idea what we're up against. I have no plan, no way to protect myself, and no idea how to get out from here.

We get to the landing at the bottom of the servants'

stairwell. It leads to some kind of narrow passageway sandwiched within the structure of the house. The boy starts sprinting down it. "This way!"

"Where are we going?! What's after us?!" I call after him. Not that knowing that information is really going to help me at all right now, but it'd be nice to know *something*!

I'm immediately sorry I asked, because just down the hall, three hulking, man-shaped figures burst through the side of the wall in an explosion of plaster to block our way. Collin immediately stops, and I crash into his back, which does a pretty good job of stopping me in my tracks as well.

The three freakishly large dudes are less than fifty feet away. They're in black suits, black button-down shirts, open collar, no tie. And they're wearing sunglasses (at night!). They see me and their jaws, packed with fangs, open far too wide while they let out blood-chilling snarls in perfect unison.

Oh, fuck me. They're *vampires*.

I straight-up scream.

I've never actually met a vampire in person, but here are the deets: They're crazy-strong, really fast, can soak up a ton of damage before even starting to slow down, have claws (!), travel in packs, and yes, if they get to you, they will eat you. (Or *drink* you, if you want to be pedantic.) Unlike what you see in the movies, they aren't cute and sparkle-y, or suave and sexy. They are feral beasts and have legit bloodlust, so there's no reasoning with them if they consider you prey.

The undead creatures charge at us, claws out, hissing

like pissed-off cats. In TV shows, vampires have full-on super-speed, turning into mere blurs when they move. And okay, vampires are fast, but if they were *that* fast, there wouldn't be any humans left in this world—just little drops of blood flecked all over the place, left over from the turbo-undead apocalypse. But even twice as fast as a normal human is still hella quick, especially when it's coming for a chubster like me who would be lucky to hit twelve miles an hour in a hot sprint.

I turn back for the servants' stairs. (Maybe I can make it through the locked hallway door above and then down the other stairwell before they get me? Or try my luck on the third floor instead?) (Yeah, I don't like my chances, either!) Then I see it. A rotten, short plank of wood hanging loose between a couple beams inside the scaffolding of the wall. I yank it out as hard as I can and pray it'll have an edge sharp enough to sub for a wooden stake. (Which I'm pretty sure is one of the things that actually *does* work against vamps.) (And yeah, I don't like my chances with this plan, either!)

But Collin grabs my arm and points behind the vampires, who have stopped about halfway to us. "Alvin, look!"

I follow his finger to see a very big man with a very big shotgun now stepping through the hole in the wall the vamps made. He's got a full-on Kevlar duster. Knee-high ass-kicking boots. Thick black Kevlar pants. High-tech night-vision goggles. And his massive biceps, chest, and thighs stretch out all that shiny cowhide like freaking sausage casings. I swear it's like he enters the hallway in slo-mo. You can practically hear the Terminator music swell around us.

Only one kind of dude would walk toward vampires with that kind of swagger.

He's a Monster Hunter.

Monster Hunters are another part of the paranormal world I've only heard about, and you'd think his surprisingly timely arrival would be a good thing. I do have a pressing monster problem at the moment, after all.

But let's not forget—I'm a monster, too.

He sees the vampires. He sees me. And he barks out, "Hey!"

Before the vampires can even get out another one of their terrifying snarls, he blasts one full in the chest. And shockingly, the vamp immediately crumples, which means that whatever buckshot he's carrying, it ain't the kind you can get at Walmart. I know at this close range, the spread of any pellets shouldn't extend wider than a few inches, but it's so goddamn loud, I still crouch my ass down into as tiny a ball as I can against the corner of the hallway wall. And just for good measure, I also wrap my arms around up and over my ears. It would be just my luck to die from a ricochet of anti-paranormal ammunition.

Collin, though, just stands there, *smiling* at the Hunter as he blasts a hole in the head of another vampire that was stupid enough to run at him. This time, some of the shot travels on through, creating an explosion of brick shrapnel just a few feet from the kid's side. He doesn't even flinch.

"*Dude!*" I hiss at Collin, eyes wide, pointing rapidly to the ground next to me.

"Ah!" he says. "Sorry, lad! Of course!"

He plops himself down next to me, but instead of cowering and covering his head like a sensible person, he throws an arm around my shoulders and hugs me close. Then he starts *stroking my hair with his fingers*! Gah!

"It's going to be okay, Alvin. It's going to be okay. Trust me, this fella's class!"

No. It is not going to be okay, because once this dude gets through the vampires, I'll have officially moved on from the frying pan portion of this misadventure directly into the *fire*.

You see, Ms. Stryker might hunt monsters, but she's not actually a Monster Hunter (capital M, capital H). From the little that Mom told me, these dudes are members of ancient clans that have dedicated their lives to exterminating supernatural threats. They are the primary reason the population of supernatural beings in the world is so small. For a Monster Hunter, there's no such thing as choosing "to live a normal human life." The only good paranormal is a dead paranormal. Unlike for the fae, she didn't have to give me any specific advice to steer clear of them, because they were the bogeymen of *almost every single one* of her bedtime stories to me. (Yes, my mother told me horror stories to "help" me get to sleep. It took me forever to realize it was to get me to stop asking her to tuck me in at night.)

Monster Hunters aren't paranormals, but somehow, they've found a way to massively boost their human capabilities. They're strong and fast, and they heal quick, too. They're supposedly masters of all forms of weaponry (which are almost always enhanced to be lethal to magical creatures like yours truly). And if that's not bad enough, word on the street is that they can *smell* paranormal blood.

This is an absolute nightmare.

I need to get out of here. Right now.

6

BLAM! THE FINAL VAMPIRE BITES THE DUST. I DON'T even bother to look back to see if the undead creature was able to get anywhere near the badass Monster Hunter before it was cut down. Instead, I jump to my feet and run for the stairs in a blind panic.

"Wait!" Mr. Terminator yells, voice deep and gruff, clearly expecting complete compliance.

I am not waiting. I book it down the hallway, still gripping the shard of wood.

Collin jogs alongside, having no trouble keeping up. "Alvin? What are you doing?"

I ignore him and almost get to the first stair, but the Monster Hunter is so fast, he swings himself in front of me before I can even put a single foot on that OSHA disaster and grabs my shoulders, fully stopping me. He's well over six feet. I am child-sized compared to him.

"Slow down, buddy. You don't need to run. I got 'em."

He's less than a foot away from me, his shotgun shoved into some kind of back holster peeking out from under his duster. Without even thinking, I shove back hard against his chest with both of my palms, dropping the stake and using all my strength to try to get out of whatever his "paranormal-creature-smelling" range might be. But at this point I'm a sweaty mess, I've got the weak-ass muscles of a committed couch potato, and his grip is so strong, I don't go anywhere.

In response, he pulls me in tight, into a full-on hug. (Oh, my God! What's with all the hugs, scary strangers?!)

"Breathe. *Breathe*! You're safe. I promise."

He squeezes me tighter. I *can't* breathe. I am so going to die.

I stop fighting him, and let my body go limp. His hands return to my shoulders. He holds me up, arms extended a bit, so he can get a good look at me with those night-vision goggles. He then jerks his head back with surprise. "*Hm*," he says.

And there it is. Game over. He now knows what I am. I drop my gaze, totally telegraphing my plan to knee him in the balls, but it doesn't matter because our bodies are still so close, I don't think I could pull it off. I am screwed!

Desperately, I look over at Collin—who the Monster Hunter is completely ignoring, by the way—wondering if the blond boy has any dance steps to get me out of *this* one.

But he's just standing there, smiling at the two of us. He then gives me an encouraging nod, like "You've got this!"

Thanks, dude.

I'm so caught up with my latest freak-out that I almost miss what the Hunter says next. "Wait. Are you like me?"

I turn back to him. *Um, what?*

"Um, what?" I say.

He lets go of my shoulders and points at the broken piece of wood I dropped on the floor. "Are you a vampire hunter?"

My jaw hangs stupidly.

He then gives my short, pudgy body another once-over with his eyes. "And… is it just you here?"

Well, at least he's *polite* about his absolute and total disbelief that I would have any chance against a vampire. And he doesn't seem to see Collin at all. Which, now that I think of it, probably means that Collin is a ghost. That *would* explain how the Irish boy knew about the servant's stairs, and maybe even how he's creating the phantasmal images without magic. Of course, I can't usually see dead people, let alone trip over them—fed or unfed, that's not part of the incubus power set—which means I've probably just figured out what the artifact in my pocket does. For all the good it'll do me right now.

The Monster Hunter seems to be expecting an answer, so I say, "Uh, yeah. Just me."

His brows scrunch. "I'm a Hunter with the Peralta Clan. Who are you with?" His voice is deep and gruff, like he doesn't use it much.

I'm not a good liar. I know this. But I also know that if you're going to lie, you want to keep as many real details as you can. You're much less likely to forget what you said, and when you do lie, you can really make it count.

"I'm not a Hunter. Not like you. I'm training to be a magic-using paranormal investigator. I started an investigation, looking for a missing girl, and wound up here. I honestly didn't know there would be vampires. The wood was kind of... an improvised thing."

His shoulders visibly relax as I start to make sense in his world. "*Right*. Well, I've been tracking these vamps for a while. Then I heard a scream." His brows scrunch. "You can use magic?"

Okay... He's clearly not a man of many words, but it sounds like he *might* be buying what I'm selling. It doesn't seem like he suspects what I am, anyway, at least not yet—which could give me a chance. Monster Hunters might hate paranormals, but when it comes to protecting other humans, they like to think of themselves as heroes. Time to lean into that so he doesn't look at me any more closely.

I take a step away from him, glance down, and scrub the back of my neck bashfully.

"A little. Just passive stuff. I'm not very good. If you hadn't shown up, I would have been toast." I widen my eyes and try to straight-up channel helpless, innocent victim. "I can't thank you enough, dude. You *saved* me."

The hint of a smile breaking above his valiantly strong jaw tells me I'm right on target. He tilts his head and takes me in again. I know what I must look like: short, baby-faced, sweaty hot mess—just who he'd expect to need extra help in a crisis. (What can I say? Sometimes being pathetic can work for you.)

He clasps my shoulder again with his strong grip (Gah! What is with all the touching?!) and straight-up grins. Underneath those night-vision goggles, it's frightening. "Don't feel bad, bro. Been in a few tough spots myself." His eyebrows raise slightly. "Hold on! Shoulda checked. You hurt?" The fingers of his free hand reach up and quickly slide over and under my chin, which causes me immediately to jerk back in shock.

Dude! Why are you feeling up my face?!

"Sorry…" he says, quickly withdrawing his hand, embarrassed. "I just… *Vampires*, you know…"

Right. He just wants to make sure I don't turn *into* a monster. Because I'm *totally* not a monster *right now*. And I just need to put his mind at ease about that.

"Oh, yeah, right…" I mumble, terrified that this is going to be the moment he'll catch me out. Who knows, maybe Hunters can sense paranormals through their pores?

I tentatively expose my neck, feeling hella vulnerable, and he glides his fingers smoothly, back and forth, over the veins around my throat. He's quite thorough and very focused, taking several seconds, even gliding his fingertips around the back of my head. His huge arm muscles flex, and I'm surprised at how soft this gruff warrior's touch is. It feels like he's handling fine china. It doesn't even tickle. But this "bite check" goes on for so freaking long, my heart starts to hammer, which he *has* to feel under my skin.

But if he does, he doesn't say anything, except "You're clean." He finally removes his hands with a small pleased smile. But then he just stands there, head cocked a little to the left, gazing at me with those night-vision specs, clearly in no rush to leave.

Crap! Does he know? Why is he just staring at me? Gah!

Time to go!

"Good, good," I sputter out, feeling the beet-red flush in my cheeks and taking a few more steps away from him.

"So, uh... *Thank you* for the rescue and everything, but it's late, and I really should *bounce*..."

He startles a little, like I just woke him from a daydream. "Oh. Right. Of course. I should get you out of here."

Before I can protest, his hand is on my back, and he's guiding me through the hole in the hallway wall into what looks like what was probably a dining room, and then out a vacant pantry to the fenced back yard. The solid wooden back door is busted in, which is probably how he got inside. (Um, there were only a handful of seconds between when I screamed and when he showed up. Exactly how strong and fast is this guy?)

He then brings us over a cracked and worn brick path to what had been a padlocked entry through the iron yard fence to the main street. But before he opens it, I see the heavy lock resting on one of the fence posts, twisted open. (Oh, right. He's very, *very* strong.)

He cautiously opens the gate and leans through. After literal gunshots coming from the house, I'd expect to see a serious police presence, probably with guns of their own out. But he says, "It's clear. We're good."

Then his hand is again on my back, guiding me along, like he's my uncle and I'm five years old. The only sound is the gentle roll of lonely, late-night traffic on the distant artery of Geary Street. There aren't any cops. Doesn't look like any of the neighbors have even turned on a light. Does the magic of the house muffle gunshots, too?

I glance back at Collin, fully expecting him to be trapped at the boundary of the fence. I'm no ghost expert, but Stryker mentioned once that hauntings have very specific limits, usually defined by the property line of wherever the person died. But he trots right out after us.

Seeing me catch his eye, he grins and gives me a wink. "See? Told you it would all work out! He's class, isn't he?"

Well, looks like the dangerous Monster Hunter has got the ghost vote! But not all of us are dead… yet.

Once we're on the sidewalk, I quickly twist and wheel myself out from under his hand and, backing away, quietly say, "Okay. Thank you *so much*. Seriously. I'm going to go find the bus now, or maybe call an Uber. But really, this was great and—"

He raises his palm, clearly expecting me to stop talking. Which I do.

"I'll drive you," he says. His voice is low, practically a growl, and he makes it feel like an offer I can't refuse.

Maybe I should just run. But he's faster than me. And he's got a freaking shotgun in the holster on his back.

Before I can debate any more about it, his hand is right back there on my shoulder, leading me down the street.

"This way," he says.

I debate about arguing with him and pitching a fit. Asserting my autonomy as, you know, an actual grown-ass man who can get himself home all by himself. But considering how committed he seems to be to providing door-to-door service, that would probably make me look even more suspicious.

At this point, he's either on to me or he's not. If he is, there's no getting away. I can't outrun him, and since he's walking down the middle of the street in Arnold Schwarzenegger combat gear, he doesn't seem at all worried about anyone thinking he's an active shooter. If he wanted to, he could just blow my head off. But if he's not on to me, and I push too hard, he might start to wonder why I'm so eager to get away from the hero who just saved my life. I'm supposed to be grateful and trusting, right? The more I protest, the more he'll be tempted to question the story that I, myself, put into his head. It's my own damn fault for feeding into his stupid ego!

In the PI world, very rarely is "rolling with it" the smart play. But it's kind of feeling like the *only* play right now.

We get to his car, which he parked a block and a half away from the house. It's a late-model tank-like black SUV with dark windows. (Because of course he rides like the freaking US Special Forces!) He unlocks the passenger side, and I slide into the front seat before he slams the door, leaving me in a tight, enclosed space where even *I* smell my own anxiety sweat. Soon to be with a highly trained Monster Hunter who might sniff me out at any second. And where I literally have nowhere to hide.

Well done, Alvin. Well done.

7

Before he takes the driver's seat, the Monster Hunter chucks his night vision goggles in the back, slides out of his Kevlar duster, then carefully places his shotgun with its back scabbard holster in the footwell behind me. (Within easy grabbing distance, I'm sure!)

The duster gets folded and put over the goggles on the back seat next to Collin, who now sits inside, gaping out his (still closed) window with the eager expression of a dog on day trip to the park. That he's made it into the car at all is hella strange. I don't care how liberally old San Francisco drew those property lines, we're over a block and a half away from the front lawn of that corner mansion! He really shouldn't be able to exist this far away from the house, not if he died there! I'm beginning to wonder if now *I'm* the thing he's haunting. Could the watch be some kind of ghost magnet?

The Monster Hunter drops into the driver's seat next to me, and for the first time, I get to see his face without the high-tech optics. And let's just say, it's not what I expected. First of all, he's young. Like still-in-his-twenties young. Black hair, dark skin. (He said he was part of the "Peralta clan," so what does that mean, Mexican ancestry? Portuguese? Maybe a mix?) And his chiseled, clean cut, perfectly symmetrical features look like they should belong to a fitness influencer with a million followers, not a cut-throat warrior. He does have one small scar on his left eyebrow, but it just makes him look more... *dashing*, I guess. What I'm trying to say is that this paranormal-killing-machine is actually really freaking handsome. Super-model handsome. Much, much hotter than any Monster Hunter has any right to be.

And no, for the record, that doesn't mean I want to pounce on him right now. Chances are he's still going to murder me, which is kind of a boner-kill, you know? But I don't do well around cute guys in general, so his Instagram thirst-trap looks are just one more reason for me to feel completely freaked out. Because, you know, I needed something else to freak out about tonight. Thank you, Universe!

I realize I'm full-on staring, which (crap!) he totally just noticed, so I follow Collin's lead and quickly turn my head to look out the window. Maybe I can just do that the whole way home, avoid any conversation, and—

His hand grips my knee, and it's all I can do not to squeak and leap up in fright. (Let's be real: I actually do both those things.) I then glance over at him through the corner of my eye, and he's looking at me with a smile that smolders with amusement. (Dude, your fingers are inches away from my inner thigh! How do you expect me to react?!)

"Still a little tense after those vamps, huh? Let's get you home. What's your address?"

I force myself not to hyperventilate while I debate about whether I should lie about this. I probably should just give him some corner near my bus line and hoof it from there. But somehow I just *know* he'll want to watch me go into my building, to make sure I "make it back safely." And anyway, it's like 3:30 in the morning by now and, to be honest, I just want to crawl into my own bed, pull the covers over my head, and pretend I never was born.

"I'm, uh, at Jones and O'Farrell." I get the words out, but my throat is so tight, it's sounds like I'm having a second puberty.

"All right."

He removes his hand (thank you!), but then reaches over me, bicep grazing my nipple (!), bringing our faces *inches* apart (!!), so he can pull my seatbelt around me and snap it in. (OMG, *dude!* I swear, I'm really not five years old!)

I'm now literally locked in place.

He responds to my look of terror with a wink. "Safety first, right?" (It's like he's *enjoying* messing with me!) Then he sticks out his massive hand for a handshake, his smolder-grin broadening. "I'm Rafa."

His teeth are perfectly white and straight. Because of course they are.

Well, I'm in it for keeps now. I have to keep playing along. After jerking forward way too quickly and triggering the seatbelt (*Yep! I'm trapped!*), I manage to shake his hand, doing my best to give him a firm grip. (The kind I figure he's used to from his other paranormal-slaughtering bros.) I don't even bother trying to make up a name. I'm so spun up at this point, there's no way I'd get a false one out in time without looking suspicious.

"I'm Alvin," I croak, before clearing my throat. "Nice to meet you. Thank you again, uh, for everything."

Crap. My voice is so high-pitched, I might as well be five!

But he just gives me another wink and says "Nice name." He then starts the car, gliding it smoothly onto the street with polished confidence. "So, if you don't mind me asking, how old are you?"

Seriously, the last thing I'm up for is chit-chat at this point. And the more I say, the more I risk tipping him off. So I keep it short.

"I'm twenty-two."

"Oh. Nice. *Good.*" I cock an eyebrow at that (it's clearly weird, right?!) so he adds. "You just looked… younger."

Of *course*, I did! Now I can't help asking: "And how old are you, dude?"

"Twenty-three." He gives me another one of those smolder-smiles. "Never met a paranormal investigator before. One of my uncles worked with one, though. In Chicago. Said he could do crazy shit. Shoot fireballs, turn invisible, that kind of thing."

"Uh-huh," I say, wishing *I* could turn invisible.

I'm expecting him to ask me about what kind of spells I can cast (um, zero!), but he actually just keeps going. Drops a whole string of sentence fragments about how this uncle from back East ("Stewie"—more distant cousin than uncle, apparently) and this Chicago PI took out a small army of goblins. I got the impression before that he didn't talk much, but here he is, practically giving me a full soliloquy. It's like he's trying hard to be casual. (As casual as a killing machine can be, anyway.) Or worse, like he's trying to hide something.

My anxiety cranks up a notch. What if this is all an act, and he *does* know what I am? Maybe he wouldn't want to murder me in his car. That'd make an awful mess, right? But I'm sure they have lovely, easy-to-clean dissection rooms back at Monster Hunter Central. Better to put me at ease in the moment so I go there quietly, right?

(And okay, I know I'm probably overreacting! If I'm being honest, he hasn't done anything, except be *overbearingly* nice to me. But I'm telling you, there's an edge in his voice that makes me feel like something else is going on here, so I can't help but stew with my head spinning around and around questions like: "What is this dude's deal?" "What does he really want with me?" And "How exactly can I throw myself out of the car without giving him any warning?") My anxiety is so freaking triggered, I need to grab my own fingers to keep from nervously tapping on the arm rest.

"Psst, Alvin! Tell him you just want to help people!"

I snap out of my fear spiral and notice Collin is leaning over my shoulder from the back seat, practically hissing in my ear. I must have been spacing out for a bit there. Rafa is glancing over at me, eyebrows raised, clearly having asked me a question.

I really, really, really don't want to seem weird to this Monster Hunter right now. And I have no idea what he asked me so, as instructed, I say, "Um, you know, I just want to help people?"

That seems to have been the right thing to say because Rafa chuckles, pleased. "Cool. *I* was born into the family business, but you actually sought it out on your own? That's fire. When did you find out you had magical talent?"

"Good job!" Collin says. "Now tell him, 'When I was fifteen, I realized I could sense magic, and it wasn't long after that, I wondered if there was some way I could use what I could do to make a difference.'"

That is, of course, totally not true. I was *born* with the ability to sense magic, and it was only after meeting Stryker a few months ago that I got this idea about trying to use my innate magic to help people. Collin is apparently still feeding me lines, which ordinarily would be extremely annoying. But I'm so up my own butt at the moment, I don't think I could remember what year it is, let alone the cover story I told Ms. Stryker. So, I just repeat Collin's words like I'm some TV news anchor, which gets Rafa nodding.

"Huh," he says. "You really sense magic. I know a lot of *paranormals* can do that, but I heard someplace it's super rare in humans."

Oh, crap.

My eyes must be as wide as saucers, because Collin squeezes my arm. "Don't worry, Alvin. We've got this! He's not going to go down any path we don't want him to. You just need to change the subject. Ask him why he works on his own. They almost never do that."

Sure, okay, whatever!

"Heh, heh. I guess it is kinda rare," I say. "But, uh, so is working on your own as a Monster Hunter, right?"

Rafa frowns, and his face immediately darkens. For a moment, I wonder if Collin just threw me under a completely different bus. But then he says, a bit husky "Yeah. It is." He glances down, and his eyes look… sad?

Silence then hangs in the air. We aren't talking anymore (which is a plus!) but for some reason, I feel low-key bad for bumming this guy out.

But Collin is super chipper. "Brilliant, Alvin! Now touch his shoulder and say, 'What we do. It *can* be a little lonely sometimes, huh?'"

I glare at the ghost. Where the hell is he going with this? I want to get out of this dude's car, not bill him for a therapy session. But Collin glares back with meaning, and since apparently I'm in no state to drive this crazy train I've got myself on, I ask the damn question. (But I don't touch Rafa's shoulder. No more touching with the stupid, deadly Monster Hunter!)

Yet again, the script Collin is serving up seems to work. Rafa seems surprised by my response, then smiles back at me. (Less smolder this time, more vulnerability.) "Yeah. Sometimes it can be. That's something you understand, too, huh?"

Yeah, dude, I can understand the human emotion of loneliness. You see, I really am a grown man. But obviously my reasons aren't going to be the same as someone who looks like you!

I glance away so he doesn't see my annoyance, and that's when I notice out my side window that we are now parked just a few buildings away from my apartment. We made it all the way home, and I didn't even realize! I'm so relieved, that when I look back, I'm completely caught off guard to find he's unbuckled his seat belt and is leaning closer to me.

And his expression is oddly *intense*.
And curious.
And...
Oh!

He's not *quite* in kissing range—there's still a respectful distance there—but even someone as clueless as me can tell where this is headed, though it makes *absolutely zero sense*.

I mean, what in the freaking hell of anime porn is actually going on here?! It sure can't be incubus powers. I might not have any experience using those abilities, but Mom's made it clear they aren't subtle, especially when it comes to affecting other people. Same way you'd know if you'd grabbed somebody's throat, I'd know if they were active.

"You're doing great!" Collin chimes in. "Now, tell him that yes, you *do* feel a bit lonely! And that it's actually class to meet someone else who gets that. And then casually ask if he needs to use your bathroom or something. Or no! Offer him *a glass of water!* That's better! Then throw in something casual but a little flirty like, 'I bet you must be *parched* after killing those vampires...'"

Excuse me, *WHAT?!*

I give Collin the fastest side eye on record, then squeak out to Rafa, "Well, look at that! It's my apartment building! That's me! Thank you again! I guess we'll see each other around! Take care!"

I literally sound like I'm having a heart attack, but in the space of those words, I'm still able to pop open my seatbelt and throw myself out of the SUV before he tries to get his arm around me or find some other way to keep me there.

But before I even make it around the hood, Rafa is out of the car himself and right next to me. "What's wrong?"

"Yeah, Alvin," says Collin, suddenly standing next to the Monster Hunter and looking completely baffled, "what are you at?"

The ghost then leans his entire upper body toward Rafa, eyebrows raised, and gives me a pointed, expectant glare.

What is going on?!

"I just… really have to get to bed! That's all!" I stammer, while backpedaling toward my building as fast as my blocky, little feet can manage.

Rafa keeps pace with me, his long legs having no trouble matching my speed. He's frowning. "Well, let me at least make sure you get up to your place okay."

"No!" I shout, slamming my palm on his chest. I hit way harder than I should and it stops both of us in the middle of the street.

Rafa glances down at my hand, and I swear, he actually looks a little hurt.

But if the Monster Hunter looks bummed, Collin seems he might actually have some kind of meltdown. "Alvin—are you totally blind? This gorgeous fella *wants to come up to your apartment!*"

And okay, yes, at this point, even I can tell that *whatever* Rafa wants from me right now, murder isn't on the menu. And maybe, because it seems to be opposite day, he really *does* want to see me naked, and not just to mark me up for dissection!

But it's all too much! This random, blond spirit is pushing hard for some kind of sex connection between me and the Monster Hunter, for God knows what reason (leave it to me to be haunted by a *pervy* ghost!) And, of course, the more Rafa gets to know me, the more likely he is to want to shoot me. Plus I still have to find a way to get the artifact I stole from vampires (!) to I'm-A-Royal-Asshole Elf before he decides I've broken our deal and outs me to the feds (even though I don't have his address or anything!) And finally, let's remember: I can't have sex with anyone because *there's a real chance I could kill them!*

I feel like I'm drowning. I literally can't breathe. I just need to get away!

"I'm sorry, dude! I'm really, really sorry!"

I turn and make a mad dash for my apartment building, and I'm behind the front door and in the foyer before he or Collin can get out another single, stupid word.

Once inside, back pressed against the security glass, I take a full ten seconds to slow my breathing enough so I don't straight-up pass out. Only then do I look back through the transparent barrier.

Rafa is still out there, standing in the road. He's staring at the door I basically slammed in his face. And I swear, he looks confused, lost, and sad.

Like I freaking broke this paranormal-killing machine's heart.

I mean, fuck my life. Seriously.

8

I turn away, and Collin is somehow standing just to my right. He looks at me with concern, like I might need a hug.

I do freaking need a hug. But so not from him!

I give him my most dangerous glare. "Not *one* word…" And I start stalking up the grungy stairs to my apartment.

Collin follows a step behind me, and he looks contrite. "I'm sorry, Alvin. I genuinely thought you were into him."

"And why would you think that?!" I swear if this ghost can read my innermost thoughts, I am done!

"Oh. Well, *mostly* because of your microexpressions and the way you stared. But when he rubbed your knee, I also noticed that the circumference of your penis expanded by just over 2mm—which, granted, isn't the most *reliable* metric, but coupled with how *handsome* Rafa is—"

Oh. My. God.

I stop just inside the stairwell of my floor and look

daggers at him. "Are you telling me you had your hands *down my pants* while we were in the car?!"

He folds his arms like I'm the crazy one. "No! Don't be daft. You'd *totally* feel that." His expression then softens. He reaches out, leaning in, and warmly squeezes the side of my shoulder. "You just seemed so freaked out, lad, I was worried about you! So, I kept an eye on all your biological processes to make sure you weren't going to, you know, need medical attention."

Gah!

I rip open the door and launch myself into the hallway.

"What kind of insane robot-ghost *are* you?" It's almost four in the morning, and I say this way too loud, but at this point, I don't care. I *am* done!

I shove my keys into the stupid, sticky lock my landlord will never fix, and Collin follows me into my tiny one-bedroom apartment, despite my very best attempt to slam the door on him.

"I'm not a robot. Or a ghost. At least, not really." He stands right in front of me, his chest puffed up a little. "I'm an Avatar of Knowledge. *The* Avatar of Knowledge, actually."

I stare at him for several seconds. The whole time, he just smiles back at me, like I'm his long-lost best friend, and we haven't seen each other for years. The sweet expression makes him look even cuter in that boy-next-door way of his. (Which, frankly, is just more infuriating!) Then I notice that all the cuts, bruises, and blood that were on his face before, as well as the dirt on his hands and feet, are gone.

"What happened to all the wounds you had when I first saw you?"

"Oh!" Bigger smile. "Well, I'm with *you* now, so, like, that's really healing."

"No, I *don't* know! I have no idea what you actually are! I haven't even *heard* of… What did you call yourself?"

"The Avatar of Knowledge?" he says. He winces like he's afraid I might hit him with a rolled-up newspaper.

I rip the watch nestled in the book page out of my back pocket so I can shove it under his nose. "And you're connected to this?!"

The moment I take the watch out, I get my answer. Collin disappears immediately. And that's when it hits me: Being careful not to trigger anything, not letting my skin directly touch it—all of that was pointless. The artifact is a *pocket* watch. How do you activate it? Well, apparently, you just need to stick it into one of your pockets!

So, looks like I've been using an object imbued with crazy-strong (meaning potentially crazy-*dangerous)* power for the last hour! Did I check if it was cursed? No. Did I at any point check myself to see if I was being magically screwed with? No.

Did I do any single freaking thing a real paranormal investigator would do to keep himself from getting screwed over by what in all likelihood is ancient God-tier magic?

No!

I put the watch, still cradled in the ripped book page, on the speckled-gray Formica counter of my kitchenette, and give myself a hard looking over for *any* magical residue. I start with a visual scan first (including an awkward look at my own butt in my jeans where the watch was.) I don't see anything out of the ordinary. Then I close my eyes—do I feel anything different? But, as usual, when it comes to sensing for any *real* magic inside me, I pull up "there's not any *there* there." Weak tea is weak. And it doesn't seem like any extra has been added on since the last time I checked.

Of course, curses are tricky. I can't be sure the bad juju is not just hidden or something. But Collin did disappear the moment I took out the watch. And, as far as I can tell, the appearance of this Avatar of Knowledge is the artifact's only real effect. Chances are, I'm actually clean.

I stare at the watch on the counter. Now, the smart play at this point would be to hide the damn thing in my refrigerator or maybe my oven—*somewhere* no one would look!—go to bed, and wait for the elf to pick it up. I did what he asked. In fact, I'm so on track, the Obligation he placed on me hasn't made a peep since I went inside the house. Other than working up a sweat, I got in and out of a vampire nest without being hurt at all, and there should be no way for them to trace the theft to me. If I do nothing more at this point, I'll get a cool $30,000 for less than an hour's work, and that's *after* having some of the best on-the-job training a junior paranormal investigator could get. For once in my life, I can finally come out a winner!

But… not everything adds up. For one thing, Collin knew who I was. And sure, he's an "Avatar of Knowledge," so maybe that's why. But he was actually, like, *happy* to see me when he appeared. Short, chubby, useless me. And now he's saying I healed him. Even if I had access to the full suite of incubus abilities—which I very much don't!—healing *other* people (or spirits or whatever he is!) ain't on the menu in any way, shape, or form. And if he *is* a spirit, why would he have been hurt in the first place? I mean, the dude was a bloody mess! And *terrified*. Until he saw my face…

There's a lot more here than an elf bullying a random, weak-ass incubus boy into a second-story job. Something to do with me.

Damn it!

I walk over to the watch on the counter, pick it up, paper and all, give myself three cleansing breaths to acknowledge how stunningly stupid I'm being, and then shove the wad into my back pocket again.

In an eye-blink, Collin is back, this time sitting on my ratty, third-hand polyester microfiber love seat. He's hanging his head.

"You're angry. With me." His words come out in an unhappy mumble.

Is that what I am? I was pretty pissed off before, but was it really about him? I mean, if I'm being totally honest, like Rafa, all this spirit's tried to do is help me. Does he actually deserve the full bill for my bad temper? When I have no idea what he's been through?

I suppose it wouldn't kill me to *try* to be a little nicer.

"Why were you hurt when I first saw you?" I ask.

He looks up, and gives me a sad smile. "Alvin… You don't have to worry about that. Let's talk about what I can do for *you*." He brightens a little. "I know you're not going to be able to keep me for long, but it's more than enough time to give you a few stock picks that could get you sorted with your mother for *years* after the money from the elf runs out. You'd like that, right?"

Okay. So, he knows about the elf. (And my mom!) That's, at least, a time saver. But not what I asked about.

"Collin, I first saw you when I put the watch in my pocket. You say you're not a ghost. Am I actually talking to a magical artifact here?"

"No. I'm my own person. But the watch binds me."

"So, you're, like, what? A spirit that knows everything?"

"Not *everything*. I'm not omniscient—a specific question has to be asked, and I have to *look* for the answer. I can't see the future. I can't read minds. Real-time information has strict limits, my general 'database' only gets updated once a day, and with only a couple exceptions, I can only know stuff that could be discovered through *human* senses or tools. But that's still a really broad portfolio! Magic spells, corporate secrets, advanced engineering, hidden diaries—you can pretty much ask me anything, and I'll be able to get you a true answer."

I think on that a moment. The ability to get an answer about practically *anything*. That would be… pretty incredible.

Then it hits me.

"Wait! Are you saying you can tell me where Emma is?!"

"Emma?" His brows scrunch.

"She's the daughter of a woman named Nicole Bruno who works for the CPA down the hall from me. She's missing."

"Oh!" He grins. "Ha! Of course, your first question

would be to help someone else! I *should've* known it would be!" He looks off to the side, then looks back at me. "As of my latest update, Emma Bruno was being held in the second sub-basement of the Benevolent Society of San Cipriano located in Nob Hill, and it's very unlikely she would have been moved in the last couple hours." He squares his shoulders, confident. "I can be more specific if you need me to be. Even help you draw a map."

Holy crap! Yeah, I might have hoped the Benevolent Society was a good lead. But he knows her exact location! And if I hadn't had a single clue, he could still have found her. Or any other missing person. Having Collin wouldn't just make me a good PI—with his help, I could literally become the best in the world. My mind reels over the possibilities.

But only for a moment. Because while it might feel like I've just won the lottery, he's just confirmed there's a teenage girl in the clutches of bad guys.

I frown and focus. (Do I need to concentrate when I ask the question? I do it anyway, just in case.)

"Collin, tell me, is Emma in imminent danger right now?"

He doesn't glance away this time. "No, not imminent. The vampires need her for a ritual, and they can't hurt her until they're ready to cast. They need me to help them do that, and that's not going to happen, because I'm with you."

Vampires! *Vampires* are mixed up with Emma's disappearance. That can't be a coincidence. And it would make sense why they'd need a human practitioner. Vampires are one of the few paranormals without any innate potential to cast spells. Magic is the energy of life, and being dead kinda gets in the way of that. I'm not surprised they could use an already powered-up artifact like the watch, but for a ritual, they'd need someone with actual mana. Someone weaker than them who they could control, like a kid.

And apparently, they need Collin, too.

"What do they need you for?"

"I'm not 100% sure. They want to cast a spell. Something evil. Something world changing. I don't know exactly what, because they were asking the wrong questions. And I was... deliberately not being cooperative."

"You can refuse instructions?"

"Of course! I mean, I'm trapped in the watch, and I'm not allowed to lie—or, at least, you won't be able to *hear* me if I lie—but other than that, I still have complete free will! If I don't *want* to do something, I don't have to."

"But then why would you ever—?"

Oh.

I frown and sit down next to him. I take his hand. "Collin, tell me how you got hurt before I found you."

Collin looks down at his hand in mine and his eyes seem haunted. "The watch isn't just my prison, Alvin. It's my torture cell. I do have free will. But, if you know what you're doing, you can use the artifact to cause me *excruciating* levels of pain. I try to fight it, but sometimes I just can't anymore. If you hadn't come when you did..."

I feel him shudder. It didn't look like any humans had lived in that house on Lake Street for a long time. Who knows how long the vampires had the watch? It could have been years. I then remember what he was saying when he first appeared. *I'll do what you want.* And how his face looked. Like he had fallen down an elevator shaft of broken glass. Again and again. They hurt him so bad, he was about to help them with an evil spell that could change the whole world.

And now I'm supposed to give him to the elf.

No one knows how to manipulate magic like the fae. They have no real moral code. No shame. And no love of humans. If the elf got his hands on this artifact, there is nothing he wouldn't do—couldn't do—to get what he wanted.

Crap. Well, winning was *fun*.

"Collin, tell me… Is there any way to free you from the watch?"

He looks up at me, startled. And touched. "*That's* what you want to know? I could make you rich. I could make you the most powerful mage in the world. Hell, I could make you *ruler* of the whole planet! It would take time, but I could do all that for you, and a whole lot more." His eyes soften. "I could even just answer… *personal* questions, if that's what you wanted."

Like about my dad. Who he is. How I can find him.

Uff.

Even though I have seriously mixed feelings on that topic, I'd be lying if I said I wasn't tempted. It's like I found a genie in a bottle. I'm not who I want to be. I have *a lot* of wishes I'd love to see fulfilled.

But if there's one solid rule about magic, it's that everything has a price. Even learning about my father could open a huge can of worms. Sure, there might be *some* way to ask the right questions and use the answers for good. But let's face it, I'm not that clever.

And there's just no time.

"Collin, the elf could show up at any minute, and I'm not strong enough to keep him from taking you from me. If we're going to get you free, it has to be now."

"But… what about the Obligation he put you under?"

Right. The promise I made to the elf. I can feel it again. The chains, wrapped heavy around my heart. Weighing on me with lethal intent.

I do this, and I could very well end up dead. But I've wanted to be something different my whole life. Something I could be proud of. But with what I am, *who* I am, it was never very likely that I'd become any kind of real hero. This might be the only chance I'll ever have to do something truly good. And I'm not going to sleep on it.

I should at least have time to leave a message for Stryker about where Emma is and that she's being held by vampires. My boss won't ignore that, especially if I wind up dead. What truly matters is making sure this powerful artifact doesn't fall into the wrong hands.

"Just… tell me what to do, okay?"

Collin looks down, pursing his lips and slowly shaking his head. He then rolls his eyes with a quick, amused snort. "*Feck*. You don't disappoint, do you? You're everything I could have hoped you would be." He takes my other hand in his. "So, I'm really sorry I have to disappoint *you*. I can't tell you how to save me. I don't know, and I can't know. That's part of the trap I'm in."

"Oh," I say, actually bummed that I won't be able to go through with my heroic suicide attempt. That I'm so useless that I don't even get that. (Which, I know, is kinda whack, but still…)

He turns his full body to me on the love seat, bringing our knees together. "But… there is something we do have time for. Something I've needed for a long while. Something I didn't think would ever be possible for me."

Good. Great! I can at least do *something*!

"Okay," I say, also turning and leaning in. "Tell me!"

He smiles. "This."

Collin slides his hand around the back of my neck, pulls me in, and before I can even react, full-on kisses me on the mouth.

His lips are soft. And warm. And they wrap around mine, sucking them in gently, like a little massage, before he pulls back, his blue eyes bright with happiness.

Uh, what?

WHAT?!

9

"You kissed me," I say, stupidly.

He grins. "I did. Free will, remember?"

I just sit there, wide-eyed, while my brain does the whole computer-crash, spinning-rainbow-circle thing. I feel his saliva cooling on my mouth. I mean, I can still freaking taste him!

(Mint and... fennel?)

"Why would you do that?!"

His eyes gleam, boyishly devilish. "Because you are feckin' adorable! Beautiful, actually. And since you decided to turn down Rafa, I figured I'd chance my arm."

Literally, not a single word he just said makes any actual sense.

"Chance your what now? *Beautiful?* What are you talking about? You're a spirit! And I might be a lot of things, but I'm not—"

He cocks an eyebrow. "Attractive? An absolute ride? *Lovable?*" He sharpens his gaze with a spark of anger while

I stare back at him blankly. "That sounds to me like your mam talking."

Uff.

Okay. There are probably a *million* reasons not to get involved with an all-seeing, God-tier spectral entity. But the fact that he's fully aware of things I wouldn't even tell my best friend (if I had one!), and can casually throw them in my face, has got to be one of them.

I glare at him, and he immediately raises up his palms in surrender. "I'm sorry, Alvin. It was rude of me to bring her up. But she's said so many things to you that were flat-out wrong, and she's been doing it since you were very young. It breaks my heart how it's made you see yourself."

I still have every reason to be seriously annoyed. But his expression is so caring, I find it hard to keep my grip on my anger. I continue to glare at him, though, because if I don't keep my grip on *something*, I'm going to lose my mind.

"You act like you know me. Even when you first saw me back in the house. *Why?*"

Collin purses his lips slightly and frowns. "When the watch is being used, if I'm ignored for a little bit, I can… ask questions for myself." He glances back up at me, vulnerable again. "You were the answer to one of my questions."

His words hit me somehow. I've never been the answer to *anyone's* question. And he just called me beautiful—something that's also never happened before—and seemed to mean it. Despite my best intentions, I feel my guard dropping.

"Um, what was the question?" I ask, my stomach vibrating, heart beating a little harder.

He sighs and shakes his head, but doesn't let go of my eyes. "I don't think I should tell you." Catching my wary frown, he raises his hand. "It's nothing bad! I promise! It's different meeting you in person, but I know enough to have a good idea how you'd react and I don't want to influence you. I want you to be safe."

My mind spins over that. What kind of question would put me in more danger just by knowing it was asked?

He squeezes my hands, and I'm immediately back with him. His eyes search mine, his lips pressed into a melancholy line. "Look. I get it. As far as you're concerned, I'm a stranger. Maybe I am pushing for too much, too soon. Just because I want this, because I want you, doesn't mean you're going to feel the same way."

Because I want this. Because I want you. Even if I could never act on it, I can't tell you how long I've waited for someone to say something like that to me. Someone who wasn't forced. Who meant it.

And as for my feelings... He doesn't have Rafa's big muscles or chiseled cheekbones. His face is soft, kinda like mine, and framed with gentle blond curls, which is nothing like me. There's a sprinkle of freckles across the bridge of his nose. The blue in his eyes captures light like a jewel. And his grip is warm and strong. I know he's a spirit —or something like that, anyway—but he feels *real*. Like a real boy holding my hands for the first time. The kind of boy I always crushed on in junior college and never got to have.

I'm in trouble.

I lean back, trying to create at least a little more distance on this cramped love seat. But I don't let go of those hands. And I give him the most honest response I can.

"I don't know what's going on here." My voice sounds strangely low, husky.

"Do you *want* to kiss me, Alvin?" He looks up through his eyelashes, shy, but underneath it, I can see his desire.

A desire for me. But if he does for some weird reason have actual *physical* needs, he should be getting as far away as possible! Incubi who don't know what they're doing can kill people. Sometimes they even do it on purpose, because it's more fun. I have the power to make others want me, even if they think I'm disgusting. Even if they know what I can do. It's wrong. It's awful. It's rape. Even if I've never used that power, it's what makes me a monster.

I've fought this part of myself for years, but I'm not made of stone. My control is slipping, the monster inside me straining against the bars of its cage.

I swallow thickly. "It doesn't matter what I want. I *can't* kiss you! If you really know about me, what I am, then you know it's too dangerous. I could really hurt you!"

He snorts, amused. "Alvin, of course I know what you are. But I'm not flesh and blood. You can't hurt me any more than you could hurt an idea or a dream. We can do anything you want, and I'll be fine. I promise."

Anything I want. Boy, does my mind want to spin after that statement! I've wanted to do *a lot of things.*

But I don't dare let the monster out!

"I don't know if *I'll* be fine!" My heart is racing. But I can't tell if it's the thought of waking up my incubus hunger and not being able to quiet it again, or if it's just being so close to someone who actually wants to do stuff with me. Someone so incredibly *cute* who wants to do stuff with me.

Collin leans in, and when I try to retreat, crumpling, my mid-back hits the thick powder-blue arm of the love seat. I can't go any farther.

His expression sharpens, becomes eager, *determined*. He can tell my resolve is slipping away. "I promise, I would never do *anything* to hurt you. But I want this so much. And I want it with you."

God, it's so freaking tempting. But I *know* I don't get to have this. It has to be a trick. A trap. I have to use my brain here!

"Why would a dream want me?" My voice comes out a whisper. My stomach twitches with quick, shallow puffs.

His face is now super close. I can feel his hot, sweet breath on my lips.

"Because I'm not just a dream. Because, like you, there are a lot of things I haven't been able to have. And because, whether you believe it or not, I really *like* what I see."

His lips crash onto mine, hungrier than before. There's not much room on this love seat, but he slides himself on top of me, wrapping his arms around my back, pressing his body against mine, and oh my God, it feels *really good*. It's like being totally parched, and then finally getting a tall glass of cold, sweet water. You just want to keep drinking and drinking forever.

Never in my life did I ever think I'd get to have this. Before I know it, I'm kissing back.

His lips move up to my ear, nibbling the lobe, which causes a hot, wet streak of pleasure to shoot straight down my neck and into my chest. It's just my freaking ear, but it's the most erotic thing I've ever felt. I swear I straight-up whimper.

"Tell me you want this, too, Alvin," he whispers, his breath tickling. "Please. Tell me *yes*."

I know this is flat-out crazy. He's not giving me any chance to think. He's *not* a cute boy, he's something else, and saying yes to a supernatural being has consequences. Just look at what happened with me and the elf! There's no way to know if "Collin" is his true form. This Avatar could be anything! A Lovecraftian horror. A vengeful Titan. An archdemon that someone trapped in a magical artifact for *everyone's* safety. Incubi and vampires aren't the only things that can consume you!

And maybe there *was* a moment I could have stopped this earlier. But now it's too late, because feeling him on top of me, kissing me, wanting me, feels too good, and this might be the only time in my entire life I get to have something like this. Because being deliberately seduced by a cute guy is literally every fantasy I've ever had since I was fourteen, but this is *better*, because it's actually happening. Because I'm so freaking turned on, I've lost all reason.

Whatever I'm caught up in right now, I'm not getting out of.

Because I don't want out.

"Okay," I whisper, high-pitched and hoarse, and feeling like I'm falling. "*Yes*."

10

Immediately, he's back on me—so much stronger than I expected—a crashing tidal wave in the form of a cute boy, pinning me against the corner of the love seat.

He brings his lips to the side of my neck and draws them down, slowly and sensuously, an inch away, his breath moist and searing. Teasing me by not touching me. Then he works his mouth back up, this time sucking and gently chewing. And, oh my God. He's nowhere near my dick, and yet it's so intense! It's like I feel it everywhere.

I moan in response. Not just once. It's more like a continuous stream of whimpers and cries. I literally can't keep the noises from coming out of my mouth.

His face pops up over mine. His eyes are filled with eager delight, sun sparkling on oceanic blue.

"So feckin' *adorable*," he says. His voice is almost a growl.

He then sinks his mouth back onto mine. His arms wrap around my back, squeezing me into him. And I hold him just as tightly as he sucks in my flesh, practically making me keen in response. The falling sensation returns. I feel like we're spinning, and I'm barely able to hold on. Maybe he is killing me, draining me, using me. But I don't care. His lips work relentlessly, devouring me. Making me want to *be* devoured.

I don't know how long we kiss on my love seat. It seems like just a couple minutes, but I know it can't be. I don't want it to stop, but Collin pulls off me and looks through the open square archway in the wall next to the love seat. The opening that leads to my bedroom.

"Let's move someplace a bit more comfortable," he says, with a wink.

His own cheeks are flushed red, and he's breathing heavy. (Which makes no sense for a spirit, but who the hell cares.) He leads me by the hand into the next room. Some distant part of me notes that this could be a chance to escape, to catch my breath, to think. But I just stumble after him. I want *more*.

I have almost no furniture in here. Just a crappy, chipped black dresser, a stack of PI books in the corner, and an old mattress on a spartan wooden frame I got at a garage sale. My sheets are an awful, twisted tangle. I never make my bed. But I don't even have a moment to feel embarrassed about him seeing it, because he suddenly pulls that extra-long wooly shepherd shirt over his head, which leaves him fully naked from the waist up.

I straight-up gape at him. He's got a small patch of blond hair between his pecs. I'm so instantly curious about it that before I realize what I'm doing, my fingers reach out and lace through his hair there. It's incredibly soft and fine.

He grins at me, boyishly puffing out his chest, letting me explore. Next to that blond tuft are two absolutely perfect little pink nipples, and when I tentatively circle one of them with the tip of my finger, he winces and whimpers. I quickly look up to make sure I didn't hurt him or anything, and find his eyes have melted into thin, wanton crescents.

I *didn't* hurt him. I made him feel *good*. Not with incubus powers. Just with touching him!

Well, maybe he's *not* a spirit. He said he was "his own person." I know better than most that there's a lot more to the world than meets the eye. Just because Rafa couldn't see him doesn't mean Collin doesn't have a physical form. A real body with *needs*.

I bend at the knees, place my hands on the silky soft skin under his ribs, and start sucking and nibbling that nipple like I felt him do on my neck. And even though I don't really know what I'm doing, now *he's* the one who's moaning. Which, I gotta tell you, is freaking *awesome*.

Yeah, I do want to be seduced, but there's also something really cool about taking the power back. Making him feel what he made me feel. My dick, which I now realize has been hard for the longest time, strains against the inside of my jeans in my new position. I quickly reach down to adjust it, and when I remove my hand, my palm is wet.

I wonder at it, before I realize what I'm looking at. I'm leaking pre-cum! I mean, I've *read* about pre-cum and stuff, but I've never experienced it before. But then, I've never been this turned on before.

This is what happens when people have real sex.

Collin notices me staring at my hand, that I'm momentarily distracted. He grins, stands me up and, in one gesture, peels down the zipper of my jacket all the way to my waist. I'm still wearing everything I had on when I left my apartment, including the windbreaker and the T-shirt, and those two garments don't exactly fit loose. But when you're an Avatar of Knowledge, I guess you know exactly where to pull. The outer layer drops off my shoulders and onto the floor and the shirt glides over my head and arms—both with no resistance. He has me half-naked in just a few seconds.

I don't have any hair at all on my body, except in my armpits and around my crotch. And, unlike him, I do have a tummy. I reflexively cover my now-bare chest and stomach with my arms, afraid he's going to start thinking of me as a boy instead of a man.

But it's not pity that shines in his eyes, it's eager lust. He gently moves my hands to my sides and kisses my chest, and then fiercely sucks my left nipple, sending such heavenly shudders through me, my knees straight-up buckle. I fall back onto the bed with a grunt that sounds more like a squeak.

He climbs on top of me, now kissing his way up my belly, which tickles like crazy and makes me bust out laughing. He grins up wickedly as I look over my chest at him, eyes wide, afraid he'll full-on attack all my ticklish spots now. (Damn it! I didn't even know I had those!) But instead, he rapidly surges up and lays completely on top of me, pressing *all* of himself against my body, which takes me fully out of the tickle zone and right to jesus-christ-that-feels-so-hot-and-amazing.

Is this what making out is always like? No wonder people make such a big deal about it!

His whole weight is on me, and his chest is so goddamned warm. And soft. And our bare skin pressing together is like a sex-multiplier, making everything feel so much more intense. I can feel his hard dick pushing against mine through our pants. (I actually made him hard! No magic. No incubus whammies. He's actually legit hard for *me*!) And that feeling itself is *so* hot and amazing that within seconds, I realize with alarm I'm going to shoot in my jeans. (Which would not only end what's happening between me and Collin—and I really don't want it to stop—but it would also be hella, hella embarrassing!)

But again, whether it's because of his powers or because we're just in sync, he lifts himself off me, raising his hips just in time. He then just hovers over my body, propped up with his elbows outside my arms in full plank position, his muscles straining. (Muscles a spirit wouldn't have!) He gazes into my face, pleased and happy. And yeah, all the physical stuff that's happened so far has been stellar, but it's actually when he looks at me, like he is looking at the most beautiful thing in the world, that makes my heart skip.

"Alvin, I want to make you come."

(!!!)

I suck in a quick breath. Ten seconds ago, I was terrified of doing that. And now that he's asking for it, I'm 100% onboard.

"Both of us," I manage to husk out. "*Please*."

He grins. "Dead right I can make *that* happen."

He rolls off me and slips off his soft leather boots, revealing bare feet. (Wasn't he barefoot before?) (Who cares?!) Then, bracing his upper back against the bed next to me, he tears down his rustic wool trousers. (No underwear!) His dick pops up, and when he rolls onto his knees to peel off my black Oxfords, I see it sticks up at a high angle. He's uncircumcised, unlike me, but he's so hard the tip of the head is exposed. It glistens. (He has pre-cum, too!) I just stare at him, completely mesmerized while he moves to strip me in just a few smooth motions.

Little blond hairs dust Collin's arms and legs. He doesn't have a six-pack, but his stomach is flat, and all his muscles have at least a little definition. He doesn't look like a supermodel. Instead, he looks like a regular, handsome guy my age or, maybe, a couple years younger. The kind of guy I'd totally get a crush on in the locker room of the gym, if I ever made it inside one. He's the one who's been calling me beautiful, but *damn*—I just want to stop and drink him in for hours.

But Collin doesn't have time for that. He's hovering over me in plank position again, but a little to the side so he can look down and wrap his hand around my cock. I immediately cry out, afraid I might shoot just at his touch (no one's touched me there, *ever*), but again, he knows to wait, doing nothing more than slowly peeling down the skin. The tip of my dick is full-on streaming pre-cum at this point, a continuous strand of it running from my cock to pool on the skin just below the soft shelf of my belly. (A drip from his own cock joins it, which almost sends me over the edge, but I focus!) Several seconds later, when I've finally calmed down enough for him to move, he scoops up a bunch of the warm, pale liquid from my lap and the curve behind the top of my dick. The brush of his soft fingers makes me shudder. He pulls down his own foreskin and lowers the throbbing, intensely pink head of his cock directly on top of mine. The swollen skin feels hot as a brand on me, and my breath catches. His fingers tremble a little as he wraps both of us into a firm grip. He then slides his hand up and down, keeping both our mushroom heads exposed, pressed against each other, using my own lubrication to jack us off. Each slick, tight rub of his flushed skin against my most sensitive spot shoots a zingy squeeze of pleasure straight down my shaft and deep into my lap.

It is literally the best thing ever done between two people in the entire history of the planet.

But even though this is one of the most hella intense sensations I've ever felt, my orgasm is building much more slowly than before. He really knows what he's doing. I look down, feeling completely in his power and loving it. His cock is maybe a little bit longer, and maybe I'm a little thicker, but we're actually pretty close in size. (Meaning totally average.) But his skin is so much lighter than mine, and the contrast sharply highlights every slip and slide. I just flat-out stare, mesmerized.

Then his lips are back on my mouth, and the way his tongue enters me is gentle, deep, and tender. And sure, I know this is just kissing and mutual masturbation. But his strong grip, his obvious passion, and the legit, *manly* weight of his upper body on me—it makes me feel absolutely *saturated* from head to toe with sexual arousal and sweet joy. It's building like a wave that'll drown me.

Delicious little jolts of pleasure spark up from the base of my cock, twitching my butthole—the ones that let me know an orgasm, a *powerful* one, is coming soon. My involuntary moans get louder and louder. I really want him to speed up, but he's deliberately taking his time, letting my excitement build. And instead of being frustrated, I actually am glad that he's in such control of me. He has so much more patience than I've ever had! I know that when he finally brings me over the edge, it will be the best come of my entire goddamn life.

I can feel it. Christ! Damn! It's about to happen! And I can tell from the blissful, twitching face Collin is making, he's just as close. This is so, so amazing! My mouth hangs open and I can't even make any more noise, because every muscle in my body is so tight, so ready, my breath is fully caught against my throat. Then everything starts to pull in at once, tensing in a delicious swell that contracts in toward the root of my dick—God, it'll be any second now! It's coming! It's coming! It's coming—

Whack!

Something hard and cold slams into the base of my right foot. It sends a sharp shock up my entire leg. The pain is so sudden and intense that it completely stops what was happening inside me, dead in its tracks.

My eyes spring open, and I see the elf standing there, at the foot of my bed. He's in his full armor, and his sword is drawn. From the way he's holding the blade, tilted, it looks like he just smacked me with its flat side.

He then swings the point of the sword to just above my throat, and sneers down at my helpless form with predatory amusement.

"Get up, incubus. I'm here to collect my watch."

11

Well, *fuck*.

I'm so totally shook that I just stare back at him, full tunnel vision, my jaw hanging. I huff shaky breath after shaky breath like I've just run a marathon.

The elf sheaths his blade. It doesn't look like he ever had any intention of stabbing me. He was probably just sticking the damn thing in my face to make his statement more dramatic. (God, I'm learning to *hate* the fae!)

His sneer slides into pure amusement, and his eyes rake up and down my body.

"It sounded like you were having quite the dream, Alvin. Are you imagining all the things—or *experiences*—thirty thousand dollars can finally bring you?"

I follow his gaze and start to come back to myself. I'm on my back on the bed, and it's only been a few seconds, so my cock is still super hard. Noticeably so. (Ugh!) But I'm surprised to find that it's not standing at attention in the open air, but instead is tenting up the cheap, thin fabric of my jeans.

In fact, I'm still in *all* the clothing I was wearing before! And Collin isn't on the bed with me. He's standing against the far wall of the room, completely covered again with his own rustic shepherd-boy attire. He returns my gaze, contrite.

Exactly what the hell just happened between us?!

The elf cocks a derisive eyebrow. "Are you going to need a moment?"

I glare at him. Hell yes, I'm going to need a moment! Or more like the next full *month* to understand what's really going on.

But the elf is for sure not going to give me that. I bring my knees to my chest, rolling up, and glance back over at Collin. Whatever it was we did, I have to get my shit together—and fast.

Collin, head down, continues to look over at me through his thick blond lashes, a little sad. But I see something else. *Gratitude.*

"I know you're going to have to give me to the elf, and I want you to know that it's okay. He's pure lethal, so this is the way it has to be. I'm just glad I had enough time to... well, to get to know you." He raises his head a little and gives me a shy smile. "I don't get to make many happy memories of my own. But being with you, like that, will always be one of my best."

I look back at the elf, who has moved to put a small but expensive-looking burgundy leather case on the bed next to me. He presses a button, which makes the silver latches pop open with a loud snap. He then pulls up the lid.

Inside are three large *stacks* of hundred-dollar bills.

Each one is wrapped with thick mustard-colored paper labeled "$10,000," fresh from the bank.

"You can see I'm a man of my word, Alvin. Now all that's left is for you to give me the watch and conclude our pact."

I carefully slide to my left and drop my legs over the side of the mattress. It's the side of the bed as far away as I can get from him. The side toward the double-hung window, the plastic shade still up from where I left it before work.

"And what makes you so sure I have it?" I ask, as cranky and sleepy-headed as I can make myself sound, but mostly just to give myself time to *think*.

I can feel the watch. It's still in the back pocket of my jeans.

The elf snorts a superior chuckle. "Besides being a flawless judge of character and ability? My contacts let me know it had been taken from the house." He then smiles at me, pleased. Like he's proud of me. "Despite your hesitation, I *knew* you were the right man for the job. And once this exchange is concluded, I will have more paid work for you. It will be quite useful to have an asset who fits so naturally... *under the radar.*"

I am pretty sure he just insulted me. Again. And I'm curious about who those contacts could be. But he's not going to answer my questions. The moment I get to my feet, he extends his palm out.

"But enough about the future," he says, coldly. "Alvin Alonso, *give* me what's mine."

I feel the skeletal fingers of the Obligation twist around my heart with icicle hardness. It sends a thrum of tension along my arm, making it twitch. My hand now *wants* to reach into my back pocket. Involuntarily, I step forward, meeting him at the foot of my bed. Standing so close to the elf, so close to closing the pact, the Obligation has moved from the brief, anxious, unpleasant discomfort I felt earlier to full-on *compulsion*.

I glance again at Collin. He nods back at me, a single head-tilt, eyes filled with gentle acceptance. He's 100% ready for me to give him up to this fae—a monster who's going to torture him, ceaselessly, mercilessly, to get whatever little evil thing he wants.

This boy knows me all too well. How my mom always talked me down, every chance she got. How I don't ever stand up for myself. How I fold under any kind of pressure, and retreat when things get to be too hard or intense. That I recently came up with all these big-ass dreams of being some kind of paranormal white knight, but when push comes to shove, that's all they will ever be: big dreams. Deep down, he knows I'm not someone who could ever be *anyone's* hero.

Well, *screw* that.

"No," I growl, and I keep my damn hand right where it is at my side. I don't care how strong this fae warrior is. All I'm going to give Lord-of-the-Rings is a big old helping of *kiss my ass*!

The elf's eyebrows raise with genuine surprise. "What do you mean, 'no'?"

And whether it's because of my direct refusal or because the elf is somehow actively tugging on his end of the Obligation, the compulsion surges down my arm like gasoline on fire. It hurts, and more than that, underneath the pain is layered this thick, urgent desire to give the elf what he wants, to honor the pact, *as I should*. It's a desire that if I didn't know better, I'd think was my own.

But I do know better. Growing up, my mother didn't hesitate to use her succubus powers to manipulate me. And before you reach for a barf bag or something, no, it was never sexual. She was a nightmare, but she was still my mom. Even so, well-fed succubi and incubi who know what they're doing can generate all *kinds* of powerful emotions in others that feel real. That feel like it's all you.

How many times did she make me blissfully happy about cleaning up after her, cooking for her, telling her again and again how wonderful she was? How much despair, how much pure *shame* did she make me feel when I did the slightest thing to displease her, no matter how petty or ridiculous? It never mattered how sure I'd been that she had been wrong, and that I was right to be angry with her. She would just *look* at me, and it was like the world got turned upside-down, and suddenly I felt the opposite of whatever it was I'd felt before. It took me a ridiculous number of years to figure out that she was actually using her *powers* on me. That I *wasn't* crazy. Or a bad child. Or only put here on this planet to earn her approval.

But eventually I did. I learned to sense when she was manipulating my emotions. To block it. To push back so hard with anger and hatred that she would stagger back as if burnt. I was never strong enough to actually yell at her, to tell her to go to hell, but it was enough to get her to stop, to get free.

And I do the same thing with the elf's compulsion,

not giving it an inch, creating an emotional chasm of pure fury between *it* and *me*.

"Alvin, what are you doing?" I hear Collin ask, deep concern in his voice. But I'm not looking over at him. I'm looking at the elf with fuck-you eyes. And he just stares back at me with shock. Because he knows that I should have succumbed to his power by now. And I'm not doing that.

"I *refuse* to give you the watch!" I snarl those words out with resolve, which makes the compulsion flare up hot inside me again. It sure doesn't feel good, but it has even less effect than before, because I've got its number and I'm not answering its calls no more.

The elf swoops in on me, a hawk on a mouse, and grips my shoulders, his face twisted with fury. "*How* are you refusing the call of the pact? That shouldn't be possible!"

Now it's my turn to sneer. "Really? Maybe you're not as flawless as you think you are, huh?"

"Alvin!" Collin cries out, rushing over. "This isn't a game. If you don't do what he wants, he'll really *hurt* you!"

I turn my head and glare at Collin, holding tight onto my anger against the compulsion like a shield. "I'm not just handing you over, like you're some *thing*! I won't!"

Collin's eyes widen, like I've just told him I'm going to commit suicide. Which maybe I did. I quickly glance around, looking for any weapon I could use against this fae warrior. But unless he's especially vulnerable to a pillow fight, I'm straight out of luck.

"Who are you talking to?!" the elf roars. Then he steps back away from me, quickly releasing his grip, like I might be on fire. He regards me with amazement and horror. "Are you… are you speaking to the Avatar? But that's impossible! You're too weak!"

"You keep saying that," I spit back at him. "But looks like there are more things in heaven and earth, doesn't it, douchebag?"

(I'm actually legit proud that not only am I able to whip out a real comeback, but that, since he's an elf, it's also a Shakespeare reference!) (Because you know, elves were huge in Shakespeare?) (Whatever. Trust me. It's totally badass.)

But Collin looks like he might be about to have a heart attack on my behalf. And it's only made worse when the elf draws his sword again. The fae's words drip with hate.

"Give the watch to me. *Now*." His voice is a hiss.

And that's when it hits me. A gut feeling that blooms into a full-on hunch. The elf has tried to bribe me. Threaten me. Grab at me. But that's all he's done. And if this *is* a God-tier artifact…

"You want it so bad? Then you're going to have to *take* it. It's in my back pocket."

I wouldn't have thought the elf's glare could become more murderous, but I would have been wrong. Silence stretches between us as he seethes. But he doesn't move. And even though I'm still totally screwed right now, I can't help feeling a little triumph.

I glance over at Collin. "He can't do it, can he? I need to hand the watch over voluntarily, don't I?"

The blond boy next to me looks horrified. "*Jaysus*, Alvin! Yes. You're right. He can't. And if he kills you, he'll *never* be able to use it." Now he grips my bicep with both of his hands, pleading with me. "But he can still *hurt* you, as much as he wants, until you agree to hand over the watch. And, trust me, there are worse things than death!"

As if on cue, the elf follows my eyes to Collin and says, "I don't know what the Avatar has promised you, but I am well familiar with the limits of all creatures. I will cut you, and skin you, and take you apart piece by piece, for *decades* if I must. But you will get no release until you give me what's mine!"

I'm currently holding onto a lot of anger to keep the Obligation at bay. But I gotta hand it to him, the elf warrior sure knows how to sound truly terrifying when he wants to. Mostly because I have no doubt he *will* back up his threat.

My legs tremble involuntarily. But I'm not going to give in. I'm not!

I lock my knees in place and straighten my back.

"Do your worst," I say, trying to sound tough. A lot tougher than I am. But I refuse to be "weak-sauce" anymore! Maybe it was the sex. Maybe it's because this cute boy really needs me right now. Or maybe I'm just tired of being pushed around, after experiencing it again and again for a whole freaking day. But for once in my life, I am going to stand up to a bully, even if it's the last thing I do. *This* is who I want to be. So this is who I *will* be, for as long as I can.

Collin, meanwhile, is tearing at his hair, pacing around, all while looking up and off to the right, gaze flicking back and forth. It's like he's desperately trying to track random birds speeding across the cracked plaster of my ceiling. "Jaysus, Alvin! What are you *doing*?! Feck, feck, feck, feck, feck!" he cries out. He's also terrified, it seems. But he's terrified for me.

The elf, very displeased, grips more tightly on the hilt of his sword.

"So be it," he says.

Suddenly Collin practically shouts in my ear. "Shite! I've got it! Alvin, you need to run and jump through the window! Right now!"

There is only the one window in my bedroom. It looks out onto the street. Five floors down.

I react with what I'm sure is the biggest WTF expression on my face, but I don't dare turn away from the elf and his goddamned sword. Still, my bizarre flinch seems to give the fae pause, and he lowers his weapon slightly and tilts his head to the side, scrutinizing me.

But Collin isn't stopping for nothing. "Listen here, Alvin! You wouldn't have gotten the same boost as with a flesh-and-blood person, and the sex we had wasn't completed, but I absolutely shared life force with you and it still counts as feeding! It won't last long, but you *should* have active incubus powers! You can easily handle the broken glass and the fall. And I guarantee it's the last thing he will ever expect you to do!"

I experience a strange feeling of disorientation. On the one hand, Collin just threw a whole lot of words at me super-fast, and I'm so freaked out, there's no way I should have the mental bandwidth to process them. On the other hand, it's like everything he just said immediately makes total sense. I'm able to absorb it all with deep understanding, and I just need to decide if I want to act on it or not.

The elf continues to stare at me, warily, watching my freaked-out reaction (or *reactions*, as I try to sort through all the confusion in my overheated brain), but he's clearly not able to see or hear the Irish boy at all. Instead, he pompously straightens his own back in what I'm sure he believes is a noble manner.

"So... I assume you are at last realizing the *foolishness* of your refusal and are now ready—"

Collin grips my arm again so hard, it hurts. "Alvin, it's now or never! I need you to trust me. Leg it toward the window, screaming your head off, and just throw yourself as hard as you can through the glass!"

Uh-huh.

What he's asking me to do is insane. Suicide. I'm not going to have access to any powers. I wasn't feeding off him. (I'd have felt it, right?!)

But really... what the hell else am I going to do?

I spin to my left, launch myself full-throttle at my bedroom window, and scream my soon-to-be-bloody head off.

"AHHHHHHHHHHH!"

12

I BRING MY HANDS TOGETHER IN FRONT OF MY extended arms and swan dive through the glass, shattering it into a million pieces.

Then I'm in the cold, open air. Falling to my death. And still screaming at the top of my lungs.

"AHHHHHHHHHH!"

And Collin is right there beside me the whole time, yelling in my ear. "Cover your head with your arms! Bend your knees! And try to relax—it'll distribute the impact! You've got this!"

Are you kidding me?!

Halfway down, I manage to throw my arms over my head. Then, while the ground rushes up at me faster than I would ever think possible, I feel Collin tug at my legs. "Feet out, Alvin! You want to land on your feet!"

I try to kick my legs out in the direction he's tugging, and right before I hit the cement sidewalk below, I hear him shout, "Now roll! Roll! Roll! Roll!"

I do land on my feet. Hard. I do not roll. Instead my

knees crumple, causing me to collapse in an ugly heap onto the concrete sidewalk, face-first, the sides of my elbows smashing against my cheekbones. *SMACK!* My entire body screams in pain.

But before I can even think for one second, Collin is pulling me back up into a standing position. And since I'm now guessing that everything he does is purely in my imagination (right?), in reality, I should be getting to my feet on my own. Which means miraculously nothing's broken, so I'm doing pretty damn great, considering!

I glance at my sleeves. Hot red blood soaks through gashes in my windbreaker. Not only did my arms get hammered against the concrete while protecting my face, they got pretty slashed up smashing through the window. But when I gingerly poke through the torn fabric where one of the wounds should be, it's barely there, and a moment later, it's gone. Even the glass shards seem to be left on the outside.

All the damage my body experienced completely healed itself in seconds. That's never happened before. Those are *incubus* powers! Collin was right!

I glance up at the window to see the elf sticking his head out, looking down at me. He gives me a truly annoyed eye roll and then quickly ducks back into the apartment. Apparently he's too noble to show off his own swan dive.

Collin tugs on the shredded fabric of my sleeve. "Alvin! We've got him on the back foot, but you aren't safe yet. Not by a long shot. And you won't have enough juice to outrun him for long." He scowls, thinking. "You need some wheels..." He urgently scans the road, then his eyes widen. "Class!"

He points, and one of his spectral directional arrows rolls out in front of his arm like a bright green carpet. It lights the way across the street and then curves behind the parked cars along the sidewalk. (And somehow I'm able to still see it through the obstructions.) It ultimately leads to a crap-brown late-'90s Crown Victoria that is parallel parked about two blocks away.

"Move, Alvin! And keep your head down once you get behind that row of motors, so he won't be able to see where you're going!"

For the record, I barely know how to drive, and of course I don't have the keys for some random car, but sure! Why not? Let's move!

I run forward, on top of the arrow/carpet, and unlike the last time I ran from the elf, now I really *am* like the wind! My legs whip like freaking hummingbird wings. I have no idea exactly how fast I'm going, but I wouldn't be surprised if it turned out to be thirty or even forty miles an hour. I'm up to the Crown Victoria in just a few seconds.

Damn. Active incubus powers are *fire*, no question there. No wonder paranormals like me are willing to kill for them.

Collin keeps up, no problem, and he's already created a blinking, glowing arrow that points directly at the side seam on the front passenger side door, next to the door handle.

"Grand! Now dig your fingers in there, and yank it back as hard as you can. You won't be strong enough to rip the whole door off, and that would make too much noise anyway, but you should be able to create a big-enough gap to reach in and unlock it."

Even after my burst of truly impressive super-speed, I'm skeptical. On my best day, I can barely handle carrying the bigger boxes from online delivery up to my apartment.

But I yank right where he tells me and sure enough, that part of the door tents out by almost a foot, creating a gap large enough to get my hand through. *Right on!* I reach in, unlock the door, throw myself inside, then close the door behind me, as quickly and quietly as I can.

It's just in time, because Collin says, "The elf is out of your building and searching the street." He's in the back seat, looking through the back window. "We've got a couple minutes, maybe, but at this distance, he'll be able to track you by smell. We better hurry." Another large glowing green arrow appears, and it points to the thin gap connecting the lower dash to the upper dash on the driver's side. "Go on! Rip that open!"

The thought the elf can track me like the freaking giant from *Jack and the Beanstalk* is hella disturbing, but Collin seems to know what he's doing, so I scoot forward toward the driver's seat and give another sharp tug. The lower dash cover easily succumbs to my newfound super-strength, revealing a mess of different colored wires and electrical stuff.

The tip of the glowing arrow then narrows to almost pinpoint size, directing my attention to a spot close to the edge of the dash panel now in my hand. "Okay, this'll be a bit fiddly, but you can do it. Put your thumb exactly right there. *Good.* Now wrap your fingers around the other side, grip hard, and then twist your wrist quick as you can to snap off a piece of the panel you're holding."

I do as I'm told. I'm left holding a thin strip of pointy plastic. Then I glance up at the rearview mirror and see the elf in the middle of the street. He's still a block and a half away. I don't see him sniffing the air or anything, but he's checking behind cars and, more disturbingly, *inside* cars—and he's walking in our direction. I'm so tense, the sharp little stick I'm holding shakes in my grip.

"What are we *doing*, Collin? A shard of plastic isn't going to get through his armor."

He grins back at me with mischief. "Sorry, lad. I thought it was obvious. We're hot-wiring a getaway car!"

Of course we are. Why should I stop with home burglary when I can commit *all* the crimes tonight?

Two more arrows appear and point to a red wire and a purple wire right next to the now-exposed steering column. Glowing text hovers above them: "Ignition Wire" and "Starter Wire," respectively.

"Now, take your nail, and dig it hard into the red one to get to the wire," he says. I force my sweaty fingers to remain steady and scrape until I expose the actual wire. "Good lad! Now the purple one. *Deadly!* You're doing great!"

I don't feel great. I feel like I'm barely holding it together. I glance up at the rearview mirror, still keeping my head low. The elf is less than a block away now.

"*Now,* stick the strip of plastic from the dashboard into where the key would go. Sound!"

"And that's it?" I ask, gritting my teeth and focusing on the plastic stick I've shoved into the slit-like keyhole.

It's taking serious willpower not to keep looking behind us.

Collin bites his lower lip. "Eh, no. You're actually going to need to do a couple of things pretty much at once. You're going to need to twist that plastic piece in the ignition. And… you're going to need to use a bit of magic on the exposed wires."

Magic. Right. I might see a little hitch in your perfect plan, oh great Avatar of Knowledge.

"Collin… I *can't* cast magic! I don't know how! And even if I did, I've never been able to sense any mana inside me."

Collin narrows his eyes with determination. "I'm aware, but I think you already know every living paranormal has the *potential* to cast spells. And if I'm right, this should be something you can easily do." He's trying to look encouraging, but I can hear the stress in his voice. "Just put your fingers on the exposed wire, and when I give you the nod, get fierce angry, picture blazing fire in your belly, and send it directly to your fingertips."

Uh-huh.

My *belly* is currently clenched tight with panic. I might not know much about how to use mana, but this isn't how it works. A paranormal might be able to use their innate abilities on the spot in the right conditions (like having just fed on life force), but fire-bending is *not* an incubus power. And from everything I've been told, casting a spell with mana requires serious prep ahead of time in the form of intricately designed runes. (Like Stryker's tattoos.) To picture flames while being all *grr* and *snarl* and hope that it does something in the real world—

Collin grabs my shoulder, leaning in from the back seat. "Focus, Alvin!" He shoots a glance over his shoulder out the rear window. "We are out of time!"

I look back, and the tension in my gut spikes into icy terror. The elf is just fifty feet away now. Sword out, silver plate mail gleaming in the streetlights. His eyes land on the back of our car, narrowing.

And just like with jumping out the window, Collin's giving me a choice that's not actually a choice. I trust him or I don't. I rely on what I have every reason to be sure is true (that this is doomed to fail) or I believe he knows better. It's that last thing that convinces me to try it—because of what Ms. Stryker told me this morning. She's never given me any spell-casting instruction until today but the lesson was clear: If you want to use magic, you have to believe it's going to work.

I don't know what Collin really is or what exactly happened between us in my bedroom, but one thing I *am* sure of is that this Avatar of Knowledge is some kind of miracle. And right now? I'm choosing to believe in miracles.

Letting the plastic shard hang from the ignition, I shove myself into the driver's seat. I pinch the two exposed wires, take all the anger I'm using to fight off the Obligation, add to it all the frustration I have for the elf showing up at literally the *worst possible time*, multiply that by how freaked out I am right now, and picture a blazing inferno in my belly. Then I mentally send the fire raging down my arms toward the wires.

Here goes noth—

Zzzzt!

Two bright sparks flash out from my fingertips. Then I hear the engine start to turn over.

Holy, holy crap! It worked!

"Savage!" Collin cries out. "Now, quick! Twist the steering wheel with your left hand, and the ignition with your right!"

Collin's arrows immediately move to direct my hands to new locations, so I quickly grab the steering wheel and the plastic stick and give them both a turn!

The steering wheel unlocks, and the car roars fully to life.

We did it!

No. Wait.

I did it.

Boy, do I so want to enjoy the moment, but I know I don't have time to even look behind me. The wheel is already turned. I claw into my brain for skills I haven't used since I was a teenager, grab the gear shift, press the side button, yank it into drive, and peel out as fast as I can onto O'Farrell while Collin full-on crows, now punching the roof of the car from the passenger seat. *Whack, whack, whack!* (There's another weird, smack-like sound behind us, like something hitting the back of the car, but it doesn't matter, because We. Are. Moving!)

"I *knew* you could do it! I knew it! You're *amazing*, Alvin!"

He grabs my shoulder and mashes a kiss into my cheek, crazy high. And yeah, with my luck, he probably is some kind of Cthulhu monster archdemon horror from the Beyond that just wants to devour me. But, to be honest, right now, both the kiss and what he's saying feel pretty damn good.

And I did do it, didn't I? This can't have been the result of me feeding, because fire is in no way an intrinsic incubus power. Which means it *had* to have been mana! *Wildcard* magic!

Of course, I didn't craft any runes first, which is a little weird, but it was just a little bit of power, so maybe I didn't need to. No matter what, it shows I have the potential to cast actual spells. I *can* use my magic to help people —I just need more training. And if I can create another spark and show it to Stryker, I can prove to her that I'm worth teaching—no getting drunk or laid required! This is literally a dream come true.

Two things are less dreamy, though.

One is that I am basically a city mouse. I haven't driven anything since my mom had me chauffeuring her around Vermont *six years ago*. I also didn't bother to adjust the seat's position, and whoever drove it before had at least four inches on me. So, even without Collin latching on to me, I'm all over the road. I need to work hard just to keep contact with the pedals and the wheel, while desperately trying to remember how to use them. None of it feels natural.

The second and bigger deal is what I see when I finally remember to glance at the rearview mirror. There's a sword sticking out of the rear trunk, stabbed there like freaking Excalibur. The elf's sword. And gripping onto its handle, pulling himself up from the road, is the noble warrior himself. Murder in his eyes.

I utter a very mouselike squeak, shove my foot down

as hard as I can, and floor it. The elf instantly jerks back from the acceleration, his arm snapping to full extension.

We're still on narrow city streets, though, lined with cars. There's only so fast I can go. The extra speed slows him, but it doesn't stop him. He's already pulling himself back up and will be fully on the back hood in just a few seconds.

Collin sees him, too. "Alvin, we need to get to the 101! He's strong, but if we can reach freeway speeds, we can shake him. Turn to the right *now!*"

I yank the wheel hard to the right, which causes the rear tires to skid. We almost spin out, but I just manage to make it onto Stockton toward Market. My bad driving whips the elf off the car and back out onto the road. (Yes!) He doesn't let go of his sword, though, which is still attached to the trunk. (Boo!)

There's no other traffic on this street, though, thank God, and I'm coming fast on a red light where the road spills onto Market.

"Blow through it! You're clear!" Collin yells, apparently able to see around corners. Huge arrows materialize ahead of me, twisting left on Market, then tightly twisting right onto 4th Street just a half-block down. It's a good thing it's well before dawn and we're now downtown. I'm barely keeping the car off the curbs, but at least in this part of town, the sides of the road are free of other vehicles.

The elf's head and shoulders are back above the trunk, but his hateful glare tells me he's struggling. Collin's right. If we can just get on the freeway, I should absolutely be able to shake him off.

In the meantime, I keep the pedal to the metal—knee

and elbows locked, and shoulders shoved back into the seat behind me—as we squeal around Market and race down 4th Street. A few blocks ahead, Collin forms an arrow for a wide right at Harrison that should get us up the on-ramp. We're already pushing fifty on this city street, but I'm pretty sure I can make that turn.

Or, at least, I *was* sure until the heavens open up and a full-on tropical storm starts to come down. A torrent of angry droplets crash down on the roof of the car with a drumming roar. Out of nowhere, it's raining so hard that the windshield is nothing but a rippling sheet of gray.

But of course, it's not out of nowhere. It's the elf, using nature magic. Because they can do that. (Innate power!) If I didn't hate the bastard so much, I'd say it was a clever move.

Lucky for me, I have an Avatar of Knowledge who, with a look of fierce determination and a wave of his hand, immediately creates a glowing heads-up display on the windshield that shows me where all the road obstacles are, and exactly where I need to drive. It's like a video game and, even though I'm too broke-ass and too friendless to have ever actually played any of those, it just makes *so much sense*. I don't even need to slow down.

Unlucky for me, rain does more than make you blind. It also destroys your traction. I make the turn at Harrison toward the on-ramp going nearly sixty, just straddling the outside edge of Collin's glowing lines—and almost immediately, I'm in a full skid, a mile-a-minute spin.

I scream while I tear at the wheel, the car jolts up as it jumps the curb, and then—

BAM!

The passenger side of the car smashes into one of the huge concrete columns of the overpass. The metallic screech of the impact rips through me. Everything throws forward and to the right. And since I'm not wearing a seatbelt, my head bashes hard into the side of the steering wheel.

Things are then very quiet. I don't know for how long.

When I come back to myself, it's like my ears, no, my *whole head*, is stuffed full of cotton. Sounds return, one by one. Collin is yelling something at me. The car engine is dead, but there's some kind of ticking noise coming from the front compartment. I notice the rain has stopped.

I lean back, bringing my hand to my eyes. I'm in a lot of pain. My neck, my arms, my nose… I can feel blood streaming down my face onto my chest. I think I bit my lip badly, too.

Even so, it still feels like I'm doing better than I should be. The pain is dulling. Things are stitching back together. Looks like my new healing powers are still there. *Good.*

But the mending is happening slower than before. And underneath it, there's something else. Something stirring inside my chest. Something needy. And fierce.

The Obligation?

No.

It's something I haven't felt for years. Something that I only got the barest taste of before I locked it way, way down. My incubus hunger. The part that needs to feed. A compulsion that can become so strong it would make the Obligation feel like a gentle suggestion.

How?! I'm not doing anything remotely erotic right

now. And I didn't feel anything after… *whatever* Collin and I did. I would definitely have noticed it!

Then it hits me. It's because I'm hurt. And still healing. I've never been this injured before, and I've used up all the juice I got from the sexy times with Collin. But even running on empty, there's still something fighting for my life. Something that will save me for a cost. Something I've tried to deny my whole life.

I'm going into debt—cold, hard debt—to the monster inside me.

Collin is still in the passenger seat. Grabbing at my shirt. Tugging at me. But it feels like he's at a distance.

"Alvin! Alvin! You have to get up! We have to run!"

I wish I could say that my monster puts rose-colored glasses on me when it's hungry. That as I turn to look at Collin, dazed as I am, I see all his cuteness. His sweet desire to protect me. Those boyish good looks. That I'm reminded of his gentle kisses, and how nice his touch was. That I'm filled with love and affection, hearts and flowers. And that *that's* what makes me want to have him.

But that's not how a predator's hunger works.

It's nothing like what you feel when you haven't eaten for a long time, but it is similar to the way we *look* at food. As something to be consumed. Something that's just there for your needs.

Not a person. But meat.

That's how I'm looking at Collin now. And already I can feel the tendrils of my innate power reaching out to him, trying to grip around his heart. Trying to make him want me so much he won't be able to do anything but submit, helpless as I devour all that he is.

Of course, I'm badly hurt. And weak. I have no real experience using these powers. And Collin's not even human, so there's nothing for the tendrils to latch onto, right? He's safe.

But I see the horror on his face as he realizes what's happening to me.

"Oh. Oh, *Alvin*."

He reaches out his hand toward my face. An act of tenderness that should move my heart, bring me back to myself, but it just ignites my hunger even more. This isn't a cute guy worried about me. It's prey showing weakness. And it makes me want to consume him *more*.

God, I hate that this is part of me. I hate that this is who I really am.

There's a staccato series of loud pops, then a scream of steel to my left. I drunkenly twist my head to see the elf rip off the driver's side door with his bare hands. (Well, look at that, he's even stronger than I was!) I watch him, barely able to keep my focus as he draws his sword. The fae has got blood on his own face, a nasty diagonal gash down his previously flawless cheek, and he's really, really angry.

My neck, mouth, and nose still hurt like hell. And even if I could get my muscles into gear, the passenger side of the car is smashed. The elf is blocking the only way out.

And yes, now my hunger wants to eat him, too. He *is* flesh and blood. If I drained him dry, my monster is certain it would make me feel *all* better. And if anyone deserved to be devoured, it's this guy.

But there's enough of me that's still me to realize that

that would not end well. That even on a good day, the fae don't make easy prey. And, let's face it: I'm a total wreck.

That's when things finally get clear. There is no escape. I'm absolutely at his mercy. And I don't get the impression mercy is his thing.

Sneering down at my smashed body, his glare drips with disappointment and hate. "You could have been so useful to me, incubus. But you ruined it."

He then raises his sword to strike, baring his teeth. "I swear to all the stars of the frozen night, I'm going to *enjoy* carving you up!"

13

He plunges his sword downward while I helplessly cringe, bracing for ice-cold metal to slice into my flesh when—

BOOM!

A thunderclap erupts from somewhere behind the car, and the elf twists and spins as if he were slammed in the shoulder by a fast ball. Immediately, he drops out of sight. It happens so fast, all I can do is squint stupidly at where he was standing.

Then, on the ground, next to the open driver's seat door, I hear a mewling grunt followed by short, abrasive scrapes. (The elf's armor dragging on the asphalt as he tries to get up?)

There's another tremendous, cracking roar, and the movement stops.

Heavy boots crunch toward me on the wet road, and then a very large man in a black Kevlar duster is above me, holding a shotgun. He throws a quick glance into the car and—

Oh! It's the Monster Hunter.

Rafa.

One look at me, and his eyes widen with horror. Then his expression hardens to stone as he turns his gaze down toward his feet.

I lean over, unsteady, and see the elf face-up on the ground. Large holes have been blasted into his armor at his right shoulder and left thigh, and he's barely able to cover them with trembling hands. His sword is out of reach, his expression frozen in shock. He looks pale and nauseous.

Rafa slams his boot onto the fae's chestplate, pinning him. Then he places the barrel of the long gun directly under the prince's chin.

"*Elf.* Do you acknowledge that I have bested you and that it is within my power to end your life?" Rafa speaks with formal precision. The words sound like something he's rehearsed.

The fae warrior glares back at him with hate, but says, "Aye."

Rafa doesn't move the tip of his weapon. "And so you acknowledge that if I choose to spare you, you will owe me a life debt?"

"Yes, Hunter," the elf snarls, furious. Fighting pain. "That is so."

"My price for your life is that you agree to never bring harm to myself, those I care for, or any other human for the rest of your days. And in case it's not clear, that includes my friend Alvin here."

The elf sneers and shifts his focus to me. "Oh, *does* it? *This* is your fr—"

Rafa jabs the barrel of his shotgun into the elf's throat, immediately wiping the elf's sneer away. "Do not test me, fae! After what I have seen tonight, I know you are capable of great evil. But I also believe in the possibility of *change*, and I am giving you this one opportunity to save your own skin. Do you accept my terms?"

The elf glances at me one more time. Safe bet he's reviewing every word Rafa said, searching for any loophole or technicality that might allow him to eventually rip me to pieces. (And it was a lot of words! Who knew Instagram Terminator could give such a speech?!) The elf's gaze thins for a moment, and I can't tell if he found what he was looking for or not.

He turns back and meets Rafa's eyes, voice dripping acid. "I agree to your terms. Spare my life, and I will not knowingly bring harm to you, any other human, or those I am aware you care for. And that list currently includes Alvin Alonso, whom you consider a friend. Is that *satisfactory?*"

Ah. I see what you did there.

But Rafa doesn't. Because he thinks I'm human.

The Monster Hunter nods. "Yes. It is." He steps back, removing both his gun and his boot. "As I'm sure you've realized, the buckshot I used contains cold iron. It's going to take you a long time to get it all out, which means you're not going to be able to use any magic, including teleportation." He regards me briefly before returning his attention to the elf. Angrier. "But the *smart* move for you right now would be to get as far away as possible, as fast as possible, before I change my mind."

"As you wish," the elf growls. His eyes slide to peer up

through his lashes. "Will you allow me to sheath my sword, Hunter? Or must I leave it behind?"

The malice there is almost imperceptible, and I suck in a breath, suddenly afraid. Not because I'm expecting the elf to use his weapon against Rafa in some sneaky surprise attack, but because I've heard supernatural rules can get very specific and weird. The terms of the pact between them have been finalized, and if Rafa claims more now, it could all be void. Or he could even wind up owing the elf something.

I'm about to say something—or at least try to—but it turns out I didn't have to worry. Rafa smiles, just as wise to what's being pulled. "Nice try. I already have what I need. Take your blade and go. *Now*."

The elf heaves himself up without another sound, sheaths his weapon, and gives me one last cold, venomous glare, so I know, no matter what he's agreed to, this isn't over between us. He then lurches off into the night, barely staying upright, like a drunk on the losing end of a brawl. Rafa watches him go, his back to me. The Monster Hunter is as tall and unmoving as a pillar of marble.

The moment the elf is out of sight, though, he holsters his shotgun in its back scabbard, wheels around, and falls to one knee. His fingers rush to my face, then freeze and recoil inches away, like any touch might break me. He looks anguished and much, much younger than the iron-willed action hero who had just sent a fae warrior packing, let alone the smoldering stud who less than an hour ago was trying to make his way up to my apartment.

"God. What did he *do* to you?!"

Huh. Maybe he really does like me.

And I might look like roadkill right now, but he's still as beefy and underwear-model handsome as ever. Same rugged, golden skin. Perfect cheekbones. Big muscles. And he's just inches from me now. My gut tightens, sure that my hunger is going to target him, that it will reach out its tendrils to try to control him, and then he'll *know*.

But it doesn't.

The need isn't gone. I can still feel it. But the monster inside seems more pensive, more *patient* than before. I'm using anger to hold off the Obligation, so maybe it works on the hunger, too? Or maybe it's because I've healed enough—at least enough to get my wits back—that I'm not going into any more debt?

One or both of those could be true, but the most likely explanation is that it knows this Hunter could kill me without a second thought. And in the end, if there's one thing the monster wants, it's to *live*.

Speaking of which, why didn't Rafa kill the elf? Based on my mother's stories, I thought Monster Hunters wanted to kill *all* paranormals.

"You let him go…" I rasp out.

It hurts to talk, but a quick run of my tongue along the inside of my mouth reassures me I didn't lose any teeth against the steering wheel. So, that's a win. The cut on my lip feels like it's closed, too.

Rafa's eyes slide to the side and he frowns. "I did. The fae are… complicated. They can choose to do good. Like people. And I don't kill people, if I don't have to." He returns his gaze to me, uncertain. "You think I made a mistake?"

If we're talking tactics against an immortal warrior unlikely to ever let go of a murderous grudge, then yeah, it could absolutely come back to bite him in the ass. (Or, more probably, *my* ass.) Not to mention that it seems like a very un–Monster Hunter way of seeing the paranormal world.

But in terms of my overall opinion of the man, I sure won't count it against him.

"I think you did the right thing, Rafa. And you saved me. Again." I try to smile, to make light of this heavy moment. "My hero." My barely healed split lip has other ideas. "*Ow*."

He quickly scans me from head to toe and goes back to being the gruff badass. "We need to get you to a hospital. Right now."

Hospital. *Uff.* An obviously good idea—and an ultimately very *bad* idea. (Mom taught me to avoid doctors like the plague. You never know if there's some way it could lead to the government discovering what I really am!)

I extend my arms and rotate my wrists. They're achey but not bad. I twist my neck left and right, stretching it a bit each way, while ignoring Rafa's protests not to move my spine. Things are stiff, but there's no *sharp* pain. And no headache or blurriness, so it looks like I escaped a concussion. I press my fingers gingerly against my cheekbones and then touch my nose. A little tender, but if anything was broken before, it's not now. Even the lip bite feels like it's days healed.

I gently push the Monster Hunter out of the way with my left arm and get to my feet outside the car. I'm definitely not 100%, but it looks like what was left of my incubus powers got me close enough.

"I'm a bit banged up, but it's not too bad. I think I just need, like, a shower or something." I take a few tentative steps forward.

His eyebrows raise at that, but he steps aside. He continues to hover alongside me as I walk a few paces from the car, his fingers extended just beyond his hips, ready to catch me if I outright collapse.

"That was a hell of a crash, Alvin. You *sure* you don't need to see a doctor?"

I glare at him sidelong, and try to channel his terse, tough-guy tone. "Don't like doctors."

He nods, pursing his lips with manly empathy. "Okay. I can get that. But my clan might know someone, and I promise, they won't be the type to ask any questions… you don't want to answer."

I wonder for a hot moment if he's figured out what I am. It *was* a bad crash, and I'm just walking away from it. That's not a very human thing to do, is it? He let the elf go. Could he know and actually be cool with me being a paranormal? It wouldn't make any sense for him to set me up for a trap after just saving me, right?

Either way, I can't risk getting mixed up with even more paranormal killers. I scowl at him, hiding fear behind anger. "No doctors!"

His focus on me shifts from concern to the edge of suspicion. Am I protesting too much? I stop and slouch a little, trying to appear a bit more hurt, more *human* than I am. Not hard, really, since it doesn't feel like I have any more incubus juice.

But I'm no actor. I need to change the subject, fast.

"Rafa, what were you even *doing* here?!"

I look behind the Crown Victoria and toward his black SUV, which is half on the curb a block away. I notice that the driver's side door is open like a barricade. He was probably behind it when he took his first shot against the elf. (Because that's what Monster Hunters do. They shoot paranormals. Let's *try* not to forget that part, right?)

My pointed question cuts him short. He scrubs the back of his neck, suddenly embarrassed. The words seem hard for him.

"I… didn't like how I left things. I obviously misread stuff and acted like a total ass. So, I waited in my car outside your apartment, because I wanted to apologize—which I get is totally stalker-y, and it didn't take long before I realized that. But then I saw you get thrown out the window—*and* use magic to get back up and haul ass down the street." He flashes a slight smile. "Pretty impressive, by the way. You definitely undersold what you could do." His brow knits, his whole face tensing. "After you told me no, I *know* I shouldn't have stayed, and I'm sorry. Before the window and then the elf coming after you, I was about to leave, I swear…"

He lets out a frustrated huff, running out of words, before he looks back up from his boots, ashamed. Contrite. *Vulnerable.*

And yeah, he was being more than a bit stalker-y, which is not cool. But the truth is, he came to my rescue when I needed him. *That's* why he's here. Because he's a real hero, and that's what real heroes do. And now he looks guilty about it. So for the second time this night, I'm wrestling with my own guilt for making the paranormal-killing Monster Hunter feel bad.

I sigh. Heavy. (And don't even have to fake it.)

"Dude, whatever. You saved my life…"

"Still. You didn't ask me to." He frowns, sheepish. Like he broke some badass bro code or something.

I take a breath. Time to throw this hangdog a bone. He's certainly not acting like he's on to me. It actually seems like he might think I'm some kind of kick-butt wizard, which is not the worst thing in the world in terms of a cover, even if it's not true. Either way, me being all standoffish isn't going to help anything.

I put my hand on his upper arm (since his shoulder would literally be a stretch.) "Rafa, I'm glad I didn't have to. For real."

A shy expression of delight lights up his stoic, action-hero eyes. And I have to admit it—even though he was super pushy before (and shouldn't have stayed outside my apartment!), I don't hate the fact that this Instagram-worthy superhero seems to be into me.

And that immediately makes me think of Collin, since he *had* been trying to play matchmaker between the two of us before. I'd been so shook that I didn't even notice he was gone!

I look around as non-suspiciously as I can and immediately see him, casually leaning against the smashed-up car. Collin eyes Rafa appreciatively and gives me an encouraging grin, paired with a thumbs up.

Well, heck. Looks like *he* thinks I'm safe with this guy, and he's supposed to know everything, right?

Rafa follows my gaze to the wreck. The steering column is still open, wires hanging out. "Not your car, huh?"

Oh, right! Crap! I stole a car tonight, didn't I? I forgot that, too!

I wince. "Um, actually, *no*."

That doesn't faze him at all. "Didn't think so. That was a big crash. No one out here to hear it this late at night, but there'll be police. And now it's covered with a bunch of your DNA."

Double crap! There's blood all over the steering wheel and everywhere. My *paranormal* blood.

Rafa misreads the horror in my eyes. "I'm guessing you don't have a spell for *that*, huh? Don't worry. The branch of my clan back East encountered the same problem once DNA testing became a thing. Luckily, we already had a way to get rid of evidence of paranormal activity and turns out, it works just as well on human genetic material. Hang on."

He quickly returns to his SUV, grabbing something from the glove compartment, and comes back with what looks like one of those bug foggers. "Stand back." He places it in the car, and pulls the soda can–like tab. The car immediately starts to fill with a thick mist that spills out of the driver's side door and onto the street, where the fae fell.

He puts his hand on my shoulder, guiding me away like he did at the Lake Street house. "The chemical dissolves fingerprints, and even hair, which is why you don't want to get *too* close to it." His lips quirk, amused at his own joke.

I glance at his hand and he immediately removes it, wincing.

"Sorry," he says.

But I bump his elbow gently to let him know we're still cool. (I'm sure a real bro would actually punch him in the shoulder or something—you know, *bromantically*—but I don't think I'll be able to pull it off.) His expression brightens briefly in response, but then he looks around.

"We should go. Someone could come by any minute."

"All right," I say. My apartment is only ten blocks away. I could walk it, but because I'm wanting to keep things friendly (and I *am* dead tired), I add, "Would you mind giving me a lift back to my apartment? I'd prefer not to have to hot-wire another car."

Bigger smile. "No problem."

Rafa rolls his black behemoth of an SUV off the curb, with me in the passenger seat. Collin appears behind him, in the back seat, next to the duster, shotgun, and scabbard placed where they were the last time. The Monster Hunter is back to being the strong, silent type—no questions asked. Not even why the hell an elf warrior would be throwing me out of windows and looking to stab me in the middle of the night.

That's good, because I don't *owe* him an explanation, right? Not even if he saved me. Not even if he's actually being pretty cool right now.

The smart play would be to get as far away as possible

from this big armed Monster Hunter as soon as I can. But now that I have a moment to think, the reality of what I learned from Collin less than an hour ago sets in.

Emma is being held by vampires.

She might not be in "immediate" danger, but that could change fast, especially if those vamps start getting peckish once they've realized they no longer have the watch. I do have a way to get in touch with Ms. Stryker when she's off-world in case of emergencies, but the message could take days to get to her, and depending on what she's doing, she still might not be able to come. I could instead reach out to the Feds, but that would inevitably lead to a ton of questions, ones that could be very dangerous for me to answer. (And even if I do manage to avoid getting thrown into a black site as a malignant paranormal, this is the government—by the time they got onboard, it could very well be too late.)

I'm still the best chance this teenage girl's got. A few hours ago, that would be just another way of saying that her current situation was hopeless. But Rafa plowed through those vampires in the Lake Street house like they were made of wet cardboard. And he does seem to like me.

The plan taking shape in my head is risky as hell, but what if I do nothing? Could I live with myself if Emma winds up dead? I'm never going to become the man I want to be by playing it safe all the time. And, at least for now, I have the Avatar of Knowledge. If that's not a game-changer, I don't know what is.

I can do this. I *have to* do this.

I clear my throat. "So, about that case I'm working…"

Rafa's eyes flick to me briefly, his expression steady. "The missing girl?"

"Yeah. I have some more information about that. I now know where she is." I hold his gaze to get his reaction. "She's being held at The Benevolent Society of San Cipriano in Nob Hill. By vampires."

"I think I've heard of it." His jaw tightens. "The elf mixed up in this? That why he was in your apartment?"

"Yes," I say, not lying, if not exactly telling the truth. "But thanks to you, he won't be a problem anymore. The girl's name is Emma. She has some magical talent, and the vampires need her for some big, evil ritual they can't cast on their own. I know exactly where they are keeping her in the building." I glance back at Collin, who is listening eagerly. "Or at least I can find out."

Collin nods in response, pleased.

"And you think you might need some backup..." Rafa's voice stays even, giving away nothing.

"Yeah. My boss is out of town. *Way* out of town. I don't have enough evidence to get the police involved, even if they could handle actual vampires. And, to be honest, maybe I *can* do a little more than I let on, but I'm no fighter. At best, *I'd* be backup." I chuckle in what I hope comes off as self-deprecating instead of nervous. "Ideally, backing up from a very safe distance."

His cocky smile from earlier returns. "It sounds like you could use a Monster Hunter." His face then darkens, and he frowns. "Hm."

I frown with him. "Um, is it too much to ask?"

He shakes his head. "No. Of course, I'll help. But if they're holed up in a building, a *public* building, this could be their nest. And that means there could be dozens of them. Bay Area vampires aren't like the others. They're special."

"Really? How so?" I know Stryker had tangled with a few over the years, but she never mentioned them being a particular problem. Still, if these vamps can get it together enough to try to pull off some apocalyptic ritual, that would make them special.

"They're less feral, somehow. More organized. Able to stay one step ahead. Just when you think they're gone, more pop up. It's part of the reason I came back, even when I was told not to." He clears his throat. "Let me reach out to my clan here. See if they, hm… See *how much* they can help. They might not be happy to see me, but they won't be able to ignore a nest of vampires kidnapping little girls. They'll step up."

"Are you sure?" I ask. Rafa's brow is so heavy, I feel like I've just stumbled into the middle of ten seasons' worth of Monster Hunter drama. But I don't know how much I should dig.

Rafa's confident smile returns. It's similar to the forced casualness from the last time we were in his car together. "100%. No matter what, I'll help you rescue that girl. How long before this ritual? Can we circle back this afternoon?"

"Yeah," I say. "My sources let me know she's not in 'immediate danger.' How about we meet at Joe's Café on Polk?" Joe's Café is close to my apartment and on a well-trafficked street. If his Monster Hunter buds get scary, I can at least beat a hasty retreat.

"Sounds good," he says. "I'll meet you there at two."

We pull up across the street from my building. Considering what happened, I expect to see cops or at least a bunch of shattered glass on the ground, but it's all gone. Even my window looks intact. It's probably a glamour, which means the elf is as good as ever at covering his tracks and keeping his mischief on the down-low. Since he's currently pumped full of cold iron, that means he must have done it before he came after the car. At least this time, his impressive power helps me.

Rafa extends his hand, and we exchange a very businesslike handshake. No innuendo or loaded agendas. Whatever he wanted from me before, looks like we're teammates now. And for Emma's sake, I can't say that's a bad thing.

I watch him drive away, and it's only when I'm safely back inside my apartment that I let myself feel how badly off I really am. I might be pretty much healed, but my whole body still aches like crazy. My incubus hunger is also present and accounted for, too—a low hum in the background that makes me want to get laid, soon, even though it's the *last* thing I need right now.

But the real issue is the Obligation. Rafa might have prevented the elf from actively coming after yours truly, but it didn't change the binding supernatural promise I made. And broke. That's all on me. It's still there, and I'm holding it off, but just barely. The burn, the squeezing around my heart—it's getting worse.

I grip the side of the kitchenette counter, steady my breath, and focus on keeping myself standing.

Collin touches my shoulder, concerned.

"How bad is it?" he asks.

"Bad." I straighten myself up. "I've got the Obligation under control, but I don't know for how long." I'm struck by a hopeful thought. "Wait. You're supposed to know everything, right? Any chance you know a way to get rid of this curse that *doesn't* involve handing you over to the elf?"

"I don't know *everything*, Alvin," he sniffs, but he looks guilty. He then glances up and to the right, his eyes moving back and forth. "But as far as human knowledge goes, there are only three ways to get free of a mystical pact: you can honor it, the person you owe can choose to release you… or you can die. And, just in case you're wondering, him dying before you do any of those things means it will *never* get lifted." He frowns, very unhappy. "I'm sorry. I know I put you in this situation. I wish I had a different answer."

Well, those options are definitely sucky. Luckily, I have one more magical resource I can tap. Even if it's the last thing I want to do.

"You didn't put me in this situation, Collin. I put myself in it. And if human knowledge can't help me, then I guess I have no choice."

I grimace at him, trying to make light of something that feels very heavy. "I'll just have to appeal to a *darker* power."

Collin's posture immediately stiffens because he knows exactly what I mean. Or, in this case, who. In San Francisco, there *is* one person who might know more than both Collin and Ms. Stryker about the magical world. A paranormal expert with centuries of experience. A woman with a relentless thirst to discover other people's secrets but whose services come at a very high cost.

It looks like it's time for a long-overdue visit with Mother.

14

Even though it's not even 5:30 a.m. yet, Mom answers my text immediately. Other than the obligatory rent-check conversation, I never reach out first, and never before dawn, so she knows it must be serious. Of course, the quick reply isn't because she's concerned or anything. I've probably just sparked her curiosity. She'll do literally anything to fight her boredom.

She sets a meeting for 6:30. She even says she'll cook and promises me pancakes and bacon. (Her favorite breakfast, not mine.)

I'm grateful at least that I have enough time to shower and change my clothes before I'll need to hustle out the door to get to her multi-floor penthouse condo in Pacific Heights. (I do check the window in the bedroom. Looks just as intact from the inside as it did from the outside. I don't even feel a breeze. There's definitely residual magic, but I can't tell whether that's a glamour or if he fixed the glass outright. Guess I'll find out if it suddenly wears off!)

Collin disappears the moment I step out of my pants

and into the shower, which in some ways I'm also grateful for. I'm still hurt, so having more sexy time together to recharge my healing powers probably *might* make a lot of sense, but I'm already having to concentrate to keep the incubus hunger at bay. I don't want to do anything to encourage it. And anyway, I don't even know what to make of what happened the *last* time we "got physical." Even thinking about it makes my stomach vibrate with emotion. What emotion, I'm not sure.

So, I go with my standard operating procedure and embrace denial. I have enough upcoming drama that I don't need to add any more to my plate.

The shower wakes me up. I'm not exactly a new man, but I do feel better. Once I dry off, I wipe clear a slash of steam off the mirror and check out my face. I can't do anything about the cuts and bruising around my nose and mouth, which look days healed but still visible. But I can at least fix my hair and wear a shirt that matches my pants and shoes. (Mom cares about that kind of stuff. Deeply.) I go with yet another polo (navy) and my only clean pair of beige khakis, slipping the watch into its back pocket. Collin appears next to me as I put on some brown penny loafers I haven't worn since high school.

"You don't need to do this, Alvin," he says, his expression downright mournful, but there's an undercurrent of anxiety. "I know a way to contact the elf. If you hand me over to him, you'll be free."

I ignore him. In part because the old me might have agreed. Between the Obligation crushing my insides and the murderous glare the elf gave me just an hour ago, I am feeling pretty overwhelmed. But at some point you have to decide if you have what it takes to be who you want to be. And for better or worse, now-or-never looks like it's still now.

Collin stays quiet in the rideshare over to her building and also as we ascend the elevator to the 49th floor of the Pacific Pinnacle Tower. The whole way, I try to focus on keeping my breath even—and not just because I'm fighting the Obligation.

The elevator doors open directly into the polished white marble foyer of the first floor of her condo. My mother is standing there, waiting for me. She gives me a serene smile. "Alvin. My darling son."

"Hi, Mom."

She quirks an eyebrow. "What happened to your face?"

"It had a little disagreement with a steering wheel. The wheel won the argument."

Her brows knit, baffled. "You were driving?"

"Yeah. And that's literally the *least* interesting thing that's happened to me in the last twenty-four hours!" Her eyes light up, so I know I've truly piqued her curiosity. (Which gives me at least a fighting chance to maintain control of this conversation, *if* I can make her work for it.)

I push past her. "You said something about pancakes?"

She smiles, immediately on to me and my attempt to keep her in suspense, but she looks more impressed than pissed. "I did. Batter is already made."

She glides effortlessly toward her high-end stainless-steel chef's kitchen, which gives me a chance to take in her current appearance.

Before I was born, Mom wasn't just a strong and alluring succubus. According to her, she was the strongest and most alluring succubus on the entire planet. And yeah, I'd question the source, except that she can still do things that supposedly no other succubi can, like completely change her form. Most sex demons who feed can make *some* minor alteration to their looks to attract prey—more luminous skin, slightly bigger muscles, maybe a change of eye color. But when my mother met my father, she was in the guise of a stunning Filipina TV star with inky black hair, brown eyes, and a rich, dusky complexion. Now the woman approaching her $30,000 quartz island is blonde with green irises and flawless ivory skin.

Wearing pink slippers and peach-colored lingerie—perfectly draped over her supernaturally perky breasts—she appears years younger than me. The term "barely legal" immediately comes to mind. (Her OnlyFans account is one of the top ten earners worldwide. Before the Internet, she could only "date" a few lonely, rich men at a time. Now she can bilk thousands.) And this is a pretty standard look for her. To say it was confusing growing up is an understatement. I could go on for a long time about how totally alone and isolated I felt as a boy, with everyone assuming I was Pinoy but having zero actual connection to any history or culture I could identify with. Until we got to San Francisco a few years ago, we'd move all the time, and Mom seemed to delight in choosing the most backwater, least diverse places in the U.S. to settle down in. I was always "the new kid," so both the white and Black students at school kept me at arm's length, and because I didn't know anything, I couldn't talk to the few real Filipino kids about even small-stakes stuff like food or holidays without sounding like a complete idiot. I felt like a fraud and, on top of that, to have a sexpot Mom who didn't look anything like me—and who wouldn't ever, even *once*, acknowledge to another living person that we were blood relations— (!)

Yeah, I could say more. A lot more.

But I don't have time for that.

I take a seat on one of the hard, silver-plated stools at the island, and she slides three perfectly shaped golden pancakes onto my plate, followed by three strips of crispy bacon. She lovingly pours the artisanal maple syrup on top while rounding behind me and humming something chirpy from *Snow White*, completing her pose as Mother of the Year. Then she takes the stool opposite of me, and rests her chin on steepled fingers, doe eyes wide with anticipation of me taking my first bite.

You see, I hate sweet breakfasts. And she knows it.

But I need to play my part here, so I shove in a large mouthful. "Mmm. Yummy," I say with zero enthusiasm.

She winks at me. "It always was your favorite."

You might ask why she even bothers with this low-rent form of torture. But then you don't know my mother. The chance to savor someone else's pain is literally why she wakes up in the morning. And she's made an art of walking up to the line without crossing it.

Collin is in the room with us. He's leaning against the stainless-steel SubZero fridge, lips pursed, looking like he wants to be anywhere else. (I feel you, bro.)

"So," she continues. "What could be more interesting than your very first car crash?"

"Mm," I say, taking another bite. (In fairness, the pancakes are spectacularly made—gently crispy on the outside, light and fluffy inside, just a hint of vanilla—and I am actually legit hungry. It just makes it all the more frustrating.) "Well, I was actually running from someone at the time. So, that's kinda interesting."

Her eyes narrow, her blithe expression sobering. (Good. Looks like I've got her attention.) "Running from *whom*?"

"An elf," I say, as casually as I can. "Elven royalty, in fact. Shining armor. Magic sword. The whole deal."

Her face darkens further, which is not exactly the eager, give-me-the-deets look I'd been expecting from a woman desperate for entertainment at my expense. But at least she's engaged. "And what did he want?"

"That's a long story. But it started yesterday, with him putting me under an Obligation to steal something."

I choose to lead with the part of my story most likely to piss her off: me making a deal with a fae. My hope is that she'll be so eager to hear the rest of my little tale, we'll be able to move past that pretty quickly. Still, I figured I'd at least get a brief lecture about how stupid I am, how I need to listen to her, etc. etc.

But I don't. She just gets even more serious, sucking in a breath. "And did you get it?"

I glance over at Collin, who folds his arms and glances meaningfully in the direction of the elevator. My mother's odd reaction doesn't seem wholly unexpected to him. And he really wants us to go.

But now I can't. Because she's acting like she knows something about this. And I need to know what she knows. (Without tipping her off that she has any leverage on me!)

"I did," I say, cooly. "That's why I'm here."

She realizes. "You didn't give it to him…" A smile slices up the side of her teenage-dream face. "*Clever* boy." She holds out her palm. "Can I see it?"

I cock my head to the side, willing my expression to appear neutral despite a growing sense of danger. "It sounds like you might already know what it is, Mom. Why would that be?"

"Because I'm your mother, and I know everything," she non-answers. Her fingers twitch. "Now, *can I see it*?"

"That depends," I say. "I'm still under the Obligation, and I need a way to get out of it without giving the elf what he wants and without dying. Is that something you can help me with or not?"

The old Alvin would never have dared to engage his mother in an actual negotiation. (I mean, the old Alvin wouldn't have willingly stepped into her Martha Stewart lair for anything.) But it's been a whole day of firsts. And the glimmer in her eyes lets me know that she's actually digging my *quid pro quo*, for whatever reason.

"Yes, sweetheart," she coos. "I'm more than certain I can help you with that."

I glance over to Collin, who huffs. "I can't read her mind. But based on what I'm getting from her vitals, I'm fairly sure she believes what she's telling you. That doesn't mean it'll be worth the price."

For whatever reason, the claws of the Obligation choose this moment to bite hard into my arteries. It's like the worst heartburn ever. I purse my lips to hide the pain, but right now, there's *a lot* I'd pay to be free of it.

"If I let you look at it, you *will* help me?"

"Yes," she says, agreeing much more quickly than I expected, and not moving her hand from the cold stone countertop.

I reach into my back pocket, all my senses on full alert for treachery. "To be clear, I'm not *giving* it to you, Mom. I'm just letting you examine it briefly."

Her smile broadens. "Now, *that's* my boy," she says. "It's taken you long enough to finally grow up. Don't worry, I'm just going to look at it."

I don't know what's creepier: that Mom is agreeing to help with so little fuss, or that she seems legit psyched that I'm clearly not trusting her. But there's no point in dragging this out. I remove the watch from my pocket and place it in her hand.

"Oh," she says, breathless, her eyes wide as saucers. She turns it over and over in her hand. "Oh, *yes*."

"So, you know what it is…"

"I do." She looks up at me, practically shining. "It's the key to making *all* our dreams come true, baby cheeks."

Uh-huh.

"And you also knew this was something I could get? *How?*"

She sniffs and shoots me a chiding smirk. The message is clear: I'm not going to get any information for free.

I quickly take the watch out of her hand. "Fine. Whatever. You said you'd help me, remember?" I slip it back into my pocket and Collin reappears back where he was. He looks relieved.

She rises and goes to the refrigerator, unknowingly forcing Collin to move. "I did. And I will," she says, calmly, her back toward me. "But tell me first: Are you able to use it?"

Collin shakes his head, but clearly I'm going to need to pick my battles, so I say, "Yes. I can."

After an almost imperceptible beat, she opens the fridge door, removes eggs, onions, cheddar cheese, and chicken-apple sausage, and places them on the countertop. All my favorite ingredients in a scramble. "Well, that's good, sweetheart. And it's clearly had a positive effect already. I imagine you rehearsed this conversation with the Avatar. Did it help you escape from the elf, too? Of course it did! I promise, anything you've done so far is merely scratching the surface of its potential. And with *my* loving guidance—"

Right. *That* greedy little fantasy needs to be nipped in the bud!

"We're not keeping it, Mom," I say. "I'm going to free the spirit inside it."

She freezes. But just for a second, before she fluidly continues making my all-time favorite breakfast food. Even the whole wheat toast cut into circles without the crusts.

"I see. Is that so?" She keeps her back toward me. "Then it sounds like it's time for you to tell me the *whole* story."

And so I do.

Or a lot of it, anyway. I leave out the sexy parts. And the part about me using any incubus powers. And *everything* about Emma—the last thing I want to do is put that poor girl on my mother's radar. But she gets all the major events.

I wasn't sure what part of my little tale of woe she'd latch onto first, but apparently it's the encounter with my fellow creatures of the night that spins her gears the most.

"*Tch.* Alvin! You needed a Monster Hunter to save you from *vampires*?"

"Vampires are legit dangerous, Mom!"

Her eyelids lower with long-suffering disappointment. "Vampires are human. And infected. And *dead*. If you fed, they'd be running from you."

"Well, sorry, Mom. You know I've always been a little squeamish about eating people. Just one of my little quirks, I guess." I know I shouldn't rise to the bait, but there is heat in my chest and I can't keep the edge out of my voice.

"How many times do I have to tell you? You don't need to kill them. And it's not like it *hurts*…"

She smirks her high-school-cheerleader mouth salaciously, probably thinking she's making a joke. Or maybe just enjoying my reaction. But rather than getting into another drawn-out convo about why I'll never be the incubus son she's always wanted, I grit my teeth and try to get us back on track.

"Can you help free me from the Obligation or not?"

She frowns, pensive, and twirls a chunk of pancake in a puddle of honey-hued syrup with her fork. (She took over my original plate when I got the scramble. The eggs and toast were incredible, by the way. Almost worth being here.) "And you are *determined* not to use this literal gift from Heaven for the benefit of either of us?"

"I told you. I'm going to free the spirit inside. That's

non-negotiable." I glance over at Collin, who looks back at me warmly. But he's also shaking his head like I'm a fool.

She chuckles. It's not kind. "I swear, I don't know where I went wrong that's made you so soft. You always were a weak little thing, but I did everything I could think of to toughen you up!"

I really was truly determined not to let her get to me this time. But then she says stuff like that! I feel the Obligation take a step back as my blood pressure rises up another notch. "Right. You never said you loved me. Not once. You used your powers on me, all the time. You made me your personal slave, cooking and cleaning up after you, seven days a week."

The doe eyes return, made all the more infuriating since it's on the face of a seventeen-year-old. "All things I would argue taught you important life skills, as any good parent should."

"You practically starved me for a full year so you could pass me off as some Bangladeshi refugee kid you adopted! Totally racist, by the way, and *I was nine years old*! You expect me to believe you did *that* for my benefit?"

A shrug and a sniff. "The sympathy opened important doors for us, I am not responsible for human ignorance, and it looks to me like you've recovered just fine." She gestures at my not-insignificant waistline. "All on meals paid for with *my* money, I might add."

It's been less than fifteen seconds since she's started in on me, and already my cheeks are burning. There's taut cable tension in my chest and arms, and my hands are clenched into fists. All the while she just smirks at me as if this were some game. I just want to let loose on her and say—I don't even know what! To use my newfound confidence to speak up at last! To somehow, *finally* get through to her that I needed a real mom growing up, not a monster!

But then I feel Collin's hand on my shoulder, and it's like cool water pouring onto a fire. He's not using any powers on me. He's just there, his expression meeting my anger with tenderness.

"She's not worth it, Alvin. You're miles better than her, and some part of her knows that. *That's* why she's winding you up."

That literally seems like the *least* likely explanation for my mom's behavior. But I'm sure he's right that she's doing this deliberately. And for whatever reason, his compliment still feels good. (Maybe it's just knowing that, if nothing else, *someone's* got my back here.)

Mom notices my cooldown immediately. But instead of being disappointed, she cocks her head, curious. "So, how's that Obligation feeling *now*?"

Oh. Right. Lovely.

This was all just some kind of "teachable moment" for her. Too bad for me, it was pointless.

"Better, Mom. But I already knew how to use rage to hold it off. I can't do that forever. What else you got?"

She takes me in, thoughtfully. "I think you underestimate how incredible it is that you are able to resist the Obligation at all. But you always were an ungrateful child." She crosses her arms. "If it were simply a matter of you not wanting to give the watch to the elf for whatever pittance he offered, then I'd say we should arrange to have it presented to the Dragon King. We'd need to go through intermediates, of course. We'd want to avoid his direct scrutiny. But he's been looking for the Avatar for a very long time, and even filtered through middlemen, the spoils of his gratitude would be immense."

The Dragon King! I don't know much about supernatural politics, but it's common knowledge he's the top of the food chain when it comes to the paranormal world. (Or really, *all* the paranormal worlds. Earth is supposedly just a backwater.) It's why I hoped dropping his name would get the elf to back off when he had me pinned to the wall. Mom's just given me a surprisingly useful tidbit.

I hear Collin suck in a breath beside me. Tension radiates down his arm to his grip on my shoulder. But I don't need to be an all-knowing spirit to realize how terrible a plan it is that Mom is suggesting.

"The Dragon King is supposedly even more evil than the elf, Mom. Hard pass."

"He's not evil. He's just powerful. So powerful, in fact, that even the lowliest of his functionaries could free you of the Obligation, and ensure the elf never bothers you again. And that would be the least his court could do for us!"

I scoff. "Not evil? He literally *devoured* all his kids. Like at a dinner party. Before dessert."

"Ay, Alvin! You never listen! He didn't 'devour' them. He had them killed. There's a difference."

"*No.*"

She sighs, heavy. "It doesn't matter what I say. I'm not going to be able to convince you to keep that spirit where it belongs, am I? Even if it gets us *everything* we could ever want?"

I don't dare trust it, but it's beginning to feel like maybe she's going to let me have the win on this.

I fold my arms. "You're not, Mom. Because it's the right thing to do."

She snorts with derision, then her perfectly pink jail-bait lips curl into a smile, amused at some private joke in her head. "Very well. I can still help you. But since I am not *quite* as noble as my darling son, you'll forgive me if I demand a little something in return."

And that right there would be the sound of the other shoe dropping.

"What do you want?"

"Nothing huge. Just an answer to a single question. You ask the Avatar, and then tell me what he says."

I glance up at Collin, who looks wary, but isn't shaking his head this time.

"And if I decide not to give you that answer?" I ask.

"Then I'll decide not to give you mine." There's a glimmer in her eye. "But I promise you that I actually do know how to get you what you want here. And, if you have any doubts about what I'm asking for, I'm sure the Avatar will be able to assure you that you'd be getting the better part of the exchange."

She's guaranteed up to something. But that doesn't mean she won't help. History shows that she does seem to want me to stay alive, if only so she can keep torturing me over breakfast food. And I'm pretty sure I know her tics well enough to tell if she's lying.

Collin shrugs. It's up to me, apparently.

"All right, Mom. Shoot."

She gazes at where I've been looking at Collin's

face to address him directly. She's off by an inch or two, so I know she can't see him, but still, her near-accuracy is eerie. "Avatar, I used to own a *very* special tiara with blue and white gems. I want you to tell me who has that now, and where they are keeping it."

Huh. Okay. This is the first I've ever heard about any tiara. For all I know, it's as powerful an artifact as the watch. But all she wants to know is where it is. She's not even asking how to get it. I raise my eyebrows at Collin, leaving it up to him whether he thinks he should share the information.

He's clearly not happy, but he says, "Your mother's tiara is in the possession of the aswang, Maharlika. When she is not wearing it, she keeps it in a silver box under the mattress of her human servant, Ligaya."

I repeat his response and my mother nods, very pleased. "That's a good answer, Avatar. Thank you." She returns her gaze to me. "And now, before I give my own answer, I have one more question, but this one's for you, my son. When you made your pact with the elf, what *exactly* did he ask you to get him?"

"The watch. He said it would be in that house on Lake Street."

"And you're sure he never *once* mentioned the Avatar of Knowledge."

My eyes widen, realizing. "No. He didn't. He didn't want me to know what it was." I lean in, suddenly energized. "So, you're saying if I get the spirit free, then I can just give him the watch, and we're done?"

"Yes, baby boy. If you do exactly what you seem hell-bent on doing anyway, you can just hand over the empty cage, and the elf will have no more claim on you."

I look up at Collin for confirmation. He's nodding, as impressed with her as I am. "I, eh, can't ask questions about my freedom, so it didn't cross my mind to even think about that possibility. But she's not wrong."

I turn back to my mother. "Right. Okay. But I don't actually know how to do that, Mom. You promised me a real answer that would get me out from under the Obligation."

"I did," she says. "And I pay my debts. Those markings on the outside of the watch are Celtic, which means it was created with druidic magic—and I just so happen to know that the most powerful druid in North America lives right here in the Bay Area, and she owes me a favor. Several favors, actually. If anyone can tell you how to free your spirit, it will be her." She glides over to a small pad of paper and pen next to the SubZero refrigerator and begins writing. "This is her address. I will let her know to expect you shortly."

Mom hands me the paper, and Collin glances over my shoulder at it. Flicking his eyes to the right and away, he says, "It's sound. There is a druid of some renown who lives at that address in Antioch. And, for what it's worth… she's dead right about the kind of magic that's trapped me."

So Mom just gave me a legitimate, solid lead. It's not even 8:00 a.m. yet and with BART, I should be able to get there and back before I'm supposed to meet Rafa. It will mean getting zero sleep, but if it can help me learn how to free both Collin from the watch and me of my Obligation, then I'm down for it.

"You're actually helping me," I say, fixing her with what I hope is a piercing look. "*Why?*"

She glares back, aggrieved, and repeats a familiar refrain. "Darling, I know you have willfully chosen not to believe it, but *everything* I've done for the last twenty-two years, I've done for you!"

God. It's the same old bullshit, and I'm just so sick of it. I shake my head, unable to hide my disappointment. I cross my arms and let us sit in silence for two full beats, just staring at each other.

She looks away first. Then her face softens, suddenly tired. It makes her look older somehow. "I might not have put it in words, Alvin… but you are my son, and I *do* love you." She purses her lips, meets my eyes, and her voice falls to a whisper, edged with sadness. "*Very* much."

I suck in a breath, truly surprised. She's never said anything like that to me before. What I would have done to have heard that growing up! Of course, I don't dare trust it now, but there's still part of me that *wants* to. And she has to know that.

I scan her face for the usual signs of deception, but bizarrely, she actually looks sincere. Like it pains her to admit it. And out of all the terrible and scary things that woman has said to me over the years, nothing has made her feel more dangerous.

15

I have a lot to think about on the way to the BART train.

In the last twenty-four hours, I've been assaulted and blackmailed by elven nobility. Promised to rescue a schoolgirl from vampires. Committed multiple crimes. Was saved twice by a ferocious Monster Hunter (who actually hit on me!). Got my hands on what is apparently one of the most powerful artifacts in existence. Had sex for the very first time (which turned out to be completely imaginary!). And now I'm off to meet a powerful druid to learn how to destroy the artifact's enchantment and free the spirit trapped inside.

For someone who, for over two decades, has been literally the most boring person on the planet, it's a lot to take in.

But am I thinking about any of that right now? No. Because I'm thinking about my mother. Which is just how she likes it.

Typical.

I take a seat on the BART train heading toward the druid's house in Antioch and realize this is the first moment I've had to actually *breathe*. The Obligation is still squeezing my insides with its scalding fingers every chance it gets, but I can't tell you how good it feels to just sit quietly for a few minutes.

Collin is perched next to me on the barely padded plastic double bench. He's been silent since we left Mom's penthouse. And it's not like he said a lot while we were there, either. Even though I know he's not human, now I'm afraid I've screwed up somehow with him. (Not that I have any idea how!) We have the front car all to ourselves, so I can talk to him in my normal voice without coming off like a lunatic to strangers.

"So… my mother didn't seem surprised that I had the watch or that I was able to steal it…" I begin.

"No," he says. "She did not."

"Do you know why?"

"I wouldn't expect much happens in San Francisco without her knowing," he says, sounding distracted. "Her work grants her access to many sources."

"Sure," I say. "Maybe somehow she heard the watch was taken. Even the elf said something about his contacts telling him. But it's weird that she would think that *I* could do it, right? She's always acted like I'm completely useless."

"Mm." Collin's lips are tightly pressed together.

"Any guesses why she'd believe I could?" I probe.

"A few," he says, frowning. And before I can continue our game of Twenty Questions, he raises his hand to stop me. "Your mother is dangerous, Alvin. Way more than you think."

I snort, and raise my eyebrows at him, trying to lighten the mood. "Oh, I *know*, Collin. Trust me."

His gaze hardens. "No, you don't. She's been awful to you, but before you were born, she was something else. She killed people. A lot of people."

I frown back. "You mean, when she fed?" (Mom always said that killing was more trouble than it was worth when draining humans. Drew too much attention. But maybe she didn't *always* feel that way.)

"No. I'm talking *tens of thousands*. In one go. There's a whole civilization that named their most fearsome demon after her. That was less than a hundred years before she completely destroyed them. Eisheth Zenunim, one of the Four Queens of Hell in Kabbalistic tradition, was based on her legend." He shakes his head, his jaw tight, frustrated. "I'm meant to be the cleverest thing going. I should have sorted out some way to keep you from her. And now I let her know you have the watch."

I scrunch my face, trying to square the idea of my superficial, petty mother—whose greatest concern in life is not being embarrassed by me in public—being some kind of epic, unholy terror. It's hard to accept. She did say she used to be a lot stronger before she had me, that the pregnancy drained her. That she couldn't change her form for the whole nine months, and even after getting that power back, she remains just a fraction of what she was. (Yet *another* thing that made me a terrible son in her books.) But killing thousands? Engaging in genocide?

Still, when it comes to my mom, I guess anything is possible.

"You think we shouldn't have told her about where to find that tiara?"

He snorts out a quick, dark laugh. "No. She'd have found it, anyway. We just saved her a couple years, and she'll still have to fight to get it back." He presses his shoulder against mine with affection. "Alvin, it's *you* I'm worried about."

The weight of him feels nice, even though I know it's basically just a hallucination. And now he's smiling, which feels even nicer, since it shows that he's not pissed at me or whatever. In fact, he's even worried about me.

Well, maybe I'm a little worried about me, too.

"So, how did she know I could find you? For that matter, how did the elf know? I mean, if Mom was telling the truth, even the Dragon King with all the resources in the multiverse hasn't been able to do that!"

"Fair questions, Alvin," he responds. "Another good one is why did a woman ask you to save her child from the same vampires who were using me? That's one I've been asking myself."

He's changing the subject. But, for the moment, I play along, happy to not think about my (possibly legendarily) evil mother for a moment. "Good point. And why'd that happen on the very same day the elf blackmailed me into stealing you?"

Collin nods, thoughtful. "The very same day I was finally going to give the vampires what they wanted…" He purses his lips. "I don't know the answer to that, Alvin. These aren't the kinds of questions I'm meant to ask."

"Of course, the biggest question is why me? Why am I mixed up in this? I'm literally *nobody*."

He turns to face me. "Alvin, you're not nobody! You're willing to risk your life to save Emma. You're willing to risk your life to save me. The real world isn't like in films. True bravery and self-sacrifice is a rare thing altogether."

"You know what I mean. The reason it's 'risking my life' to do those things is because I have no power. No magic. No actual skills." Time to get us back on track. I turn my own body toward the Irish boy, so he can see I need to hear the answer. Our knees touch. "Even the elf thought I was too weak. So, why wasn't my mother surprised I could work with you?"

He looks away and exhales a slow breath. "I can't read minds, Alvin. I told you." He stays silent for a beat, and I become afraid that's all I'm going to get. But then he continues. "But yes, I have an idea why she might have thought you could do that. I'm not sure, though, and I don't want to say anything until I am."

Well, that's a hell of a tease! (And not the first time he's teased me with something like this.) He can't realistically expect me to just let that lie there!

"Is it... something bad?"

Collin nods. "You might think so."

My heart sinks. So it *is* something awful. Something I don't know about myself. Something even worse than being born a monster that wants to suck the life force out of other people, and who will make them like it while he does it.

"As in... I could eventually become an evil, genocidal archdemon like you say my mom used to be?"

I'm dead serious when I say those words, so I'm surprised when he rolls his eyes and straight-up guffaws in response. "No, Alvin. You'll never be *anything* like her. You're too good a person."

"Then *what*?"

He squeezes his fingers together, pensively. "It takes two people to create a child. I think this has something to do with your father."

My blood chills several degrees. Learning about my father is something I both want and very much don't want. Mom deliberately changed the subject whenever it came up. The most I got was that he was a rich man traveling on business and they only spent one night together. You'd think I would have pushed for more details, but even as a kid, I'd feel this *sense of dread* whenever he came to mind.

Maybe there was a reason for that.

"What about him? Who…" I swallow hard, steeling myself, as a sense of panic rises in my throat. "Who was he?"

Collin's eyes flick up and to the right. He holds them there for a long pause.

His breath pushes out in a long hiss, and he shakes his head.

"I honestly don't know. No matter how many times I ask, I can't get an answer. The most likely explanation is that it's not human knowledge, and never was."

"And if my father was human…"

"Then chances are I'd know. Unless my power was being blocked by magic somehow—but I'm not sure what could do that."

"You think you know *what* he was, though…" I'm holding my breath.

"I have a hunch based on circumstantial evidence. But I could be wrong, and then I would have upset you for nothing." He looks over at me, wary. Like he's hovering over a bomb, afraid of cutting the wrong wire. "Do you still want me to tell you?"

Something deep inside me screams no.

I punt. "Whatever it is, you think Mom knows."

His lips purse, eyes narrow. "It's clear she's had suspicions about something. And now seeing you with the watch has confirmed them. I'm not sure what she can do with that information. Hopefully, nothing. But the fewer hooks this woman has in you, the better."

He's not wrong about that. And maybe he's also not wrong about holding off on telling me who he thinks my father is. For now, anyway. I mean, it's not like I don't already have enough drama in my life at the moment.

The thrumming panic inside me starts to recede.

"Whoever my dad is, you *really* think it's okay for Mom to know and for me not to?"

His face brightens—probably because he's realizing I'm letting it go. "I don't see how you knowing now would change anything. And I promise, if it becomes something I think you need to know, I will tell you. Maybe at that point, I'll have more information, so it won't feel like a bad thing at all."

Well, that at least sounds hopeful.

"All right. But you're forgetting that you're going to be set free today!" I say, just as happy to change the subject. "I mean, I should probably come up with a few smart questions to make sure Rafa can get Emma to safety, but then I'm breaking you out."

"Right." The blue in his irises darkens. "Well, that is a lovely thought."

I touch his shoulder. "You don't think this druid will have the answer?"

"I've been trapped in this artifact for ages. If there is a way to get me out, I doubt it will be easy."

My face falls a bit at that. He notices and immediately takes my hand in his, rubbing the space between my thumb and forefinger with his own thumb. (Which makes my stomach do a little jump. But not in a bad way.) He then tilts his head and squints up at me, affable, all storm clouds blown away. "But 'not easy' doesn't mean '*impossible.*' And, like I said, you're very brave for even trying. Look, we won't have to hop trains for at least forty minutes. Why don't you try to grab a bit of kip?"

"Kip." I've never heard that word before, but somehow I still understand, and the moment Collin says it is the moment it hits me. I am exhausted. It's been more than twenty-four hours since I slept. And whatever boost of adrenaline I've been riding on since facing off against Mom, it's clearly wearing off. I'm having to work to keep my eyes open.

"You're right," I say.

I take out my phone so I can set an alarm, but Collin places his hand over the screen. "You've no need for that. I can wake you up."

I glance over at him, and he grins broadly at me, all tension from earlier gone. The morning sunlight from the large, plexiglass window behind him shines through his curly blond hair, giving him a halo. His eyes gleam bright as sapphires from the light of the opposite window. I suck in a breath, a bit dazzled.

He takes my shoulders and turns me so my back is toward him. "Here. Rest against me."

I'm not entirely sure how he thinks this is supposed to work, but he pulls me back so he can lean against the wall of the train car, and I'm in his arms, my feet up on the bench. His surprisingly strong biceps flex against my shoulders as he settles me in, and I feel his tummy rising and falling against my back.

No one has ever held me. Not like this. (Hell, even the brief hugs I got today were more than I've gotten in my whole life, and those were being *forced* on me in a creepy vampire house!) So, this feels totally new and frankly really cool.

I get that I'm probably not being smart by agreeing to do this. In the real world, *I* must be the one who's actually leaning against the window frame, which would be unforgivingly solid and awkward like this. I bet it'll give me the mother of all neck cricks. But at this point, after everything I've just gone through, I don't have the energy to protest. And, if I'm being honest, being this way with Collin just feels so *comfy*.

The wool of his green shepherd shirt is thick and soft behind my head, like a pillow. I start to drift almost immediately, and my thoughts become drunk with grogginess. It makes me want to ask stupid questions. Or, at least, the one stupid question I can't let go of.

"Do you think… Do you think Mom could have actually meant it when she said she loved me?"

Collin is silent for a moment. And then his words come out as a whisper. "It's hard for me to think of anyone who really knew you not loving you, Alvin."

I smile, content. It's easily the sweetest thing anybody has ever said to me. And I really do feel so warm and safe, cuddled up here in his arms.

It's almost enough to make me forget it's not real.

16

Collin wakes me up with a hug, arms squeezing tight around my chest. His hot, moist breath brushes against my ear. It feels intimate and sweet—boyfriend stuff.

"Alvin, it's time for us to switch trains."

I sit up and stretch my neck and shoulders. I'm surprised to discover that there are no tight spots or anything. I couldn't have slept more than thirty minutes, but I feel totally refreshed. And even after we've separated and I've moved back to my side of the bench, I still feel the lingering warmth of Collin's arms around my chest.

Huh. In addition to making me feel things, can an Avatar of Knowledge also mask pain? Like maybe I actually have a wicked kink somewhere, but he's just keeping me from noticing it?

I deliberately make the choice to embrace denial and not ask questions I don't really want to know the answers to. Whatever that was, it was nice. And he looks supercute and smiley as we get to our feet. Like he really enjoyed it, too. Maybe for once in my life I can let myself enjoy something that's nice without waiting for the balloon to pop.

We exit through the side doors and head toward the standing eBART shuttle train for the final leg to Antioch, along with a handful of other commuters also switching trains. Halfway across the open concrete platform, I glance over at Collin, just to make sure he's still with me. He notices, and with a grin, playfully swings over and bumps his shoulder against mine. There's a cute little bob now when he walks that goes all the way up to his shoulders. It's almost like a swagger, but sweeter. Especially in his wool shepherd-boy outfit—he looks like some lost prince from a fairy tale, a jaunty hero on top of the world. I have to keep myself from staring.

He takes my hand after we sit down in an empty two-seater on the shuttle train. His skin is soft. I can feel the pulse in his thumb. Somehow it's as if cuddling just those few minutes on BART changed something between us. Opened something up.

It's not real, I remind myself, forcing myself to not look at him. I focus out the window at the gray strip malls along the highway, whizzing past.

But… if I *am* choosing to embrace denial, is it honestly such a bad thing to pretend that some cute boy actually likes me? That I'm on some kind of weird first date that's going really well? That I get to have *that*, just for a little bit longer?

We're quiet for the rest of the train ride and also in the Uber on the way to the druid's. Just enjoying being together, I guess. I know I should probably be peppering him with questions to prepare, but I'm too distracted by our interlaced fingers and the way the light catches the random bit of blond fuzz on his chin, and how he sits so close to me, constantly smiling, like he's living his best life. This whole little scheme of mine to free him isn't something he's allowed to help with, so he probably wouldn't be able to answer my questions, anyway.

(At least, that's what I tell myself as I relax in the back seat of the Uber and let the sides of our bodies, our shoulders and legs, press gently against each other.)

Don't pop the balloon, Alvin.

The druid's house is in the rural outskirts of Antioch, an area with rolling hills of mostly dry, yellow meadow. But it's not hard to tell when we're getting close: The grass literally gets greener, and the California oaks get taller and thicker. By the time we drive up the gravel road to a colorful, gingerbread-like cottage, we're surrounded by acres of lush foliage that feel like they've been nurtured by daily rains instead of suffering under the constant drought of the Bay Area. I step out of the car, and everything smells clean, fresh, and honeyed.

The druid is waiting for us in the rounded wooden archway of her open front door. She's middle-aged with short dark hair, and wears a dirty white T-shirt, jeans with grass stains, and thick leather gardening gloves. I've never met a druid before and, to be honest, I'd been expecting to see someone straight out of a Dungeons & Dragons campaign—you know, the big brown wool cloak with a hood, the staff, the whole nine yards. (More like Collin, I guess.) But she looks like a suburban mom coming straight from her garden. Only the peek of blue tattooed runes under the collar of her shirt implies she could be anything more.

"You must be Alvin!" she says, beaming at me. She makes a half-turn into her doorway and scoops her hand in toward herself a few times. "Come in! Come in!"

If I was surprised by her clothes, I'm even more surprised by her warmth. Mom's "friends" aren't exactly cheerful types. More like lifetime members of the Legion of Broken Toys and Despair. They never seem happy to be around her, and they barely talk to me at all. This… is new.

I glance at Collin, who shrugs, eyes scrunched with uncertainty. This is my show, apparently, and he's just along for the ride. We still hold hands as I follow the woman inside. (I try to mask it by keeping our fingers as close to my hip as I can.)

No matter how she looks, this woman wouldn't be on Mom's speed dial if she weren't crazy powerful. I figure leaning hard into pure politeness is the safest path.

"Thank you so much for seeing me on such short notice, Ms. Blackthorn." I nod at the soiled work gloves she removes and throws onto her kitchen table. "I'm sorry for interrupting your day. I'm sure you were in the middle of something."

"Nonsense! Your mother and I go *way* back. And please, call me Tara." She spins around and, before I can react, she has her hands on my shoulders, clasping them and turning me this way and that. She's taller than me by a few inches. "Look at *you*! So *handsome*. You definitely take after her!"

I feel myself actually blush. "Um... Well... Maybe less so now," I stammer out.

(Collin's no longer next to me. When I look for him, he's across the room, leaning against a glass-windowed standalone pantry.)

"Ach!" she cries, letting go, and bringing my attention back to her. "I know! That whole teenage seductress pose is a horror show, isn't it? What is she thinking?! Doesn't she realize that cougars are in right now?"

I can't help but snort out a laugh at that. "Yeah, well, when it comes to what potential boyfriends are looking for, I, um— I figure she knows what she's doing..."

"You mean *rich* boyfriends, don't you? And rich people are assholes. Why base your whole thing on what *they* want? It's not like she has any problems with money." She throws a quick wave up and down in front of me with her hand, like I'm Exhibit A. "And she's your mother! She should have stuck with her appearance while you were growing up, at least until you yourself decided to try something new. It must have been so confusing!"

Well, she's not wrong.

Hm. We've spent less than a minute together, and already... I'm kind of liking her. I glance over at Collin to get his reaction, but I can't read his expression. Neither wary nor happy to be here. He's doing that glancing-up-in-the-air thing every now and then, but it just seems to leave him looking puzzled. Like maybe our reason for being here has turned off *all* his divine insight.

I snap my attention back to Tara, not wanting to reveal that I can see Collin. My anxiety cranks back up a notch as I realize I should be focused on making small talk. She clearly seems to know exactly what my mom and I are, so I say, "Well, I've never had the power to change myself. What you see is what you get, for better or worse."

Next to the kitchen sink, there's a silver tray on the counter with a well-worn white teapot and two dainty, flowered tea cups. She's adding enormous chocolate-chip cookies from a large aluminum sheet to a china plate laid out next to the cups. From the aroma in the kitchen, they were just baked. She glances over her shoulder.

"That's right. She said you don't feed. So you don't have any incubus powers at all?"

I shrug. "I can detect magic, and I can see in the dark. That's about it."

Suddenly reminded that I do actually have a somewhat-useful power, I casually scan around the room for enchantments and the like. I should at least *check* if there are any dangers, right? There are lots of things that have a little bit of yeasty domestic magic with a unique hint of musky almond, but nothing major. Nothing like the doorway runes in the house on Lake Street that packed serious juice. Nothing on her. And all the stuff on the tray that she's putting together is completely normal.

Collin meets my eyes as I look up from the tea set. He was looking at it, too. His expression seems maybe a little calmer, more confident. Hopefully that's a good sign.

Tara steps away from the counter and comes up to me, holding the tray. I can smell the steam from the teapot. Floral and sweet. "Well I, for one, think your choice to abstain is very cool. It's too easy to rely on supernatural powers in this world, and even easier to use them to take advantage of other people. Bravo, you."

She makes me blush a second time.

"Um, thank you. It's really not a big thing." I don't love having a lot of attention directed at me. But I can't help smiling.

"Alvin, I have known incubi for much longer than you've been alive. Trust me, it is."

I bite my lip, not sure what to say to all these compliments. (Not that I don't like them!) I'm fidgeting the pad of my thumb against the side of my index finger without even realizing it. But she notices and immediately swivels toward the back screen door, saying with a legit Mary Poppins twinkle in her eye, "Well, we should get started, shouldn't we? It's such a nice day! Let's step out into the garden."

"Okay," I say, honestly relieved. And appreciative that she picked up on my anxiety. I know I'm the last person who should judge a book by its cover, but she really does seem different from my mother or anyone else I've met from her crowd. And even though I just had a big breakfast, I don't think I'd mind having two—or maybe *six*—of those richly fragrant, warm-from-the-oven cookies right now.

She takes us out to a wooden table with a slatted round top. It sits on a flat-stone patio in the middle of an expansive lawn. We're surrounded by a huge variety of plants in a riot of colors, like the entire botanical garden from the Golden Gate Park has been compressed into one very large backyard. There are cool landscaping features like a running fountain, and a white wooden lattice and arch over a stone path that leads deeper into the garden. The scent of pollen is heady and tickles my nose.

She gestures to a simple white deck chair and I sit down. She takes the chair just to my left.

"So, I understand you're here to free a spirit trapped by druids a long time ago." She pours us each a cup of tea while resting her fingers on the thin china lid of the pot.

"Yeah," I say. "I was hoping you might know a way. The spirit is the... Uh..." I hesitate, glancing up at Collin for his thoughts. He's standing just behind her. Considering my mom's reaction, I'm not sure how much I should reveal. He frowns and shakes his head.

"The Avatar of Knowledge, right?" she offers.

Ah. Okay. Mom already told her. Collin rolls his eyes, frustrated.

She holds out her hand. "May I see the inscriptions on the watch?"

Collin steps around her and comes next to me, urgent. "Mind yourself, Alvin. I know she seems nice, but I've been trying to ask questions about her history, what things she's working on, who she's worked *for*, and I'm only able to get bits and pieces. Maybe it's a druid thing, another limitation built into the artifact. But it's not *common*."

I want to ask if he thinks the fact we're trying to get him free is what's actually messing him up, but his alarm has made me cautious enough that I still don't want to tip Tara off that I have access to the Avatar. Instead, I try to nod as casually as I can, like I'm responding to her but also letting Collin know I hear him.

He's obviously aware I'm going to have to show the watch, though—we're not just here for tea and cookies—so he says, "Whatever you do, just don't keep us separated for long, yeah?"

I give one final, definitive nod, still smiling at Tara, and remove the watch from my back pocket. Collin disappears immediately, and when I reveal the latched silver timepiece in my hand, I say, "Just to be clear, I'm not giving this to you."

Her eyes flick up to me, a little baffled, and I'm immediately embarrassed at how that sounds. "I'm sorry. It's nothing personal. It's just that 'giving' is kind of a big deal with this artifact."

Her eyes soften with understanding. "Right. Giving so often *is* in this life." She winks at me. "I perfectly understand."

She doesn't remove the watch from my palm, but she does run her index finger along the golden (and, I realize now, *Celtic*) knotwork that lines the edges. She asks me to turn it over and does the same on the other side, stroking the designs.

"How does it work? Do you need to open it to access the Avatar?" Her voice is hushed.

"Something like that," I hedge, trying to at least respect Collin's warning.

"Of course. That makes sense," she says. "It's exquisite. And thousands of years old! They obviously wouldn't have had the metallurgy for *any* of this design back in prehistoric Ireland—let alone have known how to create an actual pocket watch! It must adapt to the times. Incredible!"

Yeah, sure, that is incredible, I guess. And it could be easy to get caught up in her enthusiasm—especially when it's about magic, which is something I'd love to learn more about.

But her words shake me. *Thousands* of years old?

I'm not sure why I'm so surprised. Sure, Collin *looks* my age and speaks modern English, but did I really think he was trapped by druids as some kind of spirit baby twenty or so years ago, and just grew up in the watch? Honestly, who knows how long he existed before they caught him? He could be *millions* of years old, right?

She closes my fingers around the timepiece and steps back. "This artifact is very powerful, Alvin. And for the moment, it's all yours. Are you *sure* you want to free the Avatar?"

There's a look of warning in her eyes. And even though Collin has been nothing but cool with me, something inside whispers that maybe I should listen to that warning. I haven't even known Collin a day. The truth is, there *is* a lot about him that's still a complete mystery. And not too long ago, I was at least considering the possibility that he might have been trapped in the artifact for a reason, that he could actually be some Lovecraftian horror…

"Do you think it might be dangerous to let him out?"

Her motherly smile returns, and her gaze becomes searching. "You seem like a boy with a strong moral compass who's been through a thing or two in life. What does your *gut* tell you?"

Well, my gut tells me that the handsome, young-looking dude trapped in the watch has the most adorable warm smile, and that I want to snuggle and cuddle with him on trains all day long.

My anxiety, on the other hand, tells me that I'm not exactly the best judge of character, and that my track record with cute guys who act nice to me, while very limited, is a far cry from what you'd call stellar.

But she asked about my gut, so I say, "I feel like he's a good guy. That he would never hurt anyone…"

She nods, completely satisfied. "Well, that's good enough for me!" Then she raises an eyebrow, intrigued. "And it's a 'he,' is it? So the spirit presents to you as male?"

My brows scrunch in confusion. And then just as quickly, I force myself to relax them. Right. Forget how old he is—of course, the Avatar of Knowledge might not even *be* a guy! It's a spirit! Do they even have genders?

Like everything else, how I see him could all just be an illusion he's creating to help us work better together or something. My anxiety and just overall frustration with myself (and my seemingly incurable gullibility!) ticks up one more notch.

"Of course," I say, looking away, feeling foolish. "It's an immaterial being. I guess it can appear however it wants…"

"Perhaps," she says, frowning as she hears me practically mumble those last words. She then leans in and gives my shoulder another motherly squeeze, her voice becoming more encouraging. "*Or*, now that I think more about it, maybe it *could be* male. There are stranger things in this world, and even stranger things from beyond it! Forget what I just said. I shouldn't have reacted that way about your *friend*. We are all geeky about something. For me, it's plants and old magic. Sometimes I let my mouth run away with me without thinking." She chuckles with self-deprecation.

"It's… still a good point," I say, painfully aware that

my recent choice to "embrace denial" with Collin might not have been as mature or self-affirming as I thought it was.

She stands. "Well, in any event, I think you are doing the right thing here! I also think I might know a way to help set your guy free. If you don't mind me abandoning you for a few minutes, I have something in my basement that I'm pretty sure will help!"

"No, I don't mind," I say.

She turns to go, and before I realize what I'm doing, I raise my fingers to her arm, stopping her. Touching anyone, let alone a virtual stranger, isn't like me. But if she really does have something that will work, that means I might not ever see Collin again, and whether he's anything like he appears or not, I'm going to have to deal with how it feels to lose him. It's something I hadn't really let myself think about at all, and I'm glad it'll be someone like her—someone actually kind and thoughtful, the *opposite* of my mom—who'll be here when it happens.

"Thank you. I really appreciate your help. I, uh— I don't have many friends, and it's actually really nice not to have to do this alone."

Her eyes widen, and she seems both surprised and maybe even genuinely touched. "You really are a sweet boy, Alvin. Your mother has no idea how rare and special that is."

She then gives my hand a warm pat and heads inside.

Sweet. Yeah, not a word Mom would ever use about me. Not unless she was being sarcastic, anyway. I know my guard should be raised. Still, I can't help but like this woman. Or wish, at least in a very small way, that someone like *her* could have been my mother growing up.

But that's not reality.

To stop myself from thinking truly insane thoughts, I check in with the Obligation inside me. That's the other reason I need to free this spirit, and it seems like Mom kept *that* information, at least, close to her vest. After my little nap, the compulsion is actually a bit quieter than it was before. But it doesn't feel any weaker. If anything, it feels like it's waiting for the right moment to kick me when I'm down. I wonder if maybe I should ask Tara about it. Supposedly druids have dealt with the fae for centuries. She might know things that Mom and Collin don't.

I look down at the watch that I'm still holding in my palm, an artifact that apparently is thousands of years old. I exhale a long breath through puffed-out cheeks. So, really, what *is* Collin? I don't *think* he's been trying to trick me. He acts as if he truly likes me, and I hope he knows he doesn't have to fake that to get me to help him. But even if he's not faking, let's be real a moment—what could someone like me even mean to an incorporeal, divine, *ancient* Avatar of Knowledge? Could the flirting just be some kind of game for him? Play-acting the role of a "perfect young lover" for the poor, lonely incubus boy? Nothing more than a bit of fun to temper the crushing boredom of immortality, kinda like my mom?

The thought that Collin could be *anything* like my mother instantly reminds me that I promised to stop asking myself stupidly painful questions, so I glance at the table and see my cup is no longer steaming. It looks like it's cooled down enough to drink and since, in my experience, tasty food and bev are super useful for maintaining denial, I take a big sip. It's actually not bad. Perfect temperature, anyway. Sweet with just a hint of a bitter aftertaste.

I don't drink a lot of tea, and its acrid flavor is the main reason why. (Although this tastes sharp in a different way than I've had before.) I take another sip and discover that now I actually kind of like the bitterness. It's *bracing*. (That's the word you use for tea, right?) Maybe my taste buds are growing up some? Even so, I'm not so grown-up that I'm not totally going to smash the huge pile of cookies on that dainty china plate. I grab the biggest one with my free hand, take a bite of its pure, chewy, chocolatey goodness (still warm! so soft!) and realize the two go especially well together.

Tea and cookies. I'm pretty sure that's what they have in the UK every day. Ireland, too, I bet. Not that Collin would ever have had that. Not really.

I glance down again at the artifact in my hand. I'm still so shook by Tara's reminder that Collin might be nothing like the cute Irish boy I've been kissing and cuddling (and *more*) that I consider not putting the watch back in my pocket at all. Maybe it would be easier to just set him free without some long goodbye.

Maybe the smart choice here is to just accept the obvious: that despite how he looks, Collin and I are very, very different.

I finish the cookie and wash it down with another swallow of tea to buy more time to think. I realize that *whatever* he is, I still need to ask about exactly where

Emma is in the Benevolent Society building and what the Monster Hunters will be up against when they try to save her. And I basically gave Collin my word that I'd bring him back as soon as possible. It's that last one that really decides it. In all fairness, he's done nothing wrong. In fact, it's been the opposite. Yeah, there's stuff I don't know about him and that's a little scary, but it's not right to totally ghost him just because feelings are hard and I wasn't smart enough to ask him about any of his backstory ahead of time.

I return the watch to my back pocket, and Collin immediately appears in front of me, looking very relieved. "Oh, good! There you are! Safe as houses."

Hm. Seems my theory from before was right. When he's not "active," he can't actually see what's going on around him. Could he still be awake that whole time? If so, Mom's boredom would have *nothing* on his.

But again, I don't know what he feels, and I can't know. I try to smile at his UK slang (are houses really that safe?) and raise my cup at him, not wanting to talk about what's truly on my mind.

"I'm fine. Tara continues to be cool. She even makes good tea." I take another sip and enjoy the flavor still more this time.

Suddenly, Collin's eyes widen with horror.

"Wait! God! Alvin! Stop!"

I freeze, not even swallowing, and watch Collin move his tongue around the inside of his mouth, like he's the one who just drank something. "Intensely sweet, *bitter aftertaste*... Oh, Jaysus. It's belladonna!"

I immediately spit out the tea into the cup.

"Wait, you mean the *poison*…?" I hiss, as quietly as I humanly can while at the same time freaking the hell out. Maybe it's just my saliva, but it still feels like there's a bunch of the tea left in my mouth. I try to spit out more, but my mouth goes dry.

"Yes. And from what I can tell from your taste buds, she also added a few *other* botanicals to speed the effects." He jams his fingers through his hair, clearly freaking out himself. "Oh, God! I'm so sorry! I tried to sense if the tea was dangerous when we were in the kitchen. I did! But she must be able to hide things from me!" He kneels beside me. "Tell me, exactly *how much* did you drink?"

I look down at the cup.

It's more than half empty.

17

"Um, I had a cookie, too," I say, stupidly.

Because stupid is exactly what I am. I'm apparently so desperate for someone, *anyone*, to like me, I've just assisted a perfect stranger with my own murder. Not exactly "paranormal investigator" tactical awareness there!

"Okay. Think. *Think!*" Collin is so scared for me, his arms are literally shaking while he paces rapidly back and forth, talking to himself. Then his eyes dart over to me with fierce resolve. "We've got to induce vomiting *right now*, Alvin!"

Well, good luck with that. I've never thrown up in my life, ever. Maybe it's an incubus thing, but I have literally no gag reflex. It was something I was even a little proud of, figuring how if I ever met the right guy, I could impress him with my sword-swallowing skills or whatever. Turns out it's yet another way me not being normal is coming to bite me in the ass.

"Unless you can conjure up a magic vomiting spell or something, I don't think I can do that, Collin." I'm whispering as best I can, but I'm so amped up, it's definitely a loud stage whisper.

Collin looks up and away, his eyes unfocused, and gives a quick nod, somehow knowing not to argue with me about this. "*Right*." He then looks over at a small greenhouse at the far end of the garden, away from the house, through the wooden arch and down the stone path. "There! She's growing a bunch of tropical plants and one of them is *Carapichea ipecacuanha*. Its roots are what make ipecac syrup, something that's been used for ages to induce vomiting after poisoning. We need to get in *there*!"

I have no idea how long Tara will be away, or even if this plant is going to work on me, but a bad option is better than no option. I get to my feet and notice I'm already feeling disoriented and off-balance. I don't know if that's the belladonna or the beginning of a panic attack, but I do know my mouth is hella dry. *Unnaturally* dry. Hopefully, this epi-kacka-wanna-whatever plant is juicy, or I'm not going to be able to get it down!

I start lurching along the thin slate-rock path that leads from the lawn patio. Collin takes my arm to steady me, which feels like it helps, but who knows what it's doing in real life?

"She also has *Physostigma venenosum* in there. You can use that to make the direct antidote to belladonna poisoning. It can be toxic too, and getting the right dose will be fierce tricky, but with my help, you should be able to manage it."

"Uh-huh," I husk out, completely overwhelmed. But sure, okay! The garden is getting brighter, and things are starting to blur. I don't know a lot about belladonna poisoning, but I think I heard somewhere it dilates your pupils. And maybe everything else, since I'm beginning to feel hot all over. Whatever Tara put in her brew, it's acting crazy fast.

"Um, I don't feel so good, Collin." My voice sounds rough. My tongue's too thick.

He looks over at me in that unfocused way of his, like he's seeing through me. "Ah. *Shite*. I'm not going to lie. It's bad. She's made something complex. I'm seeing multiple chemical compounds in your stomach, any one of which in larger doses could kill you. And together—"

A large metal spring creaks out somewhere behind us. It's the screen backdoor to the house opening. I've only made it about twenty paces away from the table, not even a quarter of the way to the greenhouse. I look behind me and see Tara stepping out. In front of her chest, she's holding open a thick brown leather folio of loose monastic-style illuminated illustrations on parchment. She sees me and is distracted just enough to lower the pages, revealing the top half of one. There's a drawing of a thick green leather-bound book. And on the book's cover, a complicated triangular knot symbol under large cat eyes.

Collin stops—which, since I'm leaning on him, stops me.

"Jaysus! I know that book!" he says, astonished.

"Alvin, honey, come back," Tara says, her voice full of motherly concern. "I think I've found what you need."

My head feels like it's full of cotton again, like after the car accident, except now I feel even crappier. There's part of me that knows I should keep moving away from Tara.

But based on how Collin just reacted, maybe she *is* really trying to help, and this is all a misunderstanding?

It takes me way longer than it should to realize how insane that thought is. Long enough for me to drop to one knee.

Collin grabs my arm and tries to tug me up. "C'mon, Alvin, you can't just give up! We've got to go!"

I realize he was also tugging me before, when I was just standing there, but the mental debate I was having about what to do was apparently taking up all my poison-addled mental bandwidth.

Tara puts the folio down on the table and glances at my cup. Then she looks up at me, and her expression is a mixture of realization and sympathy.

"Oh," she says. "You're feeling the effects of the tea, aren't you? I wasn't sure how much natural resistance you'd have, so I made it quite strong. I might have overdone it a little."

Right. She's not trying to help. Because she's actually a villain! (Because I don't get to have even a *pretend* cool mom for more than five freaking minutes!) With Collin's "assistance," I manage to get back up to my feet and turn away from her, but I only get a few more steps before I trip and fall heavily, face-first, into the ground next to the stone path.

Now I feel *really* sick. I've got a killer headache, and my stomach is cramping like crazy.

"I'm sorry about this, sweetie." My nose is pressed flat in the dirt, but it sounds like Tara's coming closer. "And I promise you're going to be okay. Eventually. That artifact was lost to us centuries ago, and I just need some time to convince you to do the right thing and return it."

"Don't give up, Alvin! Don't give up! Keep going!" It's Collin's voice. Desperate. It sounds so far away.

In fact, everything seems far away. Still, I need to listen to him. I try to crawl forward, and it's like my arms and legs belong to someone else. I'm at the edge of the lawn, just up to the garden proper, where there are these beautiful purple flowers towering above me. They continue on to drape over a white wooden arch that carves out a space for the stone path to the greenhouse. The purple vegetation is strangely fascinating to me right now. Probably because it's full of tart magic with a strong musky almond undertone. I hear Tara approach, and the plant's woody vines spread out and grow toward me. It's like I'm watching a time-lapse movie. It's both cool and terrifying at the same time, because I can't move to get away.

The woody vines twine all around me—my throat, chest, wrists, stomach, legs and ankles. I feebly make an attempt at fighting them, but my limbs are like jelly. The rough branches slowly twist me around and drag me up so I'm vertical again. They pull my forehead and back tight against the side of the sturdy arch. Then my arms and legs get stretched out and bound to the latticework. I'm essentially crucified.

My heart is racing, but it seems to be missing beats. Tara stands in front of me, eye-to-eye, looking very sympathetic. She's holding something in a small blue bottle.

"Well, *this* won't do! You're dying, and as you probably already know, you're no good to anyone dead. But I do have the antidote. Be a good boy and drink a little for me, would you?"

I try to focus on Collin, hoping he'll give me some guidance. I can't turn my head, but I know he must be next to me. What would he want me to do? I mean, it's hard to think of any way this situation could be any worse, but maybe I *shouldn't* drink the potion an evil witch is bringing to my lips?

But I can't see him at all. Then a bunch of sour fluid is in my mouth. She clamps my nose and mouth closed, so it's not long before I have to swallow to breathe.

And everything blooms to white.

18

I'M IN AND OUT FOR GOD KNOWS HOW LONG. I mostly just feel sick the whole time. Headache. Stomach cramps. Feverish. Tied up. I do remember hearing Tara say that there was no point in struggling. That the wisteria vines are as strong as steel.

But there's another voice, a boy's voice, talking to me. Sometimes it makes sense, but mostly it doesn't. Still, the sound of it makes me feel better.

Then, in a sudden rush, all the pain goes away. Collin is right in front of me. He's in total focus, but everything else around him is a blurry smear of color.

"Alvin! Alvin! Can you hear me?!"

He's gripping my shoulders, which really isn't necessary, since I'm still trussed up against the arbor by the woody branch-vine thingies. I realize I'm surprisingly unstressed, considering what's happening. In a good mood, even.

"Um, yeah," I mutter. "And I can see you, too."

I try my best to concentrate. I'm still hella fuzzy, but

things definitely feel a little more clear. I know where I am, anyway. (Which, for the record, seems to be about ten miles up shit's creek.)

(Still strangely not mad about it, though.)

"Ah, thank God!" he says. "I've bumped up both the acetylcholine and the endorphins in your brain, while also knocking back a bit of the dopamine. It's fighting the effects of the poison, but you're using up the reserves of your own body fast. Since you're essentially human right now, there's not a lot there. It won't buy us much time." He leans in, intense. "She's nearby, but not close enough to understand you. We've got to get you away from her!"

I squint at him. "You… can change my brain?" I'm trying to speak as quietly as possible, but my tongue is so sluggish, I'm not sure I'm actually forming words. Still, he seems to understand me fine.

"The longer you use the artifact, the more in sync we get. *If* I don't fight it, anyway. I can't affect the outside world directly, but there *are* meditative techniques that can alter neural function, and I basically just gave your subconscious a little crash course on that."

I try to wrap my head around all the bizarre ten-dollar words he's just thrown at me, and a memory of practicing Buddhist concentration meditation lurches into view. I have this vague image of being under a tree in some forest in Thailand and told to focus on my breathing, right at the tip of my nose. And doing that for a *very* long time, until I started feeling legit high. Kind of like how I'm feeling now.

Huh. I've never meditated a day in my life. I wonder if Collin can download other instructions into my head, like how to fight using kung fu, *Matrix*-style. That would be pretty frickin' cool. (Not to mention super helpful, considering how my day's been going!)

I'd kinda like to ask, but he's fully focused on getting me out of here—which, let's face it, is why he's the Avatar of Knowledge and I'm the stupid incubus boy who lets nice women poison him.

"She's only given you enough antidote so you don't die. She's looking for you to suffer, and she's going to fill you with other drugs to make you more compliant. To make you *want* to give her the watch."

Even though my tongue still isn't moving right, I am feeling more like myself in my own head. At least, more like the Alvin who stood up to an elven warrior with a big-ass sword just a few hours ago.

"I'm not going to do that, Collin."

A boyish smile flickers across his face. It's a little bashful.

"I know that. I know you won't." Then his worried frown returns. "But she doesn't. She's going to keep trying stuff on you until you break. And it's not like we're dealing with a professional anesthesiologist at a hospital. This is a mad lady feeding you toxic plants in her backyard. Eventually, she'll get the doses wrong, and it *will* kill you." He pulls his face into a fierce expression. "There's no getting around it. We're going to need to charge up your incubus powers."

My brows scrunch. "You can *do* that? Like with the… neuro-stuff?"

"No. You need to drain actual life force. *My* life force.

And that's not something I can teach you." He glances away, shy again. "It, um, doesn't work like that."

After a breath, Collin returns to me, eyes vulnerable. He tenderly brushes the back of his fingernails against my cheek. His fingertips then slide down to my neck. They tickle, but not in a bad way. More of a *nice* way.

Oh.

All my good mood instantly evaporates. Because I finally realize how truly fucked I am, and it's not the kind of fucked he's looking for.

"Collin, if you mean we have to have sex again, I'm sorry, but there's just no way!" Just for giggles, I check in with my dick—which, of course, is as limp as a wet rag. Limper, to be honest. "I mean, even if I *wasn't* poisoned, tied up, exhausted, and fighting an Obligation—my life's in danger, *your* life's in danger! Or at least your freedom from eternal torture! I know I'm an incubus, but I can't just turn my horniness on and off like a switch. I don't care how many endorphins or whatever are flooding my brain right now—sex is literally the furthest thing from my mind. I'm too freaked out!"

I expect him to tell me I need to try. That there's actually some kind of special sex demon technique guaranteed to get you hot and hard while awaiting your own execution. That, ultimately, sex is what defines me, no matter what's going on.

But he doesn't. Instead, his expression melts into pure empathy. "I know. Even if it were possible for other incubi to get in the mood here—and I really doubt it would be—it's not who you are. You aren't some kind of sex machine.

You're this sound, gentle, caring, and very *human* lad who feels so much, and I'm dead glad I found you."

He leans forward and affectionately presses the side of his face against mine. His cheek is super soft. The brush of his skin doesn't do anything for my dick. But it sends a warm pulse through me. And what he just said warms me even more.

His breath is at my ear, gentle and moist. "What we did last time gave you incubus powers for several minutes. This time, we just need a short burst to get you out of these vines and away from Tara. And you don't need a hard cock for that—you just need to *connect* with someone who really likes you."

He slides his arms around my back and pulls me forward. I feel the vines loosen, and I smoothly step down off the lattice, the restraints slipping off me. Somehow I know I must still be trapped up there, bound up tight, but it feels good to be free of the rough branches, even if it is an illusion.

We're now standing in front of each other, a foot apart, face-to-face. His sky-blue eyes are so kind, and he's got this cute puppy-dog smile. Even with being totally freaked out, I can't deny it—he looks adorable. He's so close, the smell of pine and heather from his shepherd-boy outfit fills my nostrils.

"I know you'll find this hard to believe, but you *are* very special to me. I would give anything to keep you safe. So, please, Alvin—open your heart and let me in."

He pulls me into an embrace, and without thinking about it, my arms draw around him, too. An actual, mutual hug is still a novel sensation for me, even if it is imaginary. He feels so solid. So strong. Then his lips find their way to mine.

I'm tempted to pull back. I wasn't joking about not being at all in the mood for sexy stuff. And I really don't want to see his disappointment when I don't respond how he expects.

But when he kisses me—slowly, tenderly—I don't stop him. Even though my mouth was dry before, there's just enough saliva to keep things smooth, and as his mouth caresses mine, I'm surprised to find it actually feels good. Not sexy good. Not really. But sweet good. Comforting good. Happy good. Good that this charming, loving boy found a way for our bodies to be even *closer*.

Of course, he's right that it's hard to believe he would really care about me. I mean, we've known each other for less than a day. And even if we had all the time in the world, I'm still…. *me*. I know what I am, and despite what the evil druid lady said, I'm not someone anyone would think was "special." At least, that's not something someone as beautiful as Collin would ever think. And it's certainly not something an ancient, all-knowing entity would think, either.

But he's told me what I need to do here. Just like with sparking the car to life, I need to *believe*. And let's face it, if I have any real super-power, it's gotta be embracing pipe dreams, right? And this particular flight of fancy isn't even that hard. The making out, the smiles, the strong embrace—none of it feels like some hallucination. It all feels completely real. And of course, I *want* to believe that a kind, smart, and totally cute guy could actually like me. *Does* like me. It's been part of almost every fantasy I've had since I was twelve. It's something I've wanted for as long as I can remember.

So, if I'm going to believe any lie during my last moments on Earth, sure, let it be *that* one.

Collin's breath tastes like mint and fennel, and he sure knows how to kiss. It's like he's massaging my lips with his —hard one moment, soft the next—but somehow it's still easy to follow his lead and kiss him back the same way. Like we fit together perfectly. Like it's the most natural thing in the world.

But what really feels good right now is actually happening much lower than my mouth. Not around my cock (sorry!) but instead somewhere in the center of my chest. We're hugging super close, and as we make out, there's, like, this happy little balloon inflating somewhere behind my solar plexus, just behind where his body presses against me the most.

Or maybe it's more like music. A beautiful note of music. Ringing out, high and pure inside me.

And it keeps growing, becoming more and more moving, until it feels like I'm about to burst with joy. All just from sweet kisses… Maybe what we're doing *is* less intense than the sex, but in some ways, without all the erotic distraction, it's even better. And whether it's *real* real, or just in my head, I can't deny how it's making me feel. How it makes me feel about *him*. This handsome, caring boy in my arms who drinks me in like he just can't get enough of me.

I break away and draw in close to his ear.

"I like you, too, Collin." I huff the words out, unable

to keep them in, letting myself get caught up in this impossible dream. "I really like you, too!"

He pulls back, and there is this look of surprised delight in his eyes. Like he's been waiting his whole life to hear that. And I have to tell you, to have someone look at me that way, like I'm someone worth waiting for, like I really *matter* to him——

Well, that does it. My lips plunge against his, needing all of him now. I kiss him fiercely, *deeply*, and I can feel my heart literally opening up. Letting Collin in. All the way in.

Then some dam breaks, and an ocean of delight rushes out from him into me. My whole body becomes flooded with vibrant, gooey, honey-sweet pleasure. It's totally sex-level intense—*more* than that, even—but it's not sexy. Not exactly.

It feels like love.

I'm feeding on love.

A bunch of things start to happen at once. Most of me stays focused on this beautiful kiss with this beautiful boy, and the thrill of everything he's giving me right now. (He's even making little whimpers as I suck on his lips—*happy* whimpers!—which is crazy awesome to hear.) But I also feel the poison burning out of my system. Whatever damage it did is being healed, and all the sickness that my endorphins kept me from focusing on is lifting away.

I also feel myself getting stronger. *A lot* stronger.

After what must be a solid minute of sensuous necking, of taking him in, Collin pulls back his head, and then I'm no longer hugging him, away from the arbor. I'm back, trapped against the lattice, feeling the bite of rough bark against my wrists, forehead, and neck. It's where I've been all this time.

"Jaysus," Collin says, his voice husky, breathing heavy. He's in front of me, floating just a few inches above the ground. He wipes his lower lip with the knuckle of his thumb, wantonly. "*That* went better than I expected. I really don't want it to stop. But we're out of time."

Nothing is blurry anymore. I can see Tara over his shoulder. She's dragged one of the chairs and the big table in front of me on the lawn and is finishing grinding something up on its flat wooden surface using a stone mortar and wooden pestle. She immediately notices me looking at her.

"Ah, you're finally back, are you?" she says. "That fever was *bad*, buddy. You've just been muttering pure nonsense for over an hour. I'm sure you still feel pretty crummy, and I'm sorry about that, but I will give you the rest of the antidote—*once* you agree to give me the watch, that is."

She starts walking up to me with the mortar in one hand and the blunt wooden pestle in another. It's got a lump of pale pink paste on its tip.

"Of course, maybe you'll still not want to do that since, for whatever reason, you seem to have decided the Avatar spirit is your pal. But I'm sure once I apply some of this lotus tree fruit to your skin, you'll soon see things my way."

She smiles at me. It's not at all kind or maternal.

It's the smile of a monster. Because of course it is. She's one of *Mom's* friends.

I glance back at Collin, who's slid to the side so I can see Tara clearly. He doesn't say anything. He just floats at my level, beaming at me. With confidence. With love. The same love that's now filling the muscles of my arms and legs with boundless energy.

My head is crystal clear. My thoughts are sharp. As she comes closer, I take note that both of Tara's hands are full. She is so sure I'm completely helpless, she's not taking *any* precautions.

Which makes sense, because without having fed, I'd just be a regular human boy, right? Hell, a *weak-ass* human boy, all tied up. She doesn't think I'm capable of doing anything at all to her. Not anything that would actually matter.

But she's wrong about me—at least right now.

Which means it's high time to show her what a *real* monster can do.

19

To make this work, I'm going to need to be both hella strong and hella fast. Luckily for me, I know I'm both right now.

Tightening the muscles in my neck to protect my throat, I rip my upper body forward and down in one thrust, shredding the branches around my head, neck, and arms, as well as a good chunk of the lattice I was attached to. I'm so strong, it all comes apart like wet paper. And I'm so fast, I'm able to use my free hands to rip off the vines around my stomach and legs before she even has a chance to react.

She's barely finished widening her eyes in shock when I hear Collin yell: "Now *hit* her, Alvin! Hard as you can!"

I've never hit anyone in my life, but I charge straight at her like a linebacker, left shoulder forward, yelling "AHHHH!" and trying to channel the entire fifteen minutes of football I've ever watched on TV. (Mom hosted a Super Bowl party once. The goblins ate the coffee table. I mostly hid in my room.) Tara's only able to shout

out a single word before I ram myself into her. For good measure, I smack up that stone bowl of mush she was carrying with my right hand and ram the whole thing into her face.

Let's see how *she* likes being poisoned!

Again, I'm just blown away with how strong I can be after I feed. The impact of my body slam knocks her back a full ten feet, off the lawn and into a whole bed of red, orange, and blue flowers.

But even as she's flying back in the air, I realize that despite my super-powers, I was still too slow. Apparently, one quick brush of her fingertips against the runes under her shirt was all she needed. Quick as lightning, her body stretches and transforms mid-flight. She becomes browner, furrier, and much, much bigger as her limbs tear through all her clothes in an instant.

What tumbles into the flowers isn't human.

"Oh, shite," Collin gasps. "She's turned herself into a grizzly bear!"

Other than a few furtive glances at some of the leather dudes at the Folsom Street Fair, my only *actual* experience with bears is with the stuffed teddy kind. And I guess I've seen a nature doc or two. I'm still crazy-strong, though, so I'm not sure how much trouble I'm in here. It's just a big animal, right?

But Collin seems to know. "This changes things. You're not going to be able to outrun her. She's got four-inch claws, ten times your weight. Almost three feet of height on you when on her hind legs. You're a little faster, but you won't be for long."

In the upper right of my vision, a half-filled horizontal

green bar with a black outline slides in, like a heads-up display in a video game. It's labeled INCUBUS POWER, is currently at 65%, and it's going down at least a percent a second. (Well, that's handy to know!)

The massive grizzly bear rolls up onto her feet and roars.

Okay. Gotta admit, this thing is monstrously huge. And yeah, super-powers or no, she is legit scary.

Collin picks up on my fear. "Don't worry. We are a long way from done, Alvin! You got the lotus tree paste in her eyes, which should impair her vision and will eventually have a sedative effect. And unlike with a werewolf, she's still 100% human in her head. She won't want to kill you, which means she's also going to need to be careful. A lot more careful than you need to be." He glances up to the right in his unfocused way, then twists his head over to the house. "Got it! Grab that rake over there!" He then looks back at the garden next to us. "And then swing it at the base of that little bush with the bell-like blue flowers. You'll need to use the rake to scoop it up from the roots!"

He shouts all that out super-fast, in less than a second, somehow expecting me to understand him when facing down a terrifying grizzly from ten feet away. But, of course, I do understand what he wants. Completely. Because that's how using the Avatar works. I'm not even sure he used actual words, but I just *get* it.

It also helps that the rake, which is propped up in shadow against the back wall of the house, is now glowing brightly with a big red arrow pointing to it. Ditto for the plant he wants me to scoop up in the garden.

Of course, those two things are completely across the lawn from each other. Regular Alvin would have no hope.

But there's nothing regular about me right now.

The bear and I start running at the same time. I'm going for the big garden tool, and she's coming for me, moving at least 25 miles an hour. But I'm going 40, feet whipping back and forth on the grass so fast they blur, so I get to the rake while still keeping *almost* the same distance between us. Its metal handle is long and cool.

"Now, pivot and jump!" Collin yells.

I turn to see a glowing green upside-down parabolic path arcing over the oncoming grizzly that leads to a spot just a couple yards from the glowing plant. I crouch and leap as best I can in its direction. My usual flabby thigh muscles explode with force. The bear is only a yard away from me when I spring, but I clear her head by several feet.

My legs flail in the air and I'm sure I look awkward as hell, but I also feel like I'm flying! If I weren't so terrified, I think I'd actually like it.

I land on my feet several yards behind her and just a few feet away from the blue-flowered shrub. Collin is already there, demonstrating. He's swinging his own phantasmal replica of the rake along a sweeping curve into the ground, again and again. He's showing me the exact angle I'll need to dig the plant up. I glance up and notice that the Incubus Power Bar is at 40%. And the bear is now just a few feet away. There's no time, but Collin still gives me the 411.

"The rake buys you distance, and this plant is wolfsbane. It's pure toxic, even just to touch it. You're going to shove it right in her mouth!"

Well, I certainly appreciate his optimism!

I burst forward and swing the rake sideways into the loose garden soil, easily scooping up the plant at the roots with my extra strength (while spewing a massive spray of dirt all over the place). I spin around, and the grizzly is almost on top of me. Her jaws stretch open wide, hot breath belching out, pulling strings of drool, ready to clamp down on my arm. And I realize that's exactly what Collin was counting on.

Using all my strength and speed, I throw my upper body forward and try to shove the entire end of the rake, now gripping the four-foot-wide plant, down the monster's throat. A grizzly is quick, but not quick enough to dodge me at point-blank range. And even though the rake head is bigger than the creature's jaws, I still get a bunch of the flowers, leaves, and stems deep inside her mouth before she can stop herself.

The massive bear reels back and actually pulls more of the plant off the tines with her teeth in the process. Annoyed and angry, her jaws snap open and shut, her tongue flailing as she tries to get the wolfsbane out. Then, almost immediately, her eyes widen with very human-looking horror. Looks like Tara's now recognized what I fed her! She immediately brings her claws up to try to dig out all of the poisonous plant, but a bear's paws are much bigger and clumsier than a human's. Between her jaw working and the awkward mitts, she's actually eating more of the stuff than removing it.

Collin is grinning. "Bang on, Alvin! The toxin won't

take any real effect for a few minutes, but there's no known antitoxin. She's going to need to do everything she can to get it all out. And if she goes human, her body weight will drop, and it'll just poison her worse. You've just bought us the time we need. Now, *leg it!* As fast as you can!"

I glance up again at my Incubus Power Bar and see it's at 26%. Collin creates one of his glowing, green arrow-paths to sprint on, and I book away from the grizzly and Tara's backyard at full speed.

The arrow continues on over the wooden side fence, which I assume means I'll need to leap. (Which I do—almost as high as before.) And then we're racing down the road with car-like speed, getting as far away from the evil druid lady as we possibly can.

20

I get almost a mile down the vacant, paved two-lane before the green bar in the upper right of my vision hits 0%, disappearing immediately, and I run out of juice. Ahead of me, a few cars whiz by a T-shaped intersection on a wide road. Even though we're still basically in the middle of nowhere, it looks like Collin directed me next to a major traffic corridor. I have no idea if that druid has some magical solution to the wolfsbane, but there's no way I'm going to chance going back to the BART station. I need to get away from Antioch as fast as I can.

Still riding on the last fumes of adrenaline, I use my rideshare app to book a trip all the way back to San Francisco. The cost is truly insane—well over a hundred dollars. But my account is on Mom's credit card, and after what just happened, she can honestly suck it.

I glance at the time—it's almost 12:30, an hour and a half before I need to meet Rafa. Then I crumple forward, palms on knees, as the exertion from the sprint hits me like the couch potato I truly am. Looks like I'm totally back to normal.

Collin's hand lands on my shoulder, giving me support as I huff and puff. He's beaming.

"Jaysus! You were *brilliant*."

I turn my head and smile up at him. His blue eyes sparkle back at me in the East Bay sun. He really is super-cute when he's excited. Hell, let's be real, he's super-cute all the time.

"That was all you, Collin. I just did what you told me."

He shakes his head. "No, Alvin. I mean, sure, I helped. But I've never been in an actual fight before. The previous owners always kept the watch safe and locked up, for all the obvious reasons. I tried to give you the best advice I could, but you made it all happen like it was dead easy. It was like we were in an action film! I mean, Jaysus, we just went through the scariest thing I've ever been part of, and you made it *fun*!"

Uh, I don't think *any* of that was easy—not for me, anyway—but he's not 100% wrong about the fun part. I mean, it was terrifying, but also, now that I think about it, it was kinda cool that I could actually fight off a grizzly, y'know? At least, cool with Collin there.

The car pulls up. The driver, "Dan," is an older guy. White hair. Faded brown small-check shirt over well-worn jeans. Very heavyset. His stomach spills over his ample lap. He confirms my name without even looking my way, and then we're away toward an on-ramp. After I snap on my seatbelt, he chooses to completely ignore me—which, as far as I'm concerned, is perfect. I need a little time to think.

Classic soft rock plays on the radio. Some old love song. I settle into the plush back seat and let my whole body relax. The adrenaline is finally sputtering out, and now I am *tired*. But I'm still feeling the afterglow of whatever it was that Collin and I did. *Feeding on love.* An echo of that sweet, happy note still rings inside. I want to hum along with it.

Collin takes my hand, and we're like we were on the way to the druid's. Just two boys who dig each other, sitting quietly together in the back of a car. Just *being* together.

But it's not that simple, is it? Even what he just said about having "owners" (over the centuries, I assume?) reminds me that he's not just some twenty-year-old dude who thinks I'm cute. Who could maybe become my boyfriend. Who I could even grow old with someday. He's not human at all.

Then again, neither am I.

He playfully grinds his shoulder against my bicep—aggressively snuggling in, resting his cheek on *my* shoulder, his blond curls tickling the corner of my jaw—and that gooey lovefeeling swells in my chest again. Fills my stomach, too. But I'm not feeding on him. I know now what that's like. No, this is different. This is coming all from me.

I think I could be actually falling for him. I think *that's* what this is.

Uff.

I know I'm the King of Pipe Dreams. And I know

everything with Collin is just some kind of illusion. But I'm not having to work anymore to believe we could love each other. Now I'm having to work *not* to believe in it.

My thoughts spin. This is bad. There are a million things I don't know about him. For example, I don't actually know if he really is a "him"! And even if I got great answers to every single one of my questions, I still need to free this spirit from the watch. I'm going to have to let him go. There's no way this doesn't end without me being in a world of pain. Without my heart shattered into jagged little pieces.

And yet… I don't know if I can stop myself. From falling in love, I mean. Not without more information, anyway. He's just too perfect.

I need to be smart, for once. I need to start asking the hard questions, and actually *listen* to his answers. Not let myself simply believe what I want to believe: that I get to have this, whatever this is, for free.

I inhale a deep breath and think about what I should ask first. Maybe I should start with something neutral, like, "Do you think Mom set us up?" Or maybe I *don't* make this about my mother for once, and instead ask, "So, the druid was a bust. What do you think we should do next?" Or maybe, I just cut to the *real* question on my mind: "Collin, who are you really, and why do you keep saying you like me so much?"

In other words, please tell me how I'm supposed to trust you—because I really want to!

I decide to start there. If I can't trust Collin, then really nothing else matters at this point. Of course the problem right now is that Driver Dan would hear me talking to myself like a crazy person and for sure blow up my (already questionable) star rating with Uber. That makes me wonder if there's a way to talk to Collin without anyone else hearing. Like in the back of my throat. I think I've seen that in a book or a movie or something. What's the word for that? To "subvocalize"?

It's worth a shot, anyway. I clear my throat, ready to give that a try—and that's when I get stabbed in the gut with a dozen razor-sharp blades.

Remember when I said that I thought the Obligation was waiting for the right moment to kick me in the nuts? Well, it turns out that it's hard to feel rageful when you've been hopped-up on love and your adrenaline is spent. I have nothing left in the tank to push back against the fae's magic, and it's like the Obligation *knows*.

Sharp edges explode up through the lower chambers of my heart before spreading throughout my entire body in lightning-bolt zigzags—cutting, slicing, *slashing*. Channels of corrosive burn quickly follow in their wake. They aren't real knives, it's not real acid, but it *feels* real.

And it's not just physical pain. I'm also consumed with shame, guilt, and this feeling of total self-loathing. A deep conviction that I'm nothing more than some asshole who breaks his word, and deserves whatever he gets.

Damn. If there's a hell, it's this. Physical agony trumped only by how much you hate yourself. I legit want to die.

I double over and grunt loudly. Collin immediately sits up, but it doesn't take an Avatar of Knowledge to see that I'm in big trouble.

"Alvin, what's wrong?!"

Corrosion and fire race through my veins. Shame and despair consume me. It's like there is nothing else. I can't talk. I can barely think. It was bad before. But I had no idea it had gotten this strong. The Obligation doesn't just hurt—it feels like there is actual physical damage devouring me from within.

I snuffle and wipe my nose.

A wet streak of cherry red trails the back of my index finger.

"Oh, God," Collin says, horrified.

With nothing in its way, the Obligation continues to tear through me. The pain claws down my legs, and up my neck, behind my eyes. And the self-hatred is so persuasive, it's hard to even summon the will to fight it. Because this *is* what I deserve. I should have given the elf what I promised him! And if I'm the kind of guy who won't keep his promises, then I should just straight-up die! Painfully. Awfully.

It's a testament to how powerful fae magic is that 99% of me is totally convinced by that argument. Moments ago, I was basking in love. Now I want nothing more than to end it all. To end myself.

But there's still a part of me that doesn't want that. A part of me that never will want that. And it's going to do whatever it takes to keep me alive.

The monster inside me. My hunger.

I don't know why it didn't rear its ugly head when I was poisoned an hour ago. Maybe the "other botanicals" the druid used were specifically designed to fight it. But that was then. Now the low thrum of predatory desire that's been lurking in the background throws itself hotly against the pain in my limbs and head like a herd of raging bulls—and it knows what it needs to win.

I must be straight-up moaning at this point, because the driver turns around. "Uh, sir... Are you okay?"

I look up at him with a wild expression. I'm covered in dirt from the garden. Blood is, no doubt, streaming from my nose.

His eyes widen with shock. "Jesus!"

Our gaze locks—and that's all it takes. My hunger flails out with savage, invisible tentacles and grabs hold of his soul.

Mom's always made clear that you don't have to *learn* to use your incubus power to overcome humans. That it just knows what to do. That it's the most natural thing in the world. For us, anyway.

But it doesn't feel natural. It feels ferocious.

His jaw goes a bit slack. His eyes soften. "Um..." he says. He blinks hard and twists his head, trying to fight the feeling the monster inside me is pumping into him. The need. The *desire*. I mean, I must look absolutely frightful. He probably doesn't even like boys.

But he doesn't stand a chance.

He swallows hard, turns back in his seat, and returns his eyes to the road. "I'm, uh— I'm going to pull over."

I see him glance up at a road sign, then change lanes to direct the car toward a rest stop, and I feel satisfaction, the line between the monster and me blurring. This has been a long time coming, and it looks like it will be *easy*.

The Obligation is still flaring in my guts, though. It hasn't let up. And despite being pummeled on two fronts, there's a part of me that's still me. Who I hope is the real me. Someone who doesn't want to hurt this guy. Who doesn't *want* to be a monster!

I grip hold of some of the guilt and shame from the fae magic and try to direct it toward fighting the hunger. Try to feel the wrongness of it. The wrongness of what it wants to do.

It doesn't work. That elvish guilt trip only wants one thing, and it doesn't care about anything else. It certainly doesn't care who gets hurt in the process.

My monster sniggers at how weak and helpless I am. But it'll fix that.

We're pulling into the rest stop parking lot now. It's run-down, mostly empty. There's a spot behind a thick tree, well away from the few other cars that are here. The driver glides us over there. He's breathing heavy.

Bryan Adams is on the radio now. Singing about sacrifice. Singing that he'd gladly give everything, even his own life, for love.

I desperately look over at Collin. He has to know some way to fight this. Something that will keep me from going through with it!

But his expression is no longer horrified. It's softened into something more like understanding. Like acceptance.

He's gently nodding, still right there at my side. "Alvin, listen to me. Don't be scared. I think this will help. After you feed again, you'll have more strength. You'll heal, and you'll be able to push back the Obligation."

No.

No, no, no!

We've parked. The music stops when the driver kills the engine. He unbuckles his seatbelt and turns to me. I can feel the hooks of my hunger deep inside him, pulling him toward my body.

"You're hurt," he says, snowy white brows steepled in, deeply concerned, reaching toward me. He seems genuinely moved. He turns and flips a switch at the base of the passenger seat in front of me, which causes it to swing forward, so he has more room to get closer. So he can swivel over and touch my chin with quivering fingers.

"I'm sorry," he says, as he starts to crawl toward the back. "I don't ever… uh… do *anything* like this… I want to help you…" He swallows hard, again. His breath ragged. "You're just so…" He's brushing the side of my cheekbone with the back of his fingers. "So fucking…" His face is beet red. He's leaning in toward me, this 240-pound bulk of a man, helpless as a kitten.

My hunger owns him completely.

"Don't worry, Alvin," Collin says, squeezing my hand. "This is a good thing. I'll make sure you don't go too far. I'll stop you in time."

The monster inside me straight-up laughs at that. A full-on tornado couldn't keep it from doing whatever little thing it wants. Some ghost trapped in a watch doesn't stand a chance. He won't be able to stop us.

I'm losing myself fast. The monster's desire is becoming my own. I try to gather every last bit of willpower I have to fight. To shut this down. My face contorts and winces.

The driver's face moves closer as he continues to climb into the back seat. He wants to get on top of me. My dick gets hard at that thought. Not because it's sexy. Because I'm unsheathing a weapon.

Collin notices my panic. I feel his thumb gently rub against the back of my knuckles. "Just let it happen, Alvin. It's okay. It's all going to be okay."

It's no easy feat for Dan to squeeze his way toward me. He's got, like, one knee on the edge of the driver's cushion and another on the back of the folded-over passenger seat. His palm is flayed out on the headrest next to me, supporting the rest of his mass. There's a scuffed silver wedding band on his ring finger. Sweat beads on his forehead.

"Kid, I don't know what it is about you, or why now, but I won't let anything hurt you ever again. I'm going to make you feel so goddamned good. I *promise*." Dan is now smiling. Eyes bright. Truly happy. No more struggle. He's looking forward to kissing me. To having me. To making me feel good. To having the best sex in his life. (Which he will, because unlike poor, stupid, regular Alvin, the monster in me keeps *all* his promises.)

It's that smile that finally does it. This is a good man. And my power is twisting what's good inside him into something foul. It wants to corrupt everything.

I slam my hands onto the tops of his shoulders and yell, "NO!"

In an instant, everything shatters. Both the monster and the Obligation get shoved back into their respective holes. Hard.

Driver Dan's eyes collapse into confusion and shame as he rears back his head.

"Oh! Oh, my God," he says, quickly recoiling back, released from my control. "What the hell am I doing?! I'm so… Fuck, I'm so *sorry!*"

The two of us are breathing in loud gasps. But he's still talking. "I don't know why I just did that! I mean, I'm not even— And you're bleeding! I should be getting you to a hospital!"

I don't want to talk right now. I don't want to be within a mile of anyone, to be honest. I am so full of anger. At myself—for letting it get as far as it did—and at Collin, for encouraging me.

And that's how I'm able to keep the Obligation in its place. How I'm able to find my voice again.

"It's okay," I say, husky, gritting my teeth. "Get us back on the road. I'll be fine. I just need to go home."

The driver quickly nods and glides us back onto the freeway. Back on our original route. Back to saying nothing. But he's not ignoring me. His eyes keep flitting up to the rearview mirror to take me in. He looks guilty, confused, and frightened.

I don't really know if I'll be fine. I am definitely injured. The Obligation did some damage. But not so much that I need to go to a hospital or anything. I think.

I *will* be all right. I have to be.

Collin's hand is back on mine. He looks at me, deeply worried. "Are you really okay, Alvin?"

"Don't talk to me," I hiss out, not even looking at him. I stare forward, boiling with anger. Wanting to be anywhere but here. "Just stay the hell away from me!"

He snaps his fingers back, like he's just been burnt. "Ah," he says. I hear pain in his voice.

And I'm not going to lie, I don't feel great about that. I don't want to hurt him. Not even a little bit.

But I also don't want to be a monster—and Collin

told me to give in to that part. He even tried to convince me somehow that it was a good thing!

And maybe if you're an immortal, all-knowing spirit, the math works out for that. Maybe in the grand scheme of the universe, there'd be some kind of net benefit. But it sure as hell doesn't work for me.

I was searching for a reason to believe that we weren't meant for each other. Looks like I now have it.

And I don't think I've ever felt so miserable.

21

WE ALL RIDE BACK WITHOUT SAYING ANOTHER WORD. It takes over an hour to get back to my block in San Francisco. The driver doesn't look at me when I exit the car, and I don't look at Collin, even though I know he's there, just a step behind me. Driver Dan then motors off to deal with what I just did to him, what I made him do, all on his own. I hope it doesn't mess him up too bad. But it probably will.

Once back in my apartment, I kick off my shoes and go straight for the bathroom. I drop my pants to the chipped tile floor, knowing it'll make the Avatar disappear. I don't want to put any more effort into pretending he doesn't exist, and I don't want to even touch the stupid watch to remove it.

I give myself a quick once-over in the mirror. There's dried blood under my nose, on my chin, on my polo shirt. My eyes look a bit hollow. And I'm covered in dirt. But I've been worse off. (And not too long ago!) Almost all of the bruising from the car crash is gone. And the Obligation is dead quiet for now. If I can keep it from digging into me again, I should be back to normal in a couple days.

Big "if."

I strip off the rest of my clothes and step into my second shower of the morning. Crank it up to what feels like near-boiling and try to burn off all the filth I feel.

Nothing happened, I tell myself. *I stopped it in time.*

But I know different. I might pretend the monster is something separate. That's just another pipe dream, though. It's not something "other." Something I can pretend belongs to someone else. This is who I am.

Suddenly, it all feels like too much. My mom, the druid, what I just did, Collin, the whole fucked-up night and day. What I am. Tears flood my eyes, and I let them come. I press my forehead against the peeling semi-gloss wall above the tub, and choke out wailing sobs while hot water beats down on my back. The truth is, I've never needed fae magic to convince me I should hate myself. I just need to look inside to get that answer.

I let the water stream over me for ten, fifteen, maybe twenty minutes. Have myself a good full-throated little cry. But eventually, I run out of tears, and then I'm just this pathetic, useless dude, pruning up in the shower, which doesn't change a goddamned thing.

I turn off the faucet, grab a towel, and scrape it over my face. The water did its work. I'm a long way from okay, but I'm no longer blindingly angry. I can do what needs to be done.

I finish drying off and get myself fresh clothes from

the bedroom. Dark-wash jeans. Gray sweatshirt. Athletic sneakers.

The window still looks intact. I walk up to it. I can tap on the glass.

Well, I guess some things *can* be fixed with magic.

Time to focus on the other stuff.

I get the watch from my other pants—leaving the pointless book page it was wrapped in behind—and slip it into the back pocket of my jeans, just before I sit down on my love seat. Collin appears immediately. He's way over on the other side of the room, standing in the corner between my cheapo silver plastic TV and even cheaper IKEA torch lamp. Barely glancing up at me. His eyes are red, like he's been crying, too.

We stare at each other for several seconds. Seems he's waiting for me to start.

Okay.

"Why did you tell me to give in to the monster inside me, Collin?" I ask, keeping my tone cold and steady.

"Ah, Alvin, you're *not* a monster…" His voice is soft. Full of emotion. Rough. He has been crying. "You're the opposite of that."

"Really? I was going to rape that man."

"But you didn't."

"No thanks to you."

He bites his lower lip and drops his gaze. "You were fierce sick. Probably more than you could tell. The Obligation was trying to kill you, and you needed the power to fight it." He looks back up at me. "You wouldn't have hurt him. Not in any permanent way. If you hadn't stopped it, even his memories would be happy. Not because of any mind control. Because it would have been a truly joy-filled experience for him."

I deliver my words flat and hard. "I'm not sure his wife would agree with how joyful that experience was. And I've heard the argument you're making before."

His frown deepens. "Your mom is wrong about a great many things. But not this."

"Really? So you think forcing people to have sex is fine so long as you can convince them they *liked* it?"

"I told you. You wouldn't be convincing them of something that's not real. Having sex with an incubus can be a divinely beautiful experience for a human. Healing, even. And, more to the point, you don't have to use that power to force people. Like any other strong muscle, yes, it can be used as a weapon, but it doesn't have to be that way. It wouldn't be that way with you."

This is full-on too much. I launch myself to my feet. "You don't know that! You don't know what this part of me wants to do! It *is* a weapon! It wants to consume and devour. It sees humans as food. As prey! And there's a *word* for what that makes me."

The Irish boy nods, but stays frustratingly calm. "I get that it feels predatory, Alvin. But that's because you've only let yourself feel it in desperate situations. When it's at its most primal. When it's scared. When it needs the higher parts of you—your values, your compassion—to give it guidance. To let it know that things are going to be okay."

"Things are not okay, Collin!" I march forward, and I'm up to him fast, poking his chest. "I know other incubi! I know my mother! Trust me, there's not the slightest hint of divine healing rainbows and sunshine in *anything* they do! They are killers! They *are* monsters!"

"You're not like them," he says, chin up, firm.

"You don't know me," I growl back, trying to sound as scary as I feel. I grip the thick fabric of his long wool shepherd shirt tight in my fist.

But he doesn't get scared. And he doesn't look away. "I want to. So, tell me. Tell me who you really are."

I fix my gaze on him. His eyes are soft, gentle, and searching, giving my rage nothing to bash itself against. Despite my best efforts, it starts to retreat inside me, like a large frothy wave sliding back into the ocean.

"You're never going to convince me that this power could ever be used for good."

"All right," he says.

"You're never going to convince me that there's *anything* good about this part of me!"

"All right," he says.

"You might know all the facts in the entire world, but I know more about this than you."

"Fair enough," he says.

He doesn't sound convinced. But he's not fighting me.

I let go of his shirt and turn away from him. "I'm going to find a way to get you out of the watch—to set you free—and then you can believe whatever the hell you like." My anger has spent itself. There's only enough left to keep pressure on the Obligation. But I still want distance between us. I want to push him as far away as I can.

I glance over my shoulder, and he nods, getting the message loud and clear. We stare at each other for a few beats. His expression is full of silent despair. And even sad, he looks cute. Just a sweet, lost boy, now in desperate need of a hug. It's almost enough to make me want to apologize for yelling at him.

But I don't.

His eyes flick up and away for a second, and he says, "It's time, Alvin. Rafa should already be at the café." His attention returns to me. "If you still want to go, that is."

Right. *Emma*. Here I am, all caught up in my own personal little pity party, and there's a high school girl, kidnapped, alone, in the clutches of completely *different* monsters. Ones who probably second-guess their villainy a lot less than I do.

I know there were other questions I wanted to ask Collin. A lot of them. But none of that feels important right now. Certainly not in comparison—and maybe not at all, anymore.

"Yeah, okay," I say. "Let's go."

Joe's Café is very old-school. Worn lime-green booths. Dim lighting, even at noon. Laminated menus. Paper placemats covered with an outdated neighborhood tourist map. Nothing San Francisco hipster about it. The only reason Joe's is still around after seventy years is because it's dirt-cheap, the coffee is bottomless, and they make a mean breakfast sandwich.

Rafa is sitting by the soot-caked window, glowering, so it looks like we're both in a mood. Laid out in front of him are two ice waters next to menus. His glass is three-quarters empty. He looks up the moment I enter, and his scowl melts into that smoldering little smile of his. Seems he's still, for whatever reason, happy to see me.

And now that he's in actual daylight, in actual normal clothes (heavy blue chambray shirt with a single button open at the chest, light jeans, silver sports watch, nice leather work boots), it's hard not to be happy to see him, too. Those Monster Hunter muscles are still bulging in all the right places, and his face practically glows in the soft, diffuse light from the street. He pulls off "alpha male" effortlessly and then makes it stunning with sensuous lips, piercing hazel eyes, and strong, youthful proportions.

And he's 100% human. And he seems to like me. If I were to fall for someone like him, we could actually make a life together. Get married, have kids, the whole nine yards. And he'd never, ever encourage me to give in to my monster.

Of course, we'd also never be able to actually have sex. And if he knew I *was* a monster, he'd probably just as likely blow my head off. So, there's that.

I sit across from him, and he slides over one of the menus as he takes me in.

"You're... looking better," he says.

Not a ringing endorsement, but I've essentially swapped my prior cuts and bruises for appearing as if I've just run a full marathon and then didn't sleep for a few days.

"Yeah, I am, thanks," I say, squinting down at my menu and working real hard at not coming off like an asshole while still keeping the Obligation in check with anger. The last thing I need to do is blow up this relationship, too. Collin stands next to the booth on Rafa's side. He's within easy glancing distance, but I don't have to look at him if I don't want to. And right now, I don't want to.

The blonde waitress is up to us immediately, heels clicking on the linoleum. It says DUSTY in white letters on the plastic brown rectangle on her checked apron, but that's almost certainly not her real name. She's wearing a worn frilly green diner uniform that was out of style by the '80s. (Never change, Joe.)

"Ready?" she asks, both bored and impatient. Looks like Rafa might have been surfing this booth for a while.

We both order burgers and fries. Rafa gets a cola. I go for coffee. I feel like I need it.

As soon as Dusty whisks our menus away, Rafa frowns, and I can see the gears turning. My guess is he's searching his brain to come up with some small talk for us. But since he might be the one person worse at chitchat than I am, I get right to the point.

"So, what did they say?"

His expression relaxes a moment, probably relieved from the pressure of needing normal conversation, but just as quickly, his scowl returns.

"They said no."

My eyebrows shoot up. Uhh, Emma's a human girl threatened by vampires—of all the responses I expected from Monster Hunter Central, "hard pass" wasn't one of them!

"Why? Do they think I'm making this up?"

He purses his lips and looks away. "They wouldn't even open the door. They… just won't help."

My shoulders slump. "I should have realized. I'm literally nobody. Why *would* they believe me?!" They might know Stryker, but she's out of town and wouldn't vouch for me, even if she were here. A real paranormal investigator would have a reputation. I'm just this weak-ass guy Rafa had to save, and taking on a big nest of "special" vampires on some rando's say-so has to be a huge ask.

Nicole trusted me to get her daughter safe, but she really couldn't have chosen worse. All I did was give that poor woman false hope.

"No!" he blurts, way too loud. A couple heads turn but quickly look away. Rafa is a big guy, and sensual lips or no, no one wants his kind of trouble.

He hunkers down and leans in toward me, voice much quieter. "Sorry. *No.* It's not you, Alvin. You're… fine. You're good." A frown darkens his features. The huffed-out sigh that follows does nothing to temper it.

"So, why then?" I ask.

He slumps into the rounded booth cushion behind him and folds his arms. "I think they're scared. I told you these vampires were special, and years ago, the West Coast clan was badly hurt by them. *My* clan. A lot of good people died, including my parents. I was hella young, and it's why I was sent back East. They knew I'd never let it go. That I'd want to fight. Maybe that's why they didn't want me back. But I thought they would have found their courage by now…"

"God, I'm so sorry, Rafa. About your parents. That's awful."

He raises his hand to stop me. "It was a long time ago. And it doesn't matter. What matters is that my clan made it perfectly clear they're not going to change their minds."

Rafa grinds his teeth, all his Monster Hunter cool replaced with almost teenage sullenness. And who can blame him? Now I'm even more curious about this clan. Have they just been sitting on their hands all this time, letting vampires run rampant? Have they done that for all paranormals? I mean, I didn't even know they had a presence here in San Francisco. (And you think Mom would've mentioned it. She's the one who made us move here!) I glance over at Collin, who's peering down at Rafa with sympathy. The Avatar of Knowledge could almost certainly tell me what their deal is. But Rafa clearly doesn't want to get into it, and I'm not talking to Collin anyway.

I suck in a breath. "What now, then?"

His chin lifts, but the rest of him stays in his sulky pose. "I said I'd help you, and I will. Just tell me where you think she is, and… I'll get her." His expression is resolute, but it's the opposite of confident.

"On your own? Against a whole nest of 'special' vampires?"

"You said you're not a fighter." After a beat, he sets his jaw and slowly nods his head forward in a deliberate rhythm. "Look. It's daytime. Most of them should be unconscious. I can get it done."

It sounds like he's trying to convince himself as much as me. I can tell Rafa doesn't like his odds, but suicide mission or not, he'll still do it. On my say-so.

Ugh.

He's right that I'd be useless in a fight. Not unless I feed, and I'm never going to do that again.

Still, this is my mess. I'm the one who made a promise to Nicole. And I'm the one who needs to prove to himself he can be more than a monster. Who needs to believe he can be... something better.

But if I want to do that, I'm going to need to get over myself and make the choice to be a little *less* useless.

"What if there were a way to avoid all the vampires?" I ask. "Or almost all of them, anyway. What if you could know exactly where they were the whole time you were inside the building?"

My words are for Rafa, but I'm looking at Collin as I say them. His eyes brighten.

The Monster Hunter sits up, immediately interested. "What do you mean?"

I look back at him, firm. "I mean, how much would that even the odds?"

He tilts his head and arches up his mouth with his lower lip, seeing it in his mind's eye. "A hell of a lot, actually. You saying you got some kind of spell for me, wizard?"

"Not *for* you." I try to channel what I hope comes off as paranormal investigator confidence. "I can use my magic to... talk to spirits. They can answer pretty much any question. For instance, I could draw us a whole map of the vamps' lair." I reflect on my fight with the grizzly, then the flight from the elf in the car with that heads-up display. "And that's not all. The spirits can also give me real-time updates of where everyone is. Who's guarding Emma. They could help us pick locks. Enter passcodes.

Even let us know about any nearby weapons and potential escape routes."

I give Collin a quick glance, just to make sure I'm not getting ahead of my skis. He nods back at me with confidence. He's even smiling a little.

"So… we'd do this together then?" Rafa asks. There's no skepticism in his voice.

My stomach twists with an involuntary quiver. Just hours ago, three vampires nearly ripped me to shreds. And that was before the Obligation started taking chunks out of me. Now I'm thinking of walking into a nest of, what? Dozens? More? (It looks like they've had at least a decade to increase their numbers.) And without any real superpowers, I'd be relying 100% on Collin to keep us alive. A guy I don't even want to talk to.

Of course, I could just give Rafa the watch. Collin seems to like him, and it's for a noble cause and all that. He might be happy to work with the Monster Hunter. And Rafa's seriously badass in his own right. With Collin's help, there's probably nothing he couldn't do.

I glance over at the Irish boy. He's gazing back at me with what looks a lot like pride and affection—and something inside me immediately recoils at the thought of giving him away.

Some of that has to do with not wanting to be a coward. Not wanting my newfound now-or-never courage to end with a pathetic little whimper. I know I'm not going to get another chance like this. If I really want to be more than some predatory monster, if I want to be something *good*, I can't just stay on the sidelines. I need to commit.

But that's not all of it. I'm still mad at Collin—and I'm not wrong to be—but for whatever reason, I'm also not ready to let him go. Not yet.

So, I won't.

"Yeah," I respond. "Let's get that girl out of there. *Together.*"

22

Well, I'm in it now.

After we got our burgers (greasy, a bit burnt, but they still hit), we spent an hour going over a map of the building that Collin helped me draw on the back of one of the placemats. I was able to show Rafa where Emma should be (the lowest sub-basement), as well as where potential vamps might be hanging out (pretty much all over). But there's a way in and a way out that should help us avoid any close encounters.

The thing that gets me is that we can't be 100% certain. Collin's "database update" was over twelve hours ago. The path we're planning to take could actually be teeming with vamps now, so as I make my way around the block, I keep picturing fangs and claws popping out of the dark, slashing at Rafa, slashing at me. Being outnumbered and overwhelmed by the undead. Trapped underground with no escape. It's like a nightmare, but I'm doing it to myself.

Rafa went to grab his monster hunting gear from his

truck, which leaves me all by myself as I casually stroll past the Benevolent Society of San Cipriano. Supposedly being closer to the lair will help the Avatar of Knowledge get more real-time answers, but I still feel like bait on a hook. I keep squeezing my fists.

"It's going to be okay," Collin says, leaning his shoulder closer to me as we walk side-by-side past tall gray stone steps. "You can do this, Alvin. *We* can do this."

The Benevolent Society of San Cipriano looks like the kind of building where vampires would hang. Six stories tall, granite façade the color of gravestone, dark stained-glass windows with sharp peaks, and a front door made for giants, framed by open iron gates. When I was drawing up the blueprints, Collin mentioned the style was "Gothic Revival," which apparently was all the rage back in the day, especially for a religious organization. It just looks straight-up creepy to me.

It also looks like it's closed for business. It's a little after 4:00 p.m., and both doors are closed. I don't see anyone going in or out. And, even more odd, there is no one on the street. (Maybe normals don't like the vibes here any more than I do.)

"Are you getting anything?" I ask.

"A couple humans are working inside on the first floor, doing what sounds like basic office stuff," he says. "No vampires roaming around that floor, though. I won't be able to pick up anything else until we're inside."

"And you're getting all that from my own hearing? Through all that stone?"

"That's right. Any real-time information I get comes from the owner of the watch, and as a paranormal, even if you don't feed, your senses are very acute. With a bit of practice, you'd hear the noise they were making, too. I could use my powers to show you, if you want."

He gives me a gentle smile, back to being his friendly, helpful self. And there's part of me, a tired part of me, that just wants to let bygones be bygones and let go of my anger toward him. We're about to do something crazy dangerous—not being pissy would probably make things easier. But if I dropped my guard, it would be that much easier for him to convince me not to fight my monster, particularly if things got tough. And Rafa, 100% human, 100% unsuspecting, would be right there for it to grab hold of. Just like it did with Driver Dan.

I lean into my anxiety and let it bleed into annoyance.

"No, thanks," I say, curt. "Just tell me if you get anything useful."

Collin nods and takes a half-step away, lips pursed. He knows I'm shutting him down. Probably unfairly.

I blow out a long breath, puffing out my cheeks, and try to release some of the useless fear and guilt inside me. Then I go to wait on the corner for Rafa, out of sight of the building. He arrives almost immediately, striding with determined confidence.

"Get anything new?" he asks, chomping casually on what I assume is a mint, clearly not stressed out in the least. He's thrown his Kevlar duster over his shotgun—the long gun is in its holster on his back, the butt of the weapon peeking out just over the collar of his coat—and he's carrying a massive tactical backpack slung over the other shoulder. (The pack is even bigger than Ms. Stryker's.) A large knife is strapped around his left thigh.

Creepy or not, I'm glad this out-of-the-way side street in Nob Hill is strangely barren of people. Between the black Kevlar and the military gear, he looks post-apocalyptic. The last thing we need is someone calling the cops.

"No," I reply. "We need to get in there. Then I'll know more."

"All right. Lead the way."

We're going in through the sewers. Almost a block away from the Society, there's a boutique hotel that used to be a laundry house. An old coal chute in an alley leads to the basement where Collin says a "culvert" connects directly to the tunnels under the street. Those conduits apparently lead to the sub-basement floor where Emma is being held. No vamps should be in the way since it's daytime and their resting place is one floor up. But we won't know until I'm closer.

Secret doorways and subterranean passages are, of course, very Sherlock Holmes, and there is part of me that finds it pretty darn cool that I have access to this kind of intel. But that's not the part that's puckering up as we start to act on it.

The first obstacle is a boringly modern padlock securing the chute hatch, but Rafa is able to twist it off with one hand. (Because, as a Monster Hunter, he's just crazy-strong like that.) I stick my head inside the lid and Collin confirms there's no one down there. Shoving my sneakers against the inner edges of the slide, I scuttle down feet-first into darkness.

At the bottom, I hear the faint clangs and splashes of a commercial kitchen upstairs and my paranormal vision kicks in. I'm sure everything above in the hotel is totally renovated, but down in this claustrophobic underground chamber, it's like time stood still. Ancient coal and damp tickles my nose, and I fight a sneeze. Against the opposite wall, two hulking, rusted iron things with big doors support thick chimneys that go up into the ceiling. (The original furnaces?) Some old wooden racks have scraps of rotting cloth stuck on them. Not much else is around. It doesn't look like the hotel uses this space. I wonder if they even know it's here.

The cracked concrete floor under my feet slopes down to the right, leading to a semi-circular bricked arch in that wall—the culvert, apparently. It's about three feet tall, protected by thick metal bars, and is under a sign that says FLOOD CONTROL. One of Collin's VR arrows confirms that's where we need to go.

We're not even at the scary part yet, but my heart is hammering. I just stare at the gate and shift from foot to foot, like a kid needing to go to the bathroom. Rafa, who slid down effortlessly behind me, passes by, cool as a cucumber. If anything, he looks like he's in a good mood. Engaged, anyway.

God, I'd give anything to have that level of chill!

Rafa snaps off another, much older-looking padlock guarding the access to the culvert. The heavy barred gate groans as he raises it. Rafa then removes a flashlight from his backpack and flicks it on. The torch shoots out a red beam of light, something that won't mess with night vision. (*Human* night vision. I'm pretty sure mine wouldn't be affected either way.) He crouches down and enters the half-height tunnel.

I follow and try not to let myself get crushed under the heavy iron bars when I bring them back down.

The way past the flood-control gate is sloped down and really cramped—barely person-sized—and even I need to crouch. Rafa is almost forced to crawl. Some of the stones are slippery with slime and moss. But after about fifteen feet, the half-tunnel then opens up into a larger vault where we can finally stand again. There are a bunch of other culverts and pipes along its walls and even more pungent mold smell. The chill in the air is clammy. Flowing water gurgles up ahead. Collin lets me know that beyond a large flap-like steel door in front of us (the "flow control" gate) is the main sewer.

It doesn't look like anyone has been in this little stone chamber for decades. It's dark, wet, and eerie. And maybe Rafa's finally feeling it, too, because he leans in toward me, frowning.

"Any vamps up ahead?" he asks, hushed.

I glance over at Collin for the first time since we got in here. He looks serious but unafraid.

"No," he says. "Vampires have used these tunnels under the city in the past, but to the best of my knowledge, not recently and almost never during the day. We shouldn't run into any bad guys. And there's no one within earshot."

I relay Collin's report, and Rafa steps up to the gate, the blood-red beam of his flashlight providing the only light.

"Stay close," he says. "Let me lead the way, okay?"

I nod back, hopefully not too visibly relieved.

There's no lock on the flow-control gate, and it leads

out to the main sewer tunnel. A low channel of water runs in front of us, and there is a narrow walkway on either side of the flow. Now that we're in the real sewer, I expect things to full-on stink, but while there are a few questionable foamy things floating around, it smells mostly like old rain and the sea.

The path to the Benevolent Society turns out to be a straight shot. We follow the walkway about 150 feet until Collin touches my shoulder, stopping me.

"It's here," he says. "You go up that ladder, and you'll be in the storeroom. Emma will just be down the hall."

Collin points at wide iron loops jutting out of the stone wall next to us. They are so grungy, even with my paranormal night vision, I might have missed them. The rungs lead up to a trap door in the ceiling of the sewer tunnel above. The steel hatch doesn't seem to have a handle, so it must open upward.

The way Collin just put it, this rescue sounds easy-peasy. But that's not my kind of luck, is it? And once we go through that hatch, there'll be no turning back.

"We're here," I say, my mouth dry.

Rafa nods and drops his pack to the ground. He removes a large Cordura belt rimmed with honest-to-goodness wooden stakes, two oversized semi-automatic shotgun magazines, and one industrial-sized Taser. He smoothly buckles the heavy strap around his waist. Well, at least he came prepared.

I glance into the pack he set down to see what other Van Helsing stuff he brought with him. There's a lockpick set, some glow sticks, the night-vision goggles, a Combat Application Tourniquet—and a whole bunch of bottles with cloth wicks sticking out of corks. I'm not talking one or two. There must be half a dozen. They're surrounded by bubble wrap to keep them from clinking, and when he lifts the pack back to his shoulder, swinging it toward me slightly, I'm hit with a faint whiff of gasoline.

They're Molotov cocktails. Fire bombs.

He catches my wide eyes and gives me a reassuring smile. "Don't worry, Alvin. Those bottles are a last resort. I'd love nothing more than to burn the whole place to the ground, but we're just here to get the girl out. Still, if we need to make a hasty exit, they'll come in handy."

I nod. It makes sense. But if I'd forgotten that a Monster Hunter's whole purpose is to kill all monsters (like yours truly), I'm remembering it now. Because, you know, I wasn't freaking out quite enough already.

I look over at Collin, who is frowning over at the backpack. That's concerning.

"Uh, anything else he brought I should worry about?" I duck my chin in toward my chest and lower my voice as much as possible.

He startles, then quickly pulls himself together, flashing a grin. "Oh! No. Sorry. It's not that." His eyes shoot up to the trap door. "It's just, now that we're closer, I think there's… something up there. On that floor."

"You mean something like *deadly vampires?*" I'm so keyed up, my whisper comes out a lot more hostile than I intend.

His grin becomes sheepish. "No, no, no. No vampires. The room above is totally deserted. I'm sure of it. It's actually more of a… feeling, I suppose." He shakes his head, like he's brushing aside cobwebs, frustrated with himself. "Sorry, Alvin. Don't mind me. I'm sure it's nothing."

Uh-huh.

I want to keep pushing Collin, but Rafa is finished arranging his gear and has noticed something's up.

"What's going on, Alvin?"

"The spirits sense something up there that they are being *annoyingly* vague about." I shoot Collin a look. "But they say the room is clear. No vamps."

"You think it's something we should worry about?"

Yeah! Probably! Maybe.

"The spirits say no."

Rafa shrugs. "All right. There's risk no matter what, and we're losing daylight. We'll do this careful and by the numbers. Just keep me posted if you get anything more."

"I will," I say and throw Collin another look, on the off chance he's suddenly decided to be a *little* more forthcoming. But he just smiles back open-mouthed like a freaking Golden Retriever and gives me a thumbs up.

Rafa is already up the ladder and opening the hatch. Neither he nor Emma has time for me to play Twenty Questions, and he's right, this was never going to be a slam dunk.

So I roll my eyes and climb up after him, feeling like that stupid character in a horror movie who ignores some blatantly obvious warning.

You know, just before he gets stabbed in the face with an ice pick.

23

The red beam of Rafa's tactical flashlight slices through the darkness as I wrestle my short arms and legs up the final rungs of the ladder. I'm not sure what I expected to find up here—a medieval torture rack? a wall of scalpels?— but the small room is full of neatly stacked cartons, most resting on the shelves of industrial wire racks lining the walls. Big box store labels suggest that a lot of what's here is pretty ordinary. Things like trash bags and disposable cups. But there are also razor blades and a whole lot of first aid stuff. So still plenty terrifying.

The trapdoor itself is tucked behind one of two large concrete columns. Clearly designed to be hidden, the space is too small and awkward to stack any boxes. The door's top is covered in fabric and the "handle" is merely a small cut-out section on the edge of the steel hatch underneath. Once I close it and smooth the cloth, the seam smoothly blends into the drab carpet tile floor. The dust puffing up from the edges suggests it hasn't been touched for a while.

I glance over at Collin to see if he's reacting weird to anything else now that we're up here, but he's looking calm and confident. One of his green VR arrows is pointing at the only door into the room. It's closed.

"No vampires are in the hallway, Alvin," he says. "You lads are good."

"Not even very *quiet* vampires?" I push, under my breath.

He grins. "No. At this distance, you'd smell them straight away."

Well, that's new information. I give the air a tentative sniff, but all I smell is cardboard and some kind of citrus cleaner. For better or worse, looks like I just need to trust him.

I step within whispering distance of Rafa. "The spirits say the hallway is also clear."

He nods, raises his flashlight to eye level, and smoothly opens the door into the hall. The hinges make no noise, which is a bit of luck. He glides out, crouched down like a SWAT officer. He clearly knows what he's doing here. As for me, my main goal is to not trip over my own feet as I follow a few steps behind him.

I'm surprised to find that this underground vampire lair looks more like a corporate office from the '80s than anything else. White walls, thin gray carpet. There are fluorescent lights lining the ceiling, but they're all turned off. We're at one end of the hall, facing a cargo-sized elevator. To the right, at the very end of the hall, there is a stairwell leading up, complete with that standard green-lined evacuation plaque you always see next to the doorway. To our left, the hallway goes down about 200 feet.

Collin is already up to the first door past the elevator. It stands open, swung outward into the hallway. He's looking into it like he's scanning for danger, but since I've just learned he gets his "real-time information" off of my senses, it could all just be for show. It makes me wonder what else between us has been just for show. Calling me "beautiful"? The eager way he smiled at me when I was naked in my bedroom? (When the reality is that I still had all my clothes on!)

I give my head a sharp shake and force myself to focus. I'm scared enough to want to be anywhere but here, but letting myself disassociate into some kind of lovesick rumination could literally get me and Rafa killed.

Collin gives me a thumbs-up in front of the open doorway, either not noticing or ignoring how scattered I am. Looking through the door myself, I see it's an actual standard break room. Thick gray plastic table, builder-grade tile floor, outdated cupboards, uncomfortable plastic chairs, large refrigerator. (And no, I really don't want to know what they're keeping chilled in there.)

Rafa has already scanned it and moved on, while Collin continues to stay ahead of us. He puts his ear up to the next two doors (both closed) and gives me the all-clear after each, which I pass on to Rafa with a thumbs-up when he glances back at me. We keep stalking down the hall. No point in poking our heads into rooms if we don't have to.

Collin then strides past a closed door as if it wasn't there. He's halfway to the next one before I whisper his name in the back of my throat. "Collin!"

I point at the opening he just ignored, and he just scrunches his brows back at me, baffled.

"Hold up," I whisper to Rafa, still a few feet ahead of me. "The spirits haven't cleared the next door."

The Monster Hunter stops immediately and gives me a firm nod, which at least makes me feel useful. I might be terrified, but there's a reason I'm here.

Collin backtracks to me, frowning. "Alvin, what are you talking about? There's no door there." He swivels his head up and down the hall and looks even more confused. "I mean, I suppose there *should* be..." He squints at where I'm pointing. "Oh! Jaysus! There *is* a door!"

"You really couldn't see it?" I ask, hopefully too quietly for Rafa to make out.

He stares at me blankly. "See what, Alvin?"

My stomach drops. What is going on here? He did say he was usually left behind for the dangerous stuff. Did Collin overpromise what he could do here? Can the Avatar of Knowledge actually malfunction? If that's true, this little adventure could go south very fast.

I jab my finger in the air next to him, jaw tense. "That door."

The Irish boy turns and jolts back, seeming to notice it again for the first time. (*Eek*.) "Oh, feck." He then immediately presses his ear against the gray laminate, closes his eyes, and breathes in deep through his nose. "Sorry. Uh, there's no vampires. Or anyone else inside there. It's clear."

"Stay here a sec," I say to Rafa, whose eyes hollow with wariness. We've been standing in place for several seconds, and I've been jabbing my fingers in the air and pulling God knows how many strange faces. I imagine at this point he's getting concerned his wizard might be malfunctioning. But he doesn't stop me.

I walk up to Collin and try to keep my cool. "What's the matter with you?" My whispered question comes out almost as a hiss.

The Avatar of Knowledge glances down, embarrassed. "I don't know, Alvin. This part of the wall just felt... unimportant, somehow." He meets my eyes, determined. "I'll be more careful. I promise! It won't happen again!"

Well, *that's* totally reassuring.

I want to be able to trust him. I need to be able to trust him. But even now, it's like he can't keep his attention on the door. He glances over at it, nervous, before he immediately looks away, eyes glazing over. Something's up.

Gathering my courage, I step close to the doorway and open my paranormal senses. At first I feel nothing—then a faint flavor of musky almonds fills my awareness. The only place I've ever sensed that kind of magic was at Tara's house—and it might have been what messed Collin up when we were there.

Is it druidic? Almost immediately, I'm hit with a strange ozone aftertaste, which is definitely different. Still, could Tara actually be here? Working with them somehow? That's a scary thought. But it's not like there'd be a garden in a sub-basement for her to use to attack us. (Right?) And Rafa's got a big gun. I bet he could take her.

Clearly sick of watching me stare into space, he approaches. "What is it, Alvin? Tell me what's happening."

I back Rafa and me away from the door, hopefully out of earshot. "No vamps, but there's magic past that door. I think it's druid magic. Not the kind of thing you'd expect in a vampire lair." I blow out a long exhale. I'm finding it hard to remember to breathe, because there is a non-trivial chance that *this* is where I'm going to get that ice pick to the head. But we can't ignore it. "I don't know what it is, but I think we need to take a look inside."

I wonder if Rafa's going to fight me on that, but he immediately defers to my judgment. This is a magic thing and I am the "wizard," after all. It feels nice, even if I do wind up getting us killed.

"All right. You swing the door open and then stay behind it, while I check things out," he says. "And if you've got any defensive spells, get them ready."

I don't have any defensive spells.

He removes his shotgun from its holster, seats its butt firmly against his shoulder, and holds the flashlight alongside the weapon's front grip with his left hand. I've tried my best to get up to speed on PI stuff over the last couple months, and I've done enough self-study about weapons on YouTube to finally recognize it as a Beretta semi-automatic—an efficient, badass weapon for an efficient, badass Monster Hunter. And it looks non-standard—extra-long magazines, better sights—so it's been made even more lethal.

He positions himself in front of the entryway and gives me a nod. I turn the handle and swiftly open the door. Rafa relaxes slightly instead of tensing, so I peer around the edge.

The bright red beam of his flashlight strafes down a rough stairwell carved into the bedrock. I can't see what it leads to from here. It's too long.

"Stay close," Rafa says as he slowly descends. I close

the door behind us and follow, questioning my own judgment with every step.

More than forty feet below, a small, roughly hewn archway opens into a large domed cavern. There aren't any stalagmites or stalactites or anything like that in here, but it doesn't look man-made—the walls are rough ash-colored rock and the space inside is massive, like train-station-hall large. The stairway deposits us at the halfway point along one wall, giving us a panoramic view of the vast chamber stretching equally left and right. Small battery-powered LED lanterns are mounted at regular intervals along the walls, each secured to simple aluminum brackets hammered into the natural crevices of the rock. They're positioned about ten feet apart, creating what would be an evenly spaced ring of light around the chamber when illuminated. None are lit. In the center of the cavern, just a little to the right, is a carved marble pedestal with a shallow silver bowl resting on top. (It reminds me of a birdbath, but it's probably an altar.) At the far wall opposite us, there is a raised platform, like a stage, and on it, slightly to the left, is an easel-like wooden lectern. Underneath my feet, a cool, refreshing, mountain-air quality wafts up into my awareness. It's not physical, which means it's a sign I'm near some kind of ley line, a natural wellspring of magic. According to Ms. Stryker, those can be great places to cast big magic.

But there aren't any people here. No druids. Certainly no vampires. And no magic of any kind on the altar, not even residue. Someone could be prepping for some kind of ritual here, but the party has yet to get started.

So where's the power I felt coming from?

I step around Rafa, just into the cavern, and my eyes are drawn like a magnet to the stand on the platform. It's turned at an angle, and I can just make out a large closed book on it. I can tell the binding is some kind of green hide—it shines dully against Rafa's crimson flashlight. That book is where the almond-scented, ozone-flavored magic is coming from.

I look for Collin to see how he's reacting, and I find him behind me, literally staring down at his shoes. He appears absolutely miserable, like he wants to be anywhere but here. There are a million questions I want to ask him, but not with Rafa breathing down my neck.

Looks like I need to tempt fate a bit more.

"There's a book over there," I say, trying to keep my voice steady. "That's where the magic is coming from. I… should check it out. Stay here."

He takes a step forward, still sighting down the barrel of his shotgun. "It could be a trap, Alvin. Let *me* get it for you."

I quickly place my hand on his shoulder, stopping him. It's actually quite cool that he wants to act as my human shield, and he's not wrong to be worried about nasty surprises. I've heard enough of Ms. Stryker's stories to know that evil wizards almost always protect their gear. As far as I know, Monster Hunters don't have any special protections against magic—at least not human magic—but, as a paranormal, I should have some resistance. In theory. (At least, I think Mom said that once.) Will it be enough? I have no idea. But as much as I hate to say it, I'm the best man for the job here. And anyway, I need to be able to talk privately to Collin.

"No, Rafa. It's got to be me." I give him what I hope looks like a confident smile. "This is magic stuff. Keep a lookout here at the base of the stairs and let me do my thing."

He lets go, and nods, again deferring to my expertise. (Hah!) He lowers his weapon, shifts it to his right hand, and starts to hand over the flashlight, but I wave it away and step into the cavern.

"I'm good," I say. I want to keep my hands clear, and now that I'm in the actual chamber, I can tell the enchantment has an edge to it. It feels downright alien. Hostile.

Rafa stays where he is and shines the beam behind me, lighting my way. Several steps in, I realize I probably should have taken the torch—that would have been the most human thing to do, and I've seen that the Hunter does have his own night-vision goggles—but hopefully he'll figure I'm able to see in this pitch-black room because he's lighting the way. Whatever he thinks, it's too late now.

I take a deep breath and cautiously approach the stand, half-expecting the book it cradles to leap at me with insect legs and hug my face. Collin trudges along next to me, his head still down.

"How you doing, Collin?" I murmur.

"I feel like I shouldn't be here. This feels wrong."

"Wrong like one of us could get hurt?"

"I don't know."

I pass by the altar. No runes or anything, but the bowl looks old. This wasn't made by a machine—it was hammered by skilled hands. It shines with fresh polish.

Crossing another fifty feet or so, I cautiously step up a small staircase onto the platform. It has a plywood top supported by 4x4 posts, all painted black. It looks like it was built recently—no scuffs, some sawdust around the screws, and it doesn't make a sound as I place my weight on it. I creep to the left side of the stage, making my way around to face the lectern. The book appears ancient, but it's not damaged. It's biggish—about sixteen inches wide and twenty inches long. The binding gleams with a well-maintained luster similar to fine leather. It has overlapping iridescent scales, too large for snakeskin. As I move in front of it, I can now see there's a design on the cover—an engraving in gold leaf of a large pair of cat eyes steepled over a complicated triangular knot thing—

Holy crap! It's the same book that was shown on the druid's illuminated illustration! The one that supposedly could help set Collin free.

"Collin, do you recognize this? I think it's what Tara had on one of those parchments."

He's just behind me. He glances over at the tome but immediately looks away, like it's too bright somehow. "I… think so." He closes his eyes and furrows his brow, before forcing himself to stare at it. After a moment, he says, "Yes. They wanted me to translate it. The vampires."

Well, *that's* interesting. "So, what can you tell me about it?"

Collin just shakes his head.

"Are there any traps or anything?"

A shrug—and another miserable expression.

"I'm sorry, Alvin. I can't help you. There's something about its magic… We should just go."

Boy, do I want to take that advice! The power feels low-key, but its ozone bite digs at me like an itch. It does feel dangerous. So, I just hover in front of the book, palms out, fingers flexing back and forth like a cartoon burglar over a bag of money.

"There a problem?" Rafa stage-whispers from way across the room.

He's clearly eager to come over, and there's only so quiet he can be with me at the opposite side of this enormous space. I'm wasting too much time.

I stage-whisper back, hoping our voices won't carry all the way up the stairs. The chamber creates a slight echo. "I think the vampires need this book for their ritual. Hang tight. I'm just, uh, making sure I don't set anything off when I grab it."

Total lie. I have literally no idea how to do that. But if I do screw up, I sure don't want to take Rafa with me. Someone's going to need to get Emma out of here!

I glance over at my Avatar of Knowledge, who usually has all the answers. He should know. But right now, he just looks like a carsick kid. His face is pale, his breath quick and shallow. Me hanging out next to the book certainly isn't doing him any favors. But it doesn't take an all-knowing spirit to tell me there's no way I should leave this thing behind for the vampires to use. Not to mention, it might be exactly what I need to save Collin—which is probably why it's messing him up.

Unless, of course, there really is some deadly booby trap, and *that's* what's subconsciously freaking him out.

Gah! The clock is ticking, and I'm just running in circles. The damn thing is either trapped or not! I need to either move on or I need to—

Without letting myself pinball to another thought, I

thrust out and grasp the book with both hands. The second I touch it, an outline around the gold engraving flares a bright blue.

Oh, crap.

I twist my head back, wincing, prepared to be zapped with a million volts of electricity. Or set on fire. Or just flat-out exploded.

But none of that happens. Instead, Collin immediately relaxes next to me and says. "Oh. *Oh.* Right. I know what that is. It's the *Rúna Diamra inna nDée Sen.*"

The what now?

Doesn't matter. Focus!

"That's nice. Should I be worried about this blue glow?" The light coming from the symbol on the cover hasn't stopped. If anything, it's gotten brighter. The book's magic doesn't feel any stronger, though.

"Alvin, you okay?" Rafa asks tightly, no longer whispering. He starts toward me.

"I believe that's because of me," Collin says. "Or the watch, anyway. The magic is similar in some ways. Like feeding like. It should be harmless."

"Still think I'm good!" I stage-whisper back at Rafa, my throat tight with anxiety. "Just give me a sec. Stay where you are."

Collin glances up and to the right. "I remember what this is now. It is ancient druidic magic. The book contains spells to contact and form pacts with the Old Gods." His scan freezes in place, like he's just noticed something, and his relief crumbles a bit. "They're mostly the ones that don't care about humanity—the really dangerous, vengeful powers. I don't believe it has any specific curse laid on it, though. The words themselves are so toxic, whatever magic you're sensing is just there to keep it in check."

Well, that sounds awful and scary. But Collin does seem much improved.

"You're looking a lot better."

He bobs his head, noticing the same thing. "Yeah. Sorry about all that before. This is very much not something I'm supposed to have access to. But since you're the owner of the watch…"

"…You're allowed to help me," I finish. Right. Huh. I'm not sure how evil Lovecraftian-type gods figure into getting Collin free, but based on his reaction, it seems those papers Tara brought out weren't complete BS, after all.

"I'm taking this with us," I say for both Rafa and Collin.

Rafa chucks his chin up with silent bro approval, apparently reassured by my confident tone. (And probably also by the fact that I haven't blown myself up yet.)

Collin nods, too. "Now that I know what it is, so long as I don't actively try to ask questions about it, it shouldn't affect me like before. Even when you're not touching it directly."

Good to know. I tuck the big book under my arm. The moment my skin breaks contact, the glow vanishes. Collin immediately looks away, but he doesn't look nauseous like before. Instead he confidently strides for the door.

"Right, so! Grand! Let's go save that girl!" he says as he quickly passes Rafa. Even if he's no longer actively suffering, the tome clearly makes him nervous. I cross back after him.

"All good?" Rafa asks.

"Yeah. This book was what was throwing the spirits off. But I've, uh, neutralized it. We shouldn't have any more delays." I say those things like I know what I'm talking about.

But it turns out I kinda do, because it's smooth sailing for the rest of the way down the hallway. Collin confirms there are no vamps or other nastiness behind any of the other doors and, in less than a minute, we have reached the room where Emma is supposedly being held, at the very end of the hall.

Rafa and I hang back about fifteen feet, while Collin presses his cheek against the corporate-gray laminate.

"So… is she in there?" I whisper.

"Yes!" he says, beaming. "Emma is here and very much alive. With my help and Rafa's picks, you should be able to get through the lock of the cell holding her in under twenty minutes, and we've easily got an hour of sunlight left!"

"Any vamps?"

Another big smile. "Nope!"

Rafa can't hear the Avatar's responses, but he's close enough to hear my questions, so he adds, "How about human guards? Any weapons?"

Collin's voice sounds a lot more glib than before, and his eyes aren't 100% focused. It's like he's straining a bit. The book might still be affecting him.

"Really concentrate," I say to him under my breath.

He glances over to me with a bright expression just as

he's about to open his mouth to answer Rafa's question. My urgent glare stops him. He nods, sobering, and after a steadying breath, he bites his lower lip with concentration and brings his ear to the door. Then his eyes snap open.

"Jaysus!"

"What?" I mutter, trying my best to subvocalize.

"She's *not* alone. There are others."

"Guards?" I ask.

Collin gives his head a shake. "I'm not sure... They're human. No gunpowder, but they all smell tense... Multiple heartbeats, pulse rates are elevated... At least half a dozen..."

Crap. We've been going back and forth out here, and whoever's on the other side could have easily heard. I lean in quickly to Rafa and hiss out, "The book is still messing with them. They say no vamps or guns, but there are others, and the spirits can't rule out their being human guards. Could be six or more."

I don't need to tell Rafa how compromised we might be and he wastes no time. He holsters his shotgun and smoothly removes his Taser from his belt. Then he flicks a gesture at me to open the door for him. As soon as my hand is on the handle, he's crouched and ready to spring inside.

He gives me a sharp nod. I turn the handle and whip the door open as fast as I can.

He takes a step forward, then freezes in place. "*Christ.*"

Both the Monster Hunter and the room are blocked by the door—I just see his feet under the gap—so I quickly poke my head over the edge.

It's more than twice as large as the break room at the

top of the hall. The floor is bare concrete, as are the walls and the ceiling slab. Two high-backed wooden chairs are in the center. Several cramped cells line the sides of the room, secured to all visible surfaces with heavy steel plating. Their thick iron bars immediately make me think of a dungeon.

Emma is in the cell opposite us, her solid form curled up on a dirty cot, her back against the wall, her knees wrapped with her arms. Just as Collin said, she's alive—and awake. Her wide eyes blink at us with fear.

But she's not alone. There are at least a dozen other kids here, also terrified.

And all are locked in separate cages.

24

They're all teens—eight boys and five girls, including Emma. Magic doesn't start to show in humans until puberty, and the younger they are, the easier it would be to manipulate them. Almost half look middle-school aged, and all look rough. Their skin is dirty, with lots of cuts and scrapes. Clothing torn and soiled. There are angry purple bruises on their necks.

Vampire bites. They've been fed on.

Several of them come up to the bars of their cells with eyes like saucers, whites shining red in the beam of Rafa's flashlight. Their faces are etched with fear and desolation, their breath hitching.

The room stinks of stale urine.

I glance over at Rafa, who just stares, the color drained from his face, lips parted. But he still doesn't look as horrified as Collin.

"I-I'm sorry, Alvin," he mumbles out, squeezing the tips of his own fingers white in front of his stomach.

"When we were planning this, I didn't think to— I mean, it didn't occur to me that, eh—!"

The sunshine boy runs out of words.

Collin has told me many times he doesn't know everything. That he has to look to get the answers, even for the real-time stuff. Which means there's really only one reason he didn't know that there were other kids in danger.

He didn't know because I never asked.

Hot anger flares in my gut, and I want to let myself burn in it. I was so tunnel-visioned with my "first case," I didn't take even a moment to think things through. If this ritual was so important, why wouldn't the vampires kidnap more than one kid? A real paranormal investigator would have at least done a general search for missing teens. And I had the freaking Avatar of Knowledge who could instantly answer any little question I could think of!

I can't believe I could have been so stupid! Except I can. I was so cocky, so eager to prove I could be some kind of hero, I was only thinking about myself. The real proof of my character is desperately staring back at me through the thick iron bars of a vampire dungeon. It shows clear as day that I'm way out of my depth. That I have no business thinking I can be anything more than useless.

Damn it all.

Well. I would honestly love to continue my shame spiral. God knows I deserve it. But Rafa and I are all these kids have right now.

The entire room is silent, except for a few sniffles from the younger boys. I break it.

"Collin, how long would it take to get them all out?"

The Avatar of Knowledge swallows hard. "Those cells might look old-school, but the security is modern and high-end. Biaxial tumbler lock systems, security pins, the works. The bars, steel plates, even the concrete are all reinforced with composites. They were probably built to contain paranormals. Even if you had a plasma torch, it would take more time than you have. And with just a regular set of lockpicks…"

Right. And we get just one shot at this. Get any of them out, and the vamps will know we have a way in.

But do nothing, and maybe they all die. Horribly.

This is the kind of tough call real heroes have to make —it's what I signed up for—and now I would give anything for it to be someone else's decision.

But as I turn back to Emma, the defiant girl from the park who now looks like she should be on a bus-stop poster for child abuse, her vulnerable eyes hopeless, mustard-yellow shirt ripped at the shoulder… and the little redheaded boy in the cell next to her, tears sliding down through the grime on his cheeks, stubby fingers clawing nervously at the wound on his neck… Well, there really isn't any choice.

Rafa is pale and angry, but all his Monster Hunter bravado seems to have been knocked out of him by the misery surrounding us. He seems frozen, lost. Who knows? Seeing these kids here, fed on by vampires, he might be reliving memories from what happened when he, himself, was a child. He acts all badass and I've been taking that for granted, but he's really only a year older than me, and I'm not all that much older than some of these teens. He heard my question, so he's looking to me for what we do next. Because I'm the one who's supposed to have all the answers. That's why I'm here.

So, I tell him.

"Twenty minutes a lock. That means we have time to save three. We get those kids out, and then we call in reinforcements. Your people, my boss, the police, the Feds, whatever it takes. But we take who we can now. Yeah?"

I try to say it like I know what I'm talking about and feel like a total fraud while doing it. But it's like my words lift a weight off of his shoulders. Somehow my fake confidence restores all of his.

"Yeah," he says, back stiffening, shoulders squaring, clearing his throat. "We save as many as we can."

"Give me your picks. The spirits will guide me. We're starting with Emma."

If I can't do anything else right, I'm at least going to honor my promise and get Nicole her daughter back.

Rafa doesn't argue. We head over to her cell. The Hunter drops his pack to the ground next to me and opens it wide, rifling through for the pick set. I place the book down to my left. It flares briefly blue in my fingers until I let go.

As soon as we approach, Emma takes a step back from the bars, face scrunched, not sure what to make of us. But I don't want her to be any more scared than she already is, so I try to smile and push as much confidence into my words as I can.

"Emma, my name's Alvin, and this is Rafa. Your mother sent me to get you out. And that's exactly what we're going to do here."

"My mom? She sent you?" Her voice is cracked and

hoarse. The way someone sounds after screaming all night at a concert.

I can't let myself think of the real reason right now. Rafa hands me the pick set. I try to keep my bright and breezy tone.

"That's right. I work for a private investigator who specializes in magic stuff. And Rafa here is a big, tough Monster Hunter." I force myself to meet her eyes. "I spoke with your mother yesterday, actually. She wanted me to tell you she loves you, and that she'll do anything to keep you safe."

I'm not sure why I added that last part. But they had just had a fight about her magic before she got kidnapped. I guess if it were me, I'd want to be told that my mom cared more about my safety than getting her way. It helps that in Emma's case, I think that's actually true.

And miraculously, I seem to have stumbled into saying the right thing. She brings steepled fingertips to her mouth and her eyes well up, but they're clearly happy tears. They spill out as she closes her eyes and nods, and my heart practically breaks in two.

But I don't have time to feel anything more than I'm already feeling. Even with Collin's help, I have no idea if I can actually do this. I've read about opening locks in my private-eye textbooks and seen a few YouTube videos, but I've never worked on one for real. I turn to Collin, my lips pursed with anxiety.

He's right by my elbow, and his expression is now gentle and encouraging, all horror gone. "We've got this, Alvin. This will be even easier than hot-wiring the car. Trust me."

Labeled green arrows of light appear, pointing at the hardware I need from Rafa's leather-bound case—a "#3 hook pick" and a "tension tool"—and as soon as I raise them to the keyway, a colorful hologram blooms out before my eyes with an exploded view of the lock. It looks like one of those high-end "How Things Work" animations, and above it are little speedometer-type gauges with narrow green sections that show me exactly how much pressure to use with each tool. Like with the heads-up display he created while we were driving, it's all very cool and video-gamey, and once I insert the tools, they get added to the hologram.

I immediately see why this lock is so tricky—unlike a typical five-pin cylinder where you shove up one pin at a time, here there are pairs of pin stacks on both sides that need to be put in place simultaneously. It would be crazy-tough to do even with a specialized tool, and this hook pick is just a sliver of metal with a curve at the end. It'll need to be aligned perfectly to catch both of them. On top of that, some of the pins are red herrings. Pick the wrong one and you have to start over. It'd be a nightmare for even an experienced locksmith.

But I have the Avatar of Knowledge, so more arrows pop up to guide me to exactly where I need to place my tools. And once I slip the tools in, Collin slides his arms around my sides from behind and places his warm hands on mine, gently guiding my angle.

I suck in a quick breath.

"This okay?" he asks quietly.

His lips are near my ear, but not so close that I feel his breath. His torso is wrapped around me, though. I feel his firm biceps press on the outside of my arms, and I freeze. But I'm not going to lie—with all the stress, all the pressure on me, it actually feels kinda nice to be held right now. To not be doing this alone. Despite all the recent drama, Collin literally has my back.

"Yeah," I say, my voice a hushed grunt.

He doesn't say anything more. He just applies gentle pressure with soft palms to help me position the pick at just the right slant as I follow the holographic guide. In less than two minutes, we get the first pair of pins shoved into place—click!—and the cylinder turns just slightly.

I immediately feel a rush of satisfaction, and when I glance over my shoulder, I see Collin's grinning, too, just as thrilled. Maybe I should stay angry with him. There's still no reason to think that he wouldn't encourage me to feed if the situation got desperate. But it's hard to keep believing that he's on the side of monsters when he's literally helping me save this girl.

And I don't have the bandwidth for another mental debate. Not when there are still seven more pairs of pins to go. I let out a long exhale, sending whatever beef I have with Collin out with it.

As we work to get the next pair shoved back, I can't help noticing how silent the room has become. It makes sense that Rafa would be quiet. He knows what I'm doing is delicate, and he's basically holding his breath as he aims the beam of his flashlight at the keyway. But there are thirteen other people around us. Young people who've been through hell. They *must* have heard that we'll only have time to rescue two more of them. Maybe they wouldn't beg for their lives, but still, you'd expect them to make some noise. But they're now just staring out of their cells, saying nothing.

I follow the redheaded boy's gaze toward the door. That's where these teens are focused. Their bodies are tight as bowstrings. Even Emma, who is gaping over my head as I kneel on hard stone in front of the lock. They're worried about something coming.

Maybe Rafa has the same thought. He sees where I'm looking, grabs the night-vision specs from his pack, gives me a quick nod, and moves toward the door to the hallway. He leaves his flashlight propped up on his pack, aimed at the lock. He glances outside but then shakes his head. Nothing to see.

He softly closes the door behind himself, then removes his mobile from an inside duster pocket and starts taking pictures of the kids in the cells. He doesn't use the flash, but the phone looks new enough that it should capture well enough in low light. I shoot him a questioning look.

"Evidence," he says. "Evidence others can't deny, no matter how cowardly they are." He shifts uncomfortably as he positions himself for a shot of two cells. I don't think he likes just standing around.

"Good idea," I respond. Then I turn back to the cell. "You doing okay there, Emma?"

At hearing her name, she looks down at me. "Mm-hm," she says, voice tight, clearly not wanting to make much sound. She might also be too weak to talk. Who knows when these kids last ate, let alone how much blood they lost?

I return my attention to finagling those pin stacks into place. Still six more to go. Ticktock, Alvin!

As I make my way through the next two pairs of stacks, I realize it isn't just the augmented reality visuals or even Collin's huggy, hands-on guidance that's helping me do this impossible task. Somehow, he's making my senses sharper. Or, at least, making me more aware of my own natural abilities—which is kinda cool. (Yet another superpower I didn't even know I had!) The tips of my fingers manipulating the thin metal now sense the subtlest vibration, the nerve endings almost raw with awareness. My hearing has sharpened to the point where I can detect the most faint click, the slightest misaligned scrape against the internal cylinder.

And that's how I hear the hum of an elevator descending from all the way down the hall, even before Collin speaks.

"Alvin, someone's coming down…"

I quickly jerk my head toward the entrance. Rafa closed the door behind himself, but it isn't flush with the floor. If it's a paranormal who shows up, they'll have night vision—and underground, with no windows to the outside, any light will draw attention like a flare.

"Kill the beam," I whisper. "Spirits say elevator's on its way."

I expect Rafa to protest, since it would put me into pitch dark and there's only one set of night-vision goggles. But he strides over without hesitation and switches off the flashlight.

A frightened whimper rises up among some of the kids, but they quickly hush.

Rafa returns to the door, peering back at me through the lenses wrapped around his head. They glow faintly green in my demon sight. He doesn't seem at all surprised when I reflexively (and stupidly) share a nod with him after our gaze locks.

Hopefully he thinks I have some kind of night-vision spell.

Whatever. I don't have time to worry about it. I have to keep going. I can't keep letting myself get distracted! We have to get at least *one* of these kids out!

As I smoothly slide in the next stack pair, I hear the elevator doors open and close. Then, a series of soft little taps, perfectly spaced apart in time—tip, tip, tip, tip—like a metronome wrapped in velvet, threading through the background, subtly getting louder. It's inhumanly precise, so it takes me a moment to realize they're footsteps.

"Jaysus, Alvin," Collin says. "It's a vampire. And it's coming right for us."

I turn back to Rafa and mouth "vampire" as obviously as I can. To his credit, he doesn't startle, even a little. He just gives me another head nod, removes one of the stakes from his belt, and takes a position just to the side of the door.

Everyone in the room is dead silent.

Except for their breathing. And heartbeats. And little involuntary shifts, clothing rubbing against itself, along with a million other things I can totally hear. If I pay attention, I can tell the difference between Rafa's pulse and everyone else's. It's thicker, *stronger* somehow. I can take in all of that—and I've just been aware of my enhanced paranormal senses for a few minutes. A vampire could potentially have centuries to practice.

The velvet tip, tip, tip continues, then stops for an excruciating moment halfway down the hall.

Then the footsteps become a run. Toward us.

Rafa must catch my frightened expression because his body tenses and his lips become a grim, murderous line. He pulls back the stake in his right fist to his shoulder.

Then *WHOOSH!* The door rips open and a gray suit with claws and fangs flings itself into the room in a blur. Rafa is on the creature instantly, grabbing its neck and stabbing down hard with the sharp wood. But the vampire is so fast, the weapon just brushes past the monster's shoulder, and they both go tumbling down, carried by momentum.

Hunter and vampire now roll on the floor in the center of the room, twisting back and forth furiously as Rafa tries to get on top to pin the monster in place. Both of the wooden chairs get slammed. (One even gets kicked in the air—I'm not sure by who—and it smashes into the bars on the next cell. A tall girl with long, stringy black hair flinches and stumbles back to her cot.) (She doesn't scream, though!)

The vampire is hissing like an angry cat. Rafa just seems to growl. It's an incredible racket, and I'm afraid they're going to crash into me at any minute. Obviously, I can't focus on the lock. All I can do is stare over my shoulder and hold the tension in the cylinder so when Rafa does get the upper hand, I won't lose any of the progress I made. (There are only a few more stacks to go!)

Luckily, my faith in the Monster Hunter is not misplaced. It doesn't even take long. He's strong enough that once the chairs are out of the way, he's able to twist his full weight on top of the vampire and pin both the creature's arms above its head with one hand. Then in a flash, he raises his sharp wooden stake with the other, bicep flaring with force. The vamp can do nothing but look up in terror. It's over.

Until it isn't. Because Rafa freezes, staring down, eyes wide.

For a hot second, I wonder if he's somehow been hypnotized or charmed or something. I don't know enough about vampires to rule it out.

The Hunter's eyes aren't vacant, though. Instead, they soften with confusion and recognition—and his voice comes out in a strangled rasp.

"*Dad?*"

Uh, what the what now?!

The vampire smiles, fangs hidden. "*Rafa*. Thank God you're here. You've *saved* me."

His expression is warm. Grateful. Trustworthy. Fatherly.

And, of course, complete bullshit. It has to be.

"Rafa! Don't trust him!" I cry out, as quickly as I can.

I'm desperate for him to hear me. And he does. He looks to me, confused, distraught, distracted. And that's all the creature needs.

As a Monster Hunter, Rafa is stronger than an ordinary human and he's got mad skills. But a vampire can have the strength of up to ten men and the speed of a hungry cobra. With a furious burst, it twists its torso, spinning Rafa onto his back and freeing its arms. And then before the Hunter can react, the creature hammers his forehead with the base of its palm, twice. Rafa slumps to the floor, out cold.

I stare, jaw loose, shoulders twisted around, as the vampire smoothly rises to its feet. It coolly peers down at Rafa, while it casually brushes an errant wrinkle out of its silky jacket with the back of its fingers. I'm still holding tension in the keyway with the tools.

Collin's voice is right up to my ear, and he sounds scared. "Alvin, let go of the lock. We're in trouble."

You think?

25

The vampire considers Rafa's unconscious form, his lower lip pushed up in a pout. "You know, I've done my best to keep him safe and away from all this. But I suppose this day was inevitable." He fluidly swivels on his heels to take me in. Velociraptor smile. "So... who would you be?"

Turns out Rafa's father is a handsome man. At least as far as dead guys go. He looks like he was in his early 40s when he was turned. He's got his son's strong jaw but has mocha eyes to Rafa's hazel ones. His cadaver-pale skin still retains a bit of south-of-the-border bronze. He's shorter than his son, and his muscles are more compact, but not by much. The charcoal suit with peaked lapels looks custom and drapes his form in high-class, athletic lines. There's a glimmer of ozone-tinted magic under his shirt near his throat.

"Keep him talking, Alvin. I just— I just need a minute. Feck!" Collin darts in close enough that I feel his breath now. It's ragged.

I don't think we're actually going to get a minute. But the Avatar of Knowledge is doing his looking-up-and-scanning-the-ceiling thing. Guess I'll figure it out!

The question is, how is this thing talking at all? Vampires are little more than wild animals!

But San Francisco vampires are special…

I let my hands drop from the keyway, turn, and stand up. I force my legs not to tremble.

"So, uh, are you really Rafa's father?"

It's a stupid question. And my voice literally squeaks at the end. But I need to stall, and I have no idea what else to say.

His smirk sharpens. He begins to circle the space, running an index finger casually, possessively, over the iron cages in front of the kids on one side of the room. His fingertip flicks with a dull snap from bar to bar, creating a dull metallic ring. He's in no rush. He knows he has me.

The kids recoil back against the far walls of their cells, whimpering, as he comes near.

"I am. And I do my best to keep informed about all my son's acquaintances. You, I don't know." Small half-shrug. "But you look about his flavor, if a little young." His voice becomes hard and commanding. "*Tell me who you are.*"

I don't think there's any power in his words, and something about the way he speaks feels affected, like he's putting on airs—but that doesn't stop a small, cowering part of me from wanting to tell him any little thing he wants, just so I can go somewhere and hide. (Probably in a puddle of my own urine.)

"I'm just… you know… some guy…" I sound weak. I sound like prey.

"Just some guy who tagged along with a Monster Hunter on what I can only assume is a daring and foolish rescue, hm?" He's almost finished his tour of the side cells. He takes in the locksmith tools in my hand. "Since Rafa is no longer welcome with his clan here, it would make sense he'd have to go bargain shopping when it comes to professional assistance. You're some kind of cracksman, I assume?"

Bargain shopping? I'm pretty sure I've just been insulted. (By yet another random, pompous bad guy!) And I have no idea what a "cracksman" is. (Sounds a little dirty, to be honest.) But if mocking me keeps him talking…

"Rafa never told me he was no longer welcome with his clan. At least not in so many words. So, uh, how exactly did *that* happen?" I try to look shocked. It's not hard.

The vampire stops at the corner of the room. He's only ten paces away. He chuckles, amused at my distress. "I suppose we *all* have our secrets, don't we?" His eyes narrow. "Some are, of course, deadlier than others."

And if that doesn't sound like a perfect setup right before you swoop in and bite some terrified dude's neck, I don't know what is.

But luckily, Collin seems to have finally gotten what he needed from the mothership, because he blurts out: "Right, right, right! The Molotov cocktails! Even just a little bit of your magic can ignite the wick, and vampires are vulnerable to fire! Alvin, don't think! Just bend down, grab a bottle cork-side from Rafa's pack, channel the fire in your stomach like you did in the car, and throw it directly at his torso! Right now!"

Uh-huh. This is the part where I would typically have a full-on mental freak-out about how all of that is impossible for me, and that I'm clueless about what I actually did the last time I created a spark, and that it was all probably just a fluke, and that vampires are crazy fast, and it'll be on me before I even lay a finger on one of those bottles.

But Collin just told me to not think, and when it comes to not thinking and doing something crazy, it's practically become my go-to move with him, so I quickly duck down, grab a bottle, picture fire in my belly, and chuck the damn thing (along with the hook pick!) as hard as I can dead at the vampire's chest.

And the bottle hits! Right on target, even!

It even shatters spectacularly! *BLAM!*

And absolutely nothing happens, except for me getting a huge splotch of gasoline all over this monster's obscenely expensive jacket.

He looks down at the spill, eyebrow cocked. "Seriously?" His eyes flick up to me and he appears more disappointed than pissed, the high-class air dropped. "You realize that's not how those work, right?"

"Alvin! What the hell was that?!" Collin steps in front of me, face red and incredulous. He thrusts out his hands toward my chest. "For feck's sake, do it again! And this time, actually *picture* raging fire inside you and send it to your fingertips! I mean, c'mon! This vampire is going to kill you! Get angry!"

I don't really know if anger is the most appropriate emotion for someone being attacked by the undead. Fear, horror, *despair*—any of those seem much more of a natural response. But the fact that Collin is acting surprised that I couldn't do his stupidly impossible magic trick is, indeed, a bit annoying. And when I reach back down this time, I'm not going to lie, it's mostly just to prove how positively ridiculous he's being, right before I get torn apart by a storm of claws and fangs.

Of course, there's only so much damage that Mr. Suave-and-Malevolent is willing to let his suit endure, so the second I go for another bottle, he's rushing me. By the time I'm back up—cork and wick half-slipping through my fingers—he's only a few feet away. And I don't know if it's really anger or just blind terror that fills my insides as I picture a bright flare racing from my guts to my fingertips, but whatever it is, this time my nerves jangle with hot, explosive energy. So, when my hand smashes the bottle into his oncoming stomach, there's a quick flash of light—

—and then the vampire's entire upper body explodes into a blaze of raging orange and yellow.

My eyes dazzle from the glare, and for a second I'm sure that I've been caught up in the conflagration, too, but then he leaps away from me with a soul-rending, ear-splitting shriek and is back rolling on the bare concrete floor, desperately trying to put himself out.

"Yes!" Collin exclaims, now apparently back to thinking I'm the bee's knees. "That was class, Alvin!"

The hook tool tumbled onto the ground just a few feet away. I immediately move to grab it, but Collin grips my bicep, stopping me.

"There's no time! We have to go. *Now*."

As if to make his point, my enhanced hearing picks up

running velvet footsteps upstairs. A lot of them. I suppose we haven't exactly been quiet down here.

I dash over to Rafa and shake his shoulders. "Rafa! Rafa! Wake up!"

His father pounded his head like a pile driver, so I'm not shocked to find his dense, muscular frame just flops, limp, in my hands. Icy terror trickles into my sides as I realize I might be completely on my own here. I glance over at the backpack, wondering if there's any way to Molotov cocktail my way out of here without killing all of us, including the kids. (Bet not!) But then those superior Hunter genetics must kick in, because Rafa's eyes flutter and open.

"Alvin?" He tries to focus on me.

"Vampires coming! A lot of them!"

My words are like a splash of cold water. In the space of a few seconds, he's pushed me out of the way and is on his feet—unsteady, but definitely awake. Then he sees his father on his back a few yards away, staring blankly at the ceiling, charcoal smoke rising up from his chest. A stink of acrid, burnt hair permeates the room. The suit is scorched and black. His whole body is badly charred.

The vampire's fingers twitch. Down, but not dead. (Or not *even more* dead, anyway.)

Rafa picks up the sharp stake he dropped, eyes still on his father. "The lock?" His face is cold, but I hear raspy emotion in his voice.

"I couldn't finish," I say, my own words low and rough.

We turn at the same time to Emma. She's back curled up on her cot, arms tight around her knees again, staring at the side of her cell, looking even more miserable than we found her. She knows she's not getting saved.

Collin leans into my field of view, serious and haunted. "Alvin, I'm sorry, but we are out of time. You'll be no good to any of these kids if those vampires get their hands on you!"

The Hunter squeezes his stake, now standing above the smoking monster on the floor. I step up to him.

"Spirits say we gotta go." I force the statement out. I don't want it to be true. But there has to be something we can salvage from this disaster. "If nothing else, we need to tell people what we've seen here... right?"

We both stand frozen for a moment, then Rafa nods. "Right. Let's move."

He puts his hand on my shoulder and starts to firmly and quickly guide me toward the door, like when we first met. He leaves his father on the ground, untouched.

Then I remember.

"The book!" I slip out of Rafa's grip and run back to grab it from in front of the redheaded boy's cell. I can't help glancing up when I get there. The kid's right above me, fingers wrapped around the iron, eyes pleading.

"Please... Don't go... Don't leave me here..." he says. It's barely a whisper. And it's like a scalpel slipping right into my heart.

I grab the book and turn away.

The blue glow immediately blooms out from its cover as I grip the leather in my fingertips. Vampire Dad startles, still splayed out on the floor.

"*You*," it says, its neck craning up, its blackened face incredulous. "You carry the watch?!"

I'm caught in his furious glare. The rest of its body remains fixed, but it trembles with effort, struggling to rise.

Collin snaps me out of my fear paralysis. "Vamps now in the elevator!"

"Right!" I say and pull my shit together. Even scarier monsters are on the way!

I run back to Rafa, who is standing in the doorway, fixated on his father. I can't tell if it's horror or fury I'm seeing. He's swapped his wooden stake for his shotgun, slightly raised, his right hand squeezing the pistol grip.

Then he abruptly turns.

"This way!" he barks. The shotgun sweeps over his father, but he doesn't fire. Instead, Rafa charges into the hall and, gripping the book under my arm, I stumble after him as best I can.

I don't look back at the kids. I just can't.

By the time I'm out the door, Rafa is almost a quarter of the way down the hallway. He's tons faster than my unfed, out-of-shape human body. Light from the elevator knifes into the corridor, and two vampires emerge. There's a tall biker-looking dude in full leather and a woman in what appears to be some kind of ball-gown. Without even breaking stride, Rafa snaps up his long gun one-handed to blast both center-forehead with two deafening roars, and that's all it takes—they are done.

My ears ring from the shots, but somehow, I can still hear the sound of someone or something desperately trying to press one of the buttons in the elevator. Apparently, just like the Spanish Inquisition, no one expects an armed Monster Hunter in their basement. The current occupant is looking to make a quick exit.

But Rafa has become death itself. And I'm caught between fascinated and scared shitless as he smoothly moves in front of the elevator and shoots whoever is left inside, cold, executioner-style. Then, face still blank, he jams one of his stakes into the bottom edge of the open elevator door, right at the corner of its recessed metal floor track, which locks it in place.

Meanwhile, I'm still running. I'm only about halfway down the hallway at this point.

And Collin is running next to me. "Alvin, blocking the elevator is not going to stop them. And if you try to go back to the sewers, they *will* get you. We need to go *up*!" One of his glowing arrows appears above the stairwell doorway at the end of the hall next to Rafa. It blinks. Urgently.

Well, crap.

"Rafa!" I yell, squeezing out the words from my strained lungs. "The spirits say the sewers are a death trap. The only way out is up!"

The Monster Hunter doesn't question the crazy logic of that. He just gives me a quick nod, cracks open the door of the stairwell, and glances in.

"Clear enough," he says. "Let's go!" Then he's already through.

I haven't even gotten there yet. Sweat stings my eyes, and I'm huffing and puffing to the point of nausea.

I dig deep, trying to will my stubby little legs into overdrive. Right before the stairwell, I glance into the elevator. Another dead vamp is splashed crimson against the painted white enamel back of the car. I press on and try my best not to think how *I* would feel at the end of Rafa's gun.

Rafa is already a half-flight ahead. I grit my teeth and push myself to my limit as I pound up the steps, trying to keep up with him. But the sprint down the long hall already has me completely gassed, and my legs rebel against the extra lift of a stair climb. I hear more footsteps above. Can't tell how many. But despite my terror, I'm not getting faster. I'm slowing down.

The Monster Hunter notices I'm lagging, and frowns. He stops to let me catch up.

I'm going to get us both killed.

"Rafa, I— I can't do it! I'm sorry! Just go!"

He doesn't react—just purses his lips, twists his torso, cranes his neck, and fires a shot into the stairwell shaft above, like a young god wielding lightning. A body from a couple flights up tumbles down. It hits the rails of the void with four bone-snapping clunks before it lands, crumpled, in front of us.

Then without a word, the Monster Hunter smashes his shoulder into my stomach, knocking the wind out of me. I don't even have time to freak that he's somehow figured me out because, in one smooth movement, he gets under me and lifts me up into a fireman's carry. And then he's racing back up the stairs, shotgun in one hand, me and my ass bouncing over his opposite shoulder like I weigh almost nothing.

(I do not weigh almost nothing.)

He fires a few more times ahead of us and, once we pass the first sub-basement, he starts shooting behind as well. More bodies drop. Then we burst out into what must be the ground floor of the Benevolent Society, to some kind of service hallway.

I might have needed to be carried like a hot, sweaty sack of potatoes, but Collin of course hasn't had any trouble keeping up. I see him right under me, as I continue to flop and bob on top of Rafa's back.

"Tell him to go down the hall to the left! That's the only way out!" he yells.

Rafa's shoulder holster is now jabbing me in the throat, but I choke out that instruction as best I can, and he careens us in the right direction. Since I'm literally hanging over his back, I see six vampires race out of the stairwell we just came from, skidding on the tile floor, swift as hyenas. And by the time we round the corner to that left hall, they're all over the place—the floors, the walls, even clawing along the ceiling like hopped-up lizards, each one raring to make the first kill. Rafa's shotgun is a heavily modified semi-automatic, but even with his extra magazines, he wouldn't be able to get all of them. He's already used a ton of ammo.

The Monster Hunter seems to have come to the same conclusion, so he full-on sprints to the fire door in front of us, no longer turning and firing. The door is closed, but he has so much momentum, he knocks it half-off of its hinges with just his elbow. *BANG!* It hangs, askew, shuddering as we whip past it.

The doorway leads to a large cavernous lobby of marble and wood. Rafa nimbly spins, taking in the new surroundings. No corporate office or industrial dungeon set here. It looks like what you'd expect the lobby of a wealthy, hundred-year-old philanthropic society building to look like. There are glass doors into conference rooms, wide stone steps leading to the upper floor, a gold art-deco elevator, and in the center of the room is an elderly female receptionist in a pilled pink wool top who I clock as pure human. She gasps with terror and ducks under the desk. Opposite from where we are, I take in the backside of the massive metal front doors I saw from the street.

Collin's big glowing arrow shows that's where we need to go.

But we aren't going to make it. A dozen vampires spew out through the door behind us, some racing along the floor while others scramble around the top of the doorway. Rafa's not going to outrun them, especially not carrying me. He fires back one more shot into the wrecked entrance to try to discourage these monsters, and then I'm unceremoniously dumped as he takes a knee so he can rip off his night-vision goggles and reload with a thick metal magazine from his belt. But the wild shot only slows them for a tick, and God knows how many more are on the way. We're going to need something that changes the rules of this game, or we're toast.

Luckily, some of the stuff you see in monster movies is actually true.

While Rafa takes another shot, I race for the doors. They're big, they're heavy, but it's still business hours and, as luck would have it, they're not locked. Just as the bloodsuckers are about to overrun Rafa, I rip one of the doors open with a desperate pull and the whole lobby floods with light.

It's late afternoon in San Francisco and okay, maybe

the *west* part of the city has fog. But we're downtown in early November, so it's clear skies all the way. Even at the beginning of sunset, there's still enough ambient sunlight to do real damage. Two vampires who had swooped around to flank Rafa immediately shriek and start pinwheeling back, red smoke billowing from their skin. The others in front of Rafa raise their arms to block the purifying light reflecting off the polished marble floor. And after a second, they, too, start to crisp just from the spill. Then all are in full retreat.

But apparently bloodsuckers like to keep their friends close. A completely human security guard I totally missed in the corner moves toward me, hand on his baton.

"Rafa! Let's go!" I call out.

The Hunter, gulping in air himself now, heaves himself back to his feet, leaving the goggles behind. He swivels, sweeping his shotgun over the guard. It stops the man, hands raised, as Rafa passes. Rafa grabs my arm, and then we're outside in the open air, running down the street.

Leaving behind a bunch of helpless kids at the mercy of a nest of enraged vampires.

26

Everyone stays grim and silent as I lead us to Stryker's office. The suite is magically protected. We'll be safe there.

It's more than I can say for the children we just abandoned.

"How many of those kids are going to get killed because of what we just did?" My voice is like gravel.

We're riding up the Aston Building's rickety 1920s elevator. I've turned my head away from Rafa to look directly at Collin, not even trying to hide that I'm talking to an invisible being.

Collin's chest sags, avoiding my eyes. "I don't know. I can't see the future." It's a clear cop out, so he mumbles. "But the vampires were badly hurt. A lot of them."

"And they'll need fresh blood to heal…" There are rocks in my stomach. "How many of the kids are required for their ritual?"

Collin shakes his head, then briefly glances at the ancient tome still under my arm. "I can't remember what was in the book. Even what the exact ritual is. It doesn't stay with me."

"So it could just be one? The rest could be expendable?"

He nods.

I turn to Rafa, in case he has any questions. He just stares forward, jaw tight. He's still gripping his shotgun. I kept close to him on our way over here, tried to use my body to hide the weapon. There was hardly anyone in the Financial District, but for all I know, someone's already called the cops on us. Would serve me right.

The elevator doors open with their usual clatter. The metallic sound echoes louder against my heavy mood. No one's here on a Saturday evening, so the hallway is dim and empty as I usher us to the office of Sarah Stryker, Paranormal Investigator. (An *actual* hero.) Once I close the door behind us, the protective runes around the frame and windows trace in with a lavender sheen that only I can see. The taste of sour apples fills my mouth. No one with malevolent intent will be able to enter.

As Collin would say, we'll be grand.

There are a lot of things that I want to do right now. Cry. Kick something really hard. Scream at the top of my lungs. Check in with Rafa, who is just standing by the door, arms hanging at his sides like a zombie.

But there's only one thing I should be doing. And I should have done it from the start.

I unlock Stryker's office and step inside. On the shelf of one of the large oak bookcases rests a long, thin black box full of small bones. It's one of the more benign trophies Ms. Stryker claimed from a clutch of evil wizards some years back. She never really had any need for the thing until I became her intern. A couple months ago, she taught me how to use it "in case of absolute emergency."

It's evil, foul magic that feels greasy on my palms as I place the bog wood container on her desktop. I draw back my arms and reflexively rub the tips of my fingers together to reduce the slimy sensation. It's only when I flick my gaze down to check for actual physical residue that I see the blood. My right hand has several cuts. Small bits of glass from the Molotov cocktail I shoved into the vampire are embedded in my skin. The cuff of my gray sweatshirt is crusted with streaks of rusty burgundy. Didn't notice it before. Now that I do, the little wounds sting.

Again, serves me right.

(No burns, though.)

"You should use the first aid kit in the second drawer to clean those up. They could go septic." Collin is next to me. Concern pinches his face.

I ignore him and reach inside the box. The little bones —mostly metacarpals and mostly human—are more or less uniform in size and are currently interlocked in a jigsaw pattern. But they can be arranged into letters, which is what I do, removing the few I don't need and ignoring the impression of needle-like grubs burrowing into my fingers with every touch. Ms. Stryker was fairly sure whatever effects this artifact could have on me wouldn't be permanent.

I don't have enough bones to get fancy, so I spell things out as succinctly as possible:

BIG VAMPIRE NEST

KIDS IN DANGER

ME TOO
HELP

I almost leave out the "me too," but whether I deserve to be saved or not, my gut tells me it'll make her respond faster.

I don't expect to get that response anytime soon. Not only is time screwy between the different planes of existence, but she'd have to notice that her own bone box changed, and it's probably shoved way down in her Go Bag. She might not even have it with her.

It could literally be days before she gets the message, which means this is just the start of calling in the cavalry. Vampires will be too much for regular cops, so I'll have to figure out how to get the Feds involved. Ideally without outing myself as a predatory demon—but those kids can't wait, so it doesn't really matter what happens to me.

I'm honestly not even sure who to call, though. Does the Department of Homeland Security have a hotline I can pull up on Google? I turn to ask Collin when the bones in the box begin to shift and softly click against each other. Startled, I peer over the edge to see each one in motion, rotating and sliding into new positions. Some of the bones I removed even leap over the sides of the container to join their macabre friends.

Finally, they settle into words:
MEET AT MY HOUSE NOW
DONT CONTACT ANYONE ELSE
HELP ON THE WAY

I stare at the yellowed skeletal fragments for a long moment, not sure what to make of them. I know Ms.

Stryker's home address—it's in Hunter's Point—but I've never been there.

"Why wouldn't she want me to contact anyone else?" I ask, glancing at Collin. "Why would she even mention that?"

His eyes flick up to the side for a couple seconds, before he looks back at me and shrugs.

"Haven't a clue, Alvin. Maybe she's not sure who we can trust?" He doesn't speak with his usual chipper confidence. I can't tell if that's because he's skeptical, or if he's just as shell-shocked from the vampire lair as I am.

But whatever, this is still unequivocally good news, right? In fact, it's exactly what I need: a real expert, a real hero, swooping in to clean up my mess. I should be clicking my heels, and any hesitation I feel must be because I know, after this, she'll for sure be done with me. Children are going to get badly hurt because of my incompetence. Because I had the selfish arrogance to think I could handle this on my own without any guidance, any supervision. Whatever else happens, my dream of being a paranormal investigator is over.

But that doesn't matter. And it doesn't matter why she'd want to keep this on the down-low. Ms. Stryker will know what to do. She always knows what to do. And if she were here, she certainly wouldn't need to explain her reasoning to the foolish intern who got himself in way over his head.

I straighten up from the desk and move toward the door. "She said 'now.' So let's get moving."

Collin stops me with a gentle touch. "Please just take the first aid kit from the desk. I'll help you sort that wound on the way." When I frown, he adds, "Rafa's a bit cut up, too."

And that's why he's the Avatar of Knowledge and I'm just a stupid incubus boy—because knowing it might help someone else totally trumps my sulky desire to keep suffering.

I scowl harder and snatch the kit from the drawer. And since I already turned around, I also stash the book in the safe with the bagged demon head before locking the door behind me and joining Rafa in the reception area. (Stryker might want to see the ritual, but if this ancient tome really is what the vamps need, it's safer here behind the office wards.)

I find Rafa perched on the edge of the couch. His Kevlar duster is off. He's bent over, staring ahead, meaty forearms resting on his thighs, hands hanging down between. The shotgun rests against the couch next to him.

"Hey," I say from the doorway to Ms. Stryker's office.

He glances up at me, haunted.

"I, uh, heard back from my boss. She wants me to meet her at her house. Now. She says help is on the way."

"That's good," he replies, muted. The muscles of his face barely move. Like his arms, his features just droop.

I know I should say something. He just found out his dead dad is not so dead and is instead an evil monster—but I have no idea how to comfort him, because I've never had any actual friends. I should have asked Collin for the best way to handle this. He could have told me the right words. But it's not like I'm going to go back into Stryker's office to have a private conference with the Avatar, so I sit next to Rafa, place the kit to my side, and just state the obvious.

"You didn't know. What had happened to him, I mean."

He shakes his head, confirming. "I was always told he'd been killed. Both my parents. That the vampires were so savage, there wasn't anything left for a funeral. When they sent me back East, they said I shouldn't come back, because it would be too hard, emotionally. That there was nothing for me in San Francisco anymore. But he's been here all this time… And he sounded…" His words trail off to a whisper.

I finish for him, realizing. "…Like he used to. Like when he was alive."

Stryker's told me that some older vampires can keep up the appearance of a person for a short period, like to get themselves dressed and walk down the street with a friendly smile before they grab you. But they're still essentially animals. You couldn't have a conversation with one.

But what if that wasn't the case? And what if it was someone you knew?

"I saw it in his face, Alvin. My father. He's still *in* there." His expression is hollow with agony.

"And you think you might be able to reach him?" There's no skepticism in my voice. If it were somebody I loved who'd gotten turned? I'd want to believe I could get them back, too.

His mouth tightens into a thin line. "Those kids. *Little* kids. He locked them up. Fed off them. Hurt them." He looks over at me. "He was third in the hierarchy of our clan. One of the best Monster Hunters in the country.

Yeah, he always wanted *more* for us. And himself. More money, a better house, getting into high society, I guess, but he was *good*... A true hero..."

All of Rafa's usual stoicism is gone. He's no longer the coldly lethal Hunter. Right now, he's just this young guy who wishes he could have a parent who loves him. I might not know anything about being a hero, but that I get.

I take his hand in mine. "And he was your dad."

Tears start to brim. "Yeah. He was my dad. And there's part of me that can't help thinking... A dumb, *childish* part... It's why I didn't..." He grits his teeth.

"I would have done the same thing." Which is true—*if* I had family who loved me—and I try to say what I'd want to hear right now. "Nobody knows magic like Ms. Stryker. If there is any way to cure him, to bring him back, she'll have the answer. Why don't you come with me? She'll want to meet you, anyway."

The faintest bit of light fills his expression. "You really think it could be possible? To bring him back?"

"I don't know," I say, feeling helpless.

The reality is probably not. I can't say exactly how vampirism works, but the population is supposedly growing worldwide. I'm pretty sure that wizard council Stryker is part of would be busy spreading a cure, if there was one.

Still, this courageous, surprisingly sweet man is hurting, and based on what his undead dad said, I get the impression that, like me, Rafa doesn't really have other friends. I want to provide him some hope; that's why I put meeting Stryker out there. In the end, though, there's really only one thing I have to give.

"Look, whatever the answer is, Rafa, whatever you have to do, all I can promise is that you won't have to do it alone. No matter what, we'll figure it out together, okay?"

He brings his chin up and snuffles in a quick, ragged breath, but the tears still spill out. He turns to me and squeezes my hand tight.

"Jesus," he says. "Why do you have to be so fucking amazing?"

Me? Amazing? Hardly. And he should know that, based on what we've just gone through, but now obviously isn't the time to tell him how wrong he is.

It's probably also not the time to push him away as he leans in and brings his face up to mine.

Our eyes lock, and I see this need in him. The need to connect, to forget everything, to have something good. Right now, I guess that's another thing I can really get.

He's so close, his shuddering breath is on my lips. One second, two seconds... I don't have to have any experience to know where this might go. He's holding himself back, waiting on me.

I glance over at Collin, who's leaning against my desk, gazing back with a gentle smile. Not encouraging me. But not *not* encouraging me.

And when I return to Rafa, he's just where I left him. Inches away. And even with tears in his eyes, he really is so freaking handsome. Dark, expressive eyebrows. Flecks of amber in his irises. And those lips, so full... so damn kissable.

I get this is super messed-up. I'd totally be taking advantage. We've got much bigger fish to fry. And an incubus starting something with a Monster Hunter officially qualifies as suicidal. Me not immediately putting a stop to this is so insane I check in with my monster to see if it's somehow driving my actions, but it's as quiet as the Obligation has been.

(Who knows why? Maybe both are just giving me the space I need to tie my own noose.)

Nothing's putting any kind of whammy on my brain. Looks like Collin will be cool, either way. Whatever I choose to do, it's all on me.

So what *do* I want? I want out of my head. I want to disappear completely. I want to feel *something* that's not pain or self-hatred, if only for just a few merciful moments!

I lean forward, only a fraction of an inch—and that's all it takes.

His large hand cups the base of my skull and his mouth hungrily claims mine. And I kiss him back, all the pent-up emotion, the boiling anger at myself, driving me forward. It fuels a need for release. For oblivion.

Rafa's kisses are different than Collin's. There's stubble, and it rubs my chin and the skin above my lip raw. The making out is a lot rougher, wetter, more *urgent*. Even his jaw muscles feel strong. They work under my fingertips as I cradle his face. As I want more.

I kiss back just as forcefully. I can't get enough of his sweet, faintly minty taste, the pricking sandpaper of his skin. My teeth scrape at his lips, and I suck him in. He chokes out a high-pitched, constricted grunt. Then another. This big man is whimpering because of what I'm doing to him.

It makes me feel powerful. In control. Maybe he

started it, but now I'm the one driving this. I'm the one who gets to decide how far this goes.

It's hot. Intense. Exciting.

It feels *good*.

But I don't deserve this power. My monster might be hanging back now, but it will come for sure if I don't stop. And I've been *lying* to this guy. Lying to him about what I am. About what I could do to him. Even lying to him about what Collin is. He deserves better, especially after what he's just been through.

It doesn't matter what I think I want, because he deserves better than me.

The words are out before I even think about them:

"Rafa..." I say, pulling back, breath ragged. "I haven't been... completely honest with you."

I press my forehead against his and squeeze my eyes shut, trying to get back under my own control.

Then I realize what I just said.

Holy fuck.

If there is any statement uttered in the middle of sexy times that demands a full interrogation, that's got to be it. And it leads to questions there's no way I can answer! I don't care how guilty I feel, I can't tell him I'm an incubus. I can't even tell him I'm a paranormal. He'll strangle me to death!

Crap!

My mind races, struggling to come up with something remotely plausible. Maybe Collin will help! Maybe if Rafa questions me, I can just tell him about the watch!

My mouth opens—even though I honestly have no

idea where to start—when the Hunter places his fingertips on my lips. "Stop, Alvin. I know what you're going to say."

Uh, come again?

He blows out a sigh, cooling down. "I mean, I have a pretty good idea what it looks like to cast a spell. Or *not* cast one. And I am a Monster Hunter. It's not like I'm going to miss the signs of what you are. Not when you can see in the dark or heal from damage that should put you in the hospital for weeks. Not with… everything else."

My heart stops. I cease breathing.

My world has officially ended.

If he sees my death-spiral freak-out, he doesn't react. Instead, he continues.

"Just… if it's okay with you… can we not do this now? After my dad… I just can't…"

He removes his hand from my mouth and, after a moment, retreats into a huddle on the edge of the couch, fists in his lap. He looks so young.

"Um…" I say, throat dry. "You don't want to, um…" Kill me? Slash my throat? Blow my head off? I mean, he *knows*! What the hell do I say to that?

That little, smoldering smile of his returns. It's nothing more than a flicker, but it's there when he glances over at me. "I think you're already aware I'm not your typical Hunter. And you've been nothing but good. Wonderful, even. This whole time. We'll need to talk about it, but it doesn't have to be a thing. Just… let's not do it now, okay?"

I nod, stunned. I have no idea what is happening. He knows I'm not human. That's clear. The implication, though, is that I've carelessly given myself completely away.

Is he saying he's put together that I'm an incubus… and is somehow cool with it? Cool enough to actually risk *kissing* me?

(!!!)

Well, even if that is true, the moment for kissing (or even just sitting still!) has passed. Those kids need to be saved now. *If* they still can be. (*Crap!*)

"We should go, Rafa," I say, voice shaky. "My boss is waiting."

He gives a heavy, almost drunken nod and stands up. Like it's an unfortunate truth, but what are you going to do? And for whatever reason, he now looks a lot more like himself. His calm, confident expression has returned. Once again, the strong bro-hero who you can rely on to save the day is back.

The moment I get to my feet, he pulls me into an embrace.

It's not fast. It's not scary. But it is tight, like he can't get close enough.

"You're a good guy, Alvin," he says, lips pressed into the hair on top of my head. His nose breathes me in. A long, deep breath. "Don't ever forget that."

And the moment I hear those words, it's like a massive dam starts to crack inside me. My breath hitches, and I'm fighting my own tears. I hug him back, just as tight. I breathe him in, too—his chest is musky through the cotton chambray shirt, the scent surprisingly pleasant—and I wish with all my heart his words were true. I wish I could believe them.

But I can't, so I don't let myself cry. I just give back one more full-body squeeze and try to let the clenched sensation of our hug numb the ache inside me.

Then we part, grab our stuff, and head out the door.

You'd think that with what he just told me, with what we just did, I'd feel some sense of relief. He knows what I am, and he's acting like it's something we'll just talk out. And I have plenty of reason to believe that Stryker's going to take care of everything else.

But Rafa and I haven't had that talk yet. Not really.

And vampires could be draining those kids dry right now.

And I really have no idea what Stryker is going to say or do when I see her.

I'd love to believe that the hard part of this nightmare is over, but people are still counting on me. All those kids, Nicole, even Rafa. So, I'm not going to relax, I'm not going to let up, until I know everyone is safe.

I might never be good. But I swear on my life, I'm *done* being useless.

Thank you for reading!

Ready to see how Alvin's story ends?

The conclusion to Alvin's adventure, **Incubus Vampire Slayer** (*Alvin Alonso's Secret Files*, Book 2), is already available for your reading pleasure. Alvin's done running—now the real fun can begin!

Get it here:

https://alexwoolfson.com/incubus-vampire-slayer/

Thank you for reading!

One other really important thing...

Your voice can make a huge difference for a debut author like me. If you are enjoying this duet, **I would be incredibly grateful if you could take a moment to leave a review on Amazon.**

Reviews tell the Amazon algorithm that this book is worth recommending—and they're the best way to let me know that people actually want to read more of Alvin's adventures.

Thank you so much for your support!

About the Author

Alex Woolfson writes action-packed adventures with lovable gay heroes.

An East-Coaster who now calls the Bay Area home, Alex spent twenty years editing films and video before turning to comics, where he created the Lambda Literary Award finalist graphic novel *Artifice* and the long-running LGBTQ-superhero webcomic *The Young Protectors*.

His debut MM urban-fantasy novel, *The Reluctant Incubus*, kicks off the *Alvin Alonso's Secret Files* duet, delivering high stakes action, slow-burn romance, and queer heroes who save the world ***and*** each other.

When Alex isn't at his treadmill desk writing, you'll find him traveling the globe with his husband, on the hunt for the perfect taco.

instagram.com/alexwoolfson
facebook.com/AlexWoolfsonAuthor
tiktok.com/@alexwoolfson